TROUBLE IN PARADISE

Elise Noble

Published by Undercover Publishing Limited

Copyright © 2015 Elise Noble

r22

ISBN: 978-1-910954-02-7

Edited by Amanda Ann Larson

www.undercover-publishing.com

www.elise-noble.com

For the wonderful people of Dahab, Egypt, who have always made me feel so welcome.

CHAPTER 1

I SAT ON the floor in my living room, surrounded by the wreckage of my hopes and dreams. Scattered papers on my left side, a pile of used Kleenex on my right. The aftermath of the past day and a half.

The half-empty box of clean tissues took centre stage in front of me, and I plucked out another one so I could blow my nose.

"Callie, have you phoned the florist yet?" my mother called from the kitchen.

I gave a shuddering sniffle and swallowed down another batch of tears. "No, Mum. It's on the list."

Along with contacting the rest of the wedding guests, speaking to the caterer, getting hold of the dress designer, cancelling the hire of the vintage Rolls Royce... The list went on.

All I'd done so far was explained to the organisers at the lovely hotel we'd chosen as the venue for our wedding reception that we were no longer getting married.

The lady I spoke to had sounded suitably shocked, but quickly recovered enough to say, "I'm terribly sorry, but with only three days until the wedding, we can't give you a refund."

That was the icing on the cake. *Cake*. The tears fell harder. Of course, now there would be no cake. The beautiful three-tier affair we'd chosen together would probably be distributed at the local homeless shelter, the little bride and groom that were supposed to perch on top consigned to the dustbin.

When I said "we'd chosen," I meant my fiancé Bryce and me. No, no... My *ex*-fiancé.

My mother wandered through and put a glass of red wine down next to me.

"Darling, drink this. It'll make you feel better."

I looked at my watch. "Mum, it's only ten thirty in the morning."

"I know, dear, but desperate times call for desperate measures."

Was she saying I was desperate? No way! I was off men, forever.

"People will think I'm an alcoholic."

"No, dear, alcoholics go to meetings. You'd just be a party girl."

I looked towards the ceiling, praying for divine intervention. It was great that Mum was being supportive and everything, but I couldn't help wishing she'd do it from the comfort of her own home. That way, I'd be able to mope in peace.

"You've got to get right back into the saddle and show that no-good scoundrel what he's missing," she continued.

Oh, that was easy for her to say. She'd had plenty of practice. Brenda Shawcross was now on husband number five. Or was it six? She'd married one of them twice, claiming she couldn't quite make up her mind, and I wasn't sure whether to count that as one mistake or two.

My father had been hubby number one. He'd stuck

around long enough to saddle my sister and me with the names Persephone and Callista, and then taken off for parts unknown. The last time I heard from him, which was eight years ago, he was running a beachside bar on Santorini. The Tango Lounge. I'd googled it, and Trip Advisor gave it two stars.

I'd got the better end of the deal with the name thing, though. At least I could shorten mine to Callie. There wasn't much you could do with Persephone other than Percy, and no way did Princess P want to get mistaken for a boy. When I was four and my sister was five, she'd begged me to swap names, and I often thought that my refusal had contributed to the chip she'd carried around on her shoulder ever since.

I took a deep breath. Things could be worse. Persephone could be here too. But in a tiny miracle, she'd cried off the wedding. Apparently attending a golf tournament in Quinta do Lago with her oh-so-perfect husband was far more important than watching her only sister get married.

Or not get married, as it turned out.

"Mum, give me a break, would you?"

"Men aren't worth crying over. Especially that one. I never liked him, you know."

Oh, now she told me. I'd only been dating Bryce for six years. "He wasn't *that* bad. I mean, he had his good points."

"What were they?"

I struggled to think. Was I defending Bryce or just my own poor judgement? With hindsight, I saw that perhaps he hadn't been the greatest thing since sliced bread after all, but I hated the thought that I'd wasted six years of my life with an idiot.

Finally, I came up with, "He always left the toilet seat down."

My mother stared at me, and I wasn't sure whether to laugh or cry. So I settled for a bizarre mix of the two, and her eyes widened in alarm.

"Callie, that's—"

Saved by the bell. Or rather, by the front door opening. I winced as it slammed back into the wall, and a small chunk of plaster fell to the carpet. My friend Kat never could make a quiet entrance.

"Right, I've got a bottle of wine, two tubs of Ben and Jerry's, and a movie. And once we've finished laughing at Will Ferrell, I've got a lighter to burn Bryce's stuff," she announced.

What was it with the wine? And where did Kat think we were going to have a fire? I lived in a second-floor flat for goodness sakes.

My mother, on the other hand, thought it was an excellent idea. "I'll get spoons. And extra glasses. And we could do with some petrol to make things go up nicely."

She hustled out to the kitchen, and I tried to be the voice of reason.

"We can't burn Bryce's things. What if he wants them back?"

"Well, he should have thought about that before he decided he 'needed space,' shouldn't he?" Kat used her fingers to form little air quotes around the words.

She did have a point, I supposed. And she was only trying to help. Partly because she was my best friend, and partly out of guilt because it was she who'd introduced me to Bryce in the first place. She'd apologised a thousand times for that in the past thirty-six hours, and I kept trying to reassure her that it wasn't her fault. We'd only been sixteen at the time. How could either of us have known what a Grade A asshole he would turn into?

I still remembered the day I'd first met him. When I'd walked into a meeting of the local amateur dramatics society with Kat, there he was, standing across the room, talking with the director of the play he was about to star in. I'd thought he was terribly sophisticated because he was drinking an espresso. How shallow had I been back then?

He was two years older than me, and I'd almost died of embarrassment when he'd sauntered over and introduced himself. Of course, he'd still been plain old Brian then. The transformation into Bryce had come later, when he decided no serious actor would ever be called Brian Featherstone.

He'd kissed my hand and told me I made him think of the Bard's Ophelia, and I'd rushed home to look up who Ophelia was. The potential wife of Prince Hamlet! He thought I could be a princess? I'd gone giddy just thinking about it.

After that, it didn't take much persuading from Kat for me to join the drama group. Bryce had been the shining star, quoting Shakespeare as if he knew the guy personally. Kat tended to have small speaking parts. The lead actress's sidekick, that sort of thing. Me? I helped to make the props and carry stuff.

Sort of like a rehearsal for life, really.

Three months later, Bryce had finally asked me out. Well, what he'd actually said was, "My pal Andrew's birthday celebration is on Saturday. I'd be honoured if you would accompany me."

It didn't matter that I knew he'd already asked Mandy Smith and she'd said no because she had tickets to a Michael Jackson tribute concert. Bryce wanted me to go with him. Me!

I'd leapt at the chance, put on my best dress and my highest heels, then spent three hours holding onto Brian's beer glass while he hobnobbed with the up and coming social elite of the town that we lived in. The blisters were worth it.

He'd been my first boyfriend. And, I swore as I sat in a fort made from piled-up tissues, my last. It was at that moment I recalled Ophelia had gone mad in the end. Was that my destiny?

"Stop thinking about him!" Kat brought me back to reality by snapping her fingers in front of my face.

"I'm trying. But Bryce has been my life for six years. There're reminders of him everywhere."

"Yes, but we're going to fix that."

"Kat, we're not hauling his stuff to the park and toasting marshmallows over it."

She pouted. "Fine. But I honestly think it would make you feel better." She considered the options for a few seconds. "How about just the photos then? We could burn them in the sink."

"No! It would set the fire alarm off."

She looked at me like I'd had the best idea ever.

"The fire alarm? That's brilliant! We'd get a whole truck full of firemen. Like a home delivery of eye candy."

"I'm going to bed now."

"No, you're not. You're going to get out and live life to the fullest without Mr. Four-Syllable-Words holding you back."

I had to giggle at that. Bryce really *had* talked that way. He kept a thesaurus on his nightstand and a dictionary in the cupboard next to his box of low-sugar, high-fibre muesli so he could learn a new word every morning.

"So you're saying I should find a man who only speaks in short sentences?"

"No, I'm saying you should find a man who doesn't speak at all. He should be doing other things with his mouth."

My mouth dropped open. "You can't say that!"

"Why not?"

"My mother's in the kitchen."

"She's been married six times. You think she doesn't know about these things?"

I wanted to close my ears. I didn't discuss "these things," not even with Bryce. He was strictly a missionary man. No variation. I recalled the day when, after reading a particularly graphic romance novel, I'd suggested we might try things with me on top.

He'd stared at me, aghast. "But Callista, you wouldn't have any comprehension as to what was involved. You're just not that type of girl."

And that was that. Discussion over. I just wasn't that type of girl.

Kat must have noticed my blank expression. "Pack it in!"

"What?"

"You're thinking again."

"I'm sorry," I said, sarcasm rising to the fore. "I'll switch my brain off for a bit, shall I?"

She was oblivious. "I'm not sure you can do that. What you really need is a change of scene."

My mother hurried back in with a glass of wine in each hand. One red, one white. She handed them both to me, and I was surprised she hadn't cut out the middlemen and brought the bottles.

"A change of scene? That's a marvellous idea, Kat. Callie can come and stay with me for a while."

No, no, no. No way! "I wouldn't want to impose."

"It'll be no trouble. Your room's exactly as you left it when you moved in here."

Just what I needed—boy band posters and an abundance of out-of-date hair products. "Mum, I'll be fine here."

"Nonsense, it's settled. I'll just go and grab the ice cream."

As soon as she left the room, I turned to Kat.

"Do something," I hissed.

"Like what?"

"I don't know, but this was your idea. Fix it!"

Mum returned and plonked a bowl down in front of me. She'd been a little over-generous with her portions. Much as I loved Phish Food and Chunky Monkey, if I ate a pint of each, I'd be sick.

"Eat up, dear. Once you've finished, I'll help you to pack."

I glared at Kat with murder in my eyes.

"I-I-I've had a better idea," she stammered. "Callie can come and stay with me for a while instead. She's always said she wanted to do a bit of travelling."

I'd said nothing of the bloody sort. That was Kat's brainwave? To go and stay with her? Out of the frying pan and into the fire, as they said. Almost literally, because Kat lived in Egypt, and wasn't it about a thousand degrees centigrade out there?

This was going from bad to worse. I grabbed another tissue and blew my nose. Why couldn't they both just go home?

"Kat, I can't."

"Why not?"

A good question, and one I wasn't sure how to answer. I didn't have a fiancé I needed to stay and pander to anymore, plus I worked as a teacher, and we'd just broken up for the summer holidays. Six long weeks of nothingness stretched ahead of me, and Kat knew it.

"There's nobody to water the plants," was the best excuse I could think of.

"What, those?" Kat asked, pointing at a sorry looking yucca in the corner, which stood next to an orchid that had seen better days.

"You're full of good ideas today, aren't you, Kat?" said my mother. "I'll take the plants home with me. Dave can look after them."

Hubby number five/six was a keen gardener. Allegedly. I suspected it might have been a tactical move on his part because every time my mum asked him to do some DIY, he escaped to the potting shed.

"And you're packed for the beach already," Kat said. "You just need to pick up your suitcase."

Gee, thanks for reminding me. Bryce and I had planned to honeymoon at a couples resort in Jamaica. I'd been looking forward to that trip for months, but now the tickets would most likely sit in his wallet, unused. Hmm. I really did want to go to the beach, but did I dare to just up and leave?

My phone rang, and I recoiled in horror as I recognised the ringtone I'd assigned to Persephone.

"The Bitch Came Back" by Theory of a Deadman. I didn't want to answer it, but I had to. If I let it go to voicemail, she'd only take it as an admission of defeat.

"Callista." She used my full name as a greeting.

I returned the favour. "Persephone."

"Oh, you poor thing. When Mother called me yesterday and said Bryce had left you, I just knew I had to make the time to call this week. You must be feeling truly terrible."

"I'm not feeling great, no." I wanted to add, "mainly because you're on the phone," but I didn't dare.

She ploughed on. "I was just saying to Pierre the other week that it was inevitable. I mean, Bryce's career has been taking off since he got that understudy role in *Macbeth*. It was only a matter of time."

"What do you mean, a matter of time?" I asked through gritted teeth.

"Well, before he traded up. You have to admit you were punching above your weight, don't you? Even though Bryce was no Pierre, he still had some class."

Tears pricked the corners of my eyes. I tried to think of something to say, but no words would come out. Why did Persephone always have to make me feel so small? She never stopped reminding me of how wonderful her husband was. He was a bloody pastry chef, not the living incarnation of Apollo.

My darling sister must have heard me sniffing, like a shark smelling blood.

"Oh, don't cry. I'm sure in a month or two, when you feel able to leave the house again, you'll find someone more suitable."

Where had she learned to be so mean? I'd never been a violent person, but sometimes, I wanted to cut out her tongue. I'd had enough of her constant put-downs.

"As a matter of fact, I'm just going off on holiday. I might find myself a new man sooner than you think."

What was I even saying?

Persephone was silent for a few seconds, and then I heard a rather unladylike snort. "Oh, is Kat still there? She hasn't been filling your head with nonsense again, has she?"

"No, she's been very helpful. We're going to Egypt. I'm all packed, and I'm really looking forward to it."

Hysterical giggles threatened to burst out. *Stay calm, Callie. Just breathe.*

"Egypt? Well, it's hardly Mustique, but I suppose even people like you and Kat have to take a break somewhere. Oh, I've got to go—Pierre's calling me. We're having dinner with the Molinards tonight, and we have to pick up a gateau on the way."

With that, she hung up.

Kat grinned at me in triumph. "I'll fetch your case, shall I?"

No matter how much I wanted to, I couldn't back out now. Not when I'd told Persephone I was going. My life might have been a mess, but even so, I hated the thought of another "I told you so" phone call from my older sister.

She'd married Pierre two years ago after a whirlwind romance. Their wedding ceremony had been perfect. The sun shone, her dress was beautiful, and nobody got drunk at the reception. They lived in Paris in their perfect apartment on a perfect street with their perfect daughter, Annie.

Nothing ever went wrong in Persephone's life.

We couldn't be more different.
I reached for the tissues again.

CHAPTER 2

"DRINKS, SNACKS? ANY magazines?"

The oh-so-perky voice of one of the cabin crew grated in my ears as she pushed her trolley down the aisle of the aeroplane, and I shifted uncomfortably in my seat. I wasn't sure who it had been designed for, but it certainly wasn't an adult human. The sun squinted over the horizon, causing an instant headache, and I pulled down the blind.

At least I had the window seat. Kat was squashed into the middle with a guy who looked as if he was more at home on a rugby pitch sitting on the other side. His knees were butted up against the seat in front, and he couldn't move his arms.

"Do you want anything?" Kat asked, gesturing towards the trolley.

I shook my head no. I felt a bit sick.

Today was supposed to be my wedding day. I should have been walking down the aisle in the local church with the love of my life before sitting down to a meal of organic roast beef and locally sourced vegetables, but instead, I was thirty thousand feet up, somewhere over the Netherlands according to the pilot.

Kat, Mum, and I had spent the last couple of days cancelling everything. By the time we'd finished, I felt as though I was drowning at the bottom of a black hole.

My dreams had been snatched away from me. I'd spent month after stressful month organising everything, and only the thought of getting married had kept me going. Now the light at the end of the tunnel had been firmly extinguished, the pot of gold at the end of the rainbow stolen by a freaking Leprechaun.

Not only that, I'd poured my life savings into my dream day, and the only thing I had to show for it was a dress that probably didn't even fit any more. With all the ice cream and cake Kat had plied me with since my world fell apart, my clothes were feeling decidedly snug. And now I was on my way to the small seaside town of Fidda Hilal, where Kat had spent the last six months working as a windsurfing instructor.

I'd been so busy with the wedding disaster, I hadn't even had a chance to find out anything about the place. Was it a peaceful retreat? Or the Egyptian equivalent of Benidorm?

"So where are we going, exactly?" I asked Kat.

"We're flying into Sharm el-Sheikh, and Fidda Hilal's eighty kilometres up the desert highway. It'll take an hour and a half to get there."

That didn't sound too bad a journey. An hour and a half was bearable. I mean, it wasn't as bad as the time Bryce had booked us a mini-break in Copenhagen and the low-cost airline we'd flown with landed us in Sweden. We'd had to take a cramped coach full of tetchy holidaymakers across the border, and by the time we'd reached our hotel, we'd missed dinner.

I couldn't wait to get to Fidda Hilal, unpack, and settle in. That way, I could go back to my moping. Kat had offered her sofa, but since she only had a one-bedroom apartment and she shared it with Mo, the wakeboarding instructor she was currently in lust with, I'd opted to stay in a local hotel instead. I didn't fancy several weeks tripping over them, and worse, I couldn't stand the thought of them closing the bedroom door and getting on with what I'd be missing.

The Coral Cove Resort was rated five stars, according to their website, and just around the corner from Kat's home. Mum had insisted on paying. A "breakup treat," she called it. I felt guilty for taking her money, but it was the best solution for everyone—at least, that's what I kept telling myself. I still half wished I'd stayed at home in bed.

"And Fidda Hilal's got a nice beach, right?" I asked.

Kat laughed. "Plenty of them. Miles and miles of golden sand, and it only rains once a year. The rest of the time, it's blue sky and sunshine."

Good thing I'd packed that extra bottle of sunscreen, then. I also had a suitcase full of the new bikinis I'd bought to wear for Bryce, as well as a few floaty cover-ups and some sparkly flip-flops. I swallowed down the lump in my throat as I thought of the beautiful brochure pictures for the Crystal Blue Hotel in Jamaica. That was where I should have been travelling to, not Fidda Hilal.

Originally, I'd tried to leave most of the swimwear behind—I'd only intended to wear it on our room's private terrace, after all—but Kat wouldn't hear of it.

"Nonsense. You need to show Bryce what he's missing."

"But he won't be there."

"That's not the point. Besides, with Facebook and Twitter, he might as well be."

Great, just what I needed—my wobbly bits being

showcased for everyone to see.

"Kat, you're not putting half-naked photos of me on the internet."

"We'll see."

Mental note: If Kat was in the vicinity, keep a towel around me at all times.

I'd tried to pack some more practical items, but Kat had taken most of them out. Despite my protests, she'd also insisted I leave in the lingerie I'd bought for my wedding night.

"You never know—you might get lucky," she'd said with a wink, pushing the pale pink lace bra and matching panties firmly back into my luggage.

Out of the question, but I was too tired to argue with her. It would be easier to toss them into the back of the wardrobe when I got to the hotel.

When we finally arrived at Sharm el-Sheikh airport, I was relieved to find our luggage had got there too. I hefted my suitcase off the conveyor belt and set it down. Tilting it onto its wheels, I trailed Kat out of the terminal, only to get stopped by a security guard.

"You need to put your bags through the machine. For X-rays."

"On the way *out* of the airport?"

He shrugged. "Is the rules."

"Just do it," Kat whispered. "Logic doesn't always take precedence around here."

Eventually, we got outside, and a wall of heat hit me. Wow. Shouts came from all sides, and I kept my head down and attempted to ignore the cries of people trying to sell me everything from a minibus transfer to foam party tickets.

Then I stopped dead.

"We're riding in that?"

Kat shrugged. "Yeah."

When she'd said it would take an hour and a half to reach Fidda Hilal, she should have added a caveat: An hour and a half *if* the taxi didn't break down.

To say the vehicle had seen better days was an understatement. I looked on dubiously as the driver put our cases in the boot and tied the lid shut with string.

"Welcome to Egypt." He opened the door for us to sit in the back, giving me a toothless grin as he did so. "I hope you enjoy."

I managed a weak smile in return. What had I got myself into? The engine started on only the fourth try, and we slowly sputtered out of the car park.

"Where's the seatbelt?" I hissed at Kat.

She glanced over her shoulder, then shrugged. "Probably somebody took them out."

Great. I hung onto the edge of my seat as we joined a dual carriageway, went the wrong way around a roundabout, and finally ended up on the road out of town.

"Why does he keep tooting his horn at everybody?" I whispered. "What have they done wrong?"

"Nothing. He's saying hello—they all do it. Just don't drive with your headlights on because that's considered rude."

"But what if it's dark?"

"People are quite good at jumping out of the way. Goats too."

I groaned. This break was starting to sound like the worst decision I'd ever made. And considering I'd said "yes" to Bryce, that was a significant statement to make.

Despite having to stop at four separate police checkpoints, we made it to Fidda Hilal in an hour and a quarter, with the car *beep-beep-beeping* the entire way to tell the driver he was exceeding the speed limit. I'd be hearing that noise in my sleep. Probably the driver didn't notice, though, because he spent most of the journey on the phone.

"We are here," he announced, stomping on the brakes outside my hotel. The car backfired, and a couple of other guests standing nearby gave us dirty looks. I couldn't blame them.

Kat opened my door, and although it was dark, spotlights lit up the paved courtyard, and the place didn't look too bad. With the run of luck I'd been having, I wouldn't have been surprised to find myself on a building site.

"Are you getting out?" she asked.

"Yes." But I paused to yawn first. "I'm dog-tired."

More like dog-unconscious, actually.

I studiously looked at my feet as I wheeled my case past the other guests, heading towards the hotel reception, which was in a separate building on the far side of the courtyard. My feet sweated in my trainers as I stepped inside, and I wished I'd thought to change into a pair of flip-flops on the way.

A dark-skinned man in a white uniform rushed up to us. "I take your bags."

Kat gestured at mine. "Just that one. I'm not staying."

She only had a small backpack. I'd always envied her ability to travel light. And no matter where we went, she still managed to look more stylish than me.

Relieved of my bag, we carried on to the front desk, and once I'd given my name, the man standing behind it gave me a big grin.

"Miss Callie, we have saved one of our best rooms for you. Right next to the sea. The lady who booked it said you had been abandoned by your husband. All of us here at the Coral Cove Resort are very sorry to hear this."

Mother! I felt like banging my head on the desk. Had she told *everyone*? I'd come here to escape the pitying glances, not have people expressing their condolences wherever I went.

After entering my details into the computer, the man pressed a key into my hand and motioned for me to go with the porter, who was still standing nearby with my suitcase. Kat and I followed him out of a door at the back of the building and traipsed behind him along narrow paths that wound their way through the hotel gardens. A sweet fragrance wafted up at me from the flowers. What were those pink ones? If I took some photos, perhaps hubby number five/six would be able to tell me.

In the distance, I heard the gentle rush of the sea as waves broke on the shore. But apart from that, there was peace and quiet. The resort wasn't a traditional box-like hotel. Instead, a series of small villas dotted the grounds, all painted white, each of them only one or two storeys high.

As we got closer to my room, the sound of the waves grew louder. Monotonous yet powerful, and I found the sound soothing. A few minutes later, the porter stopped and opened up my room, which took up the whole of a single-storey villa.

"Here we have the bathroom, the TV, the closet…" The porter threw open a pair of full-height doors that led outside. "The terrace."

It was too dark to see much, but the strong smell of the sea told me just how close to the water I was. I inhaled deeply, savouring the salty tang.

"He wants a tip," Kat whispered to me.

I spun around to see the porter hovering near the door to the room. Well, suite. Mum had gone all out. I fished in my pocket, coming up with a chapstick, some fluff, and a pound coin. That would have to do until I could find a bank and get some local currency.

I pressed the money into his hand and gave him an apologetic smile. "Sorry, that's all I have at the moment."

He gave me a little half-bow. "Thank you, Miss Callie. And I am very sorry about your husband."

The receptionist had told the porter? I wanted to sink through the floor, but Kat didn't seem to notice.

"I'd better go too," she said. "When the boss heard I was coming back early, he begged me to take a course tomorrow. One of the other instructors didn't turn up for work today, and he can't afford to turn away business." She shrugged apologetically. "I could use the cash too, so I kind of said yes."

Great. My first day in a strange country, and I'd be spending it on my own. Good thing I'd brought plenty to read with me. I couldn't be upset with Kat, though. She'd been so good to me over the Bryce fiasco, and she wasn't exactly rolling in money.

"That's okay. I can sit on the beach tomorrow. Will I see you for dinner?"

"Of course. I wouldn't miss it for the world. And

we'll have to arrange a time for you to meet Mo."

Ah yes, her latest beau. She went through men at a rate of knots, and I'd been the one dishing out the tissues on a number of occasions over the years. Fortunately, she seemed to get over men as fast as she got under them, so it wasn't too much of an ordeal.

Not like Bryce and me.

We hugged each other goodbye, and Kat said she'd come to the hotel at six the next day to find me. Then she disappeared off down the path.

Once she was gone, I walked over to the terrace and stood in the open doorway, gazing into the inky blackness. Pictures of my old life with Bryce swam through my mind.

The way he always pushed his floppy fringe out of his eyes when he wanted to look at me. The soft touch of his hand on the small of my back when he'd once held the door open for me to walk into a restaurant. His habit of squinting at *The Times* on a Sunday morning when he'd forgotten to put his glasses on.

I stood there until the first tears ran down my cheeks.

"Stop it," I told myself, remembering Kat's repeated instruction.

But what I saw when I turned back to the room made me cry even harder. The king-sized bed. Two chairs at the dining table. A sofa made for snuggling up on. Through the open door of the bathroom, his 'n' hers sinks waited side by side, each with a pile of fluffy towels next to it.

I shouldn't have come to Egypt. But I was stuck there, at least for a few weeks. There was no way Mum would agree to me changing my flight home, which she'd also booked and paid for, and I couldn't afford another one myself.

I'd just have to cope. Somehow.

I threw myself onto the bed and hugged a pillow to me in the vain hope that it would help to dull the ache in my chest. It didn't. Eventually, sheer exhaustion caused me to fall into a restless sleep, but even then, there was no escape. Bryce's face haunted my dreams too.

CHAPTER 3

I WOKE THE next morning still hugging the pillow as if it were some kind of surrogate boyfriend. Was this destined to be my life?

Get out of bed, Callie.

My joints creaked as I dragged myself out of bed and into the bathroom. The headache I'd had for the last five days hadn't shifted, and my mouth tasted like the bottom of a birdcage. Or at least, what I imagined the bottom of a birdcage would taste like. I hadn't exactly checked.

I flicked on the bathroom light and groaned when I saw myself in the mirror—mascara was smeared across my face as a result of my crying jag, and my hair, normally a shiny chocolate waterfall that fell to the middle of my back, more closely resembled a bird's nest. Plus I was still wearing yesterday's clothes.

Where was my toiletry bag? I rummaged through my suitcase, and after brushing my teeth and detangling my hair, I felt a little more like a human being again.

A human being who just wanted to crawl back into bed, pull the covers up over my head, and hide from the world.

Hold on. What was stopping me? *Nothing.* Kat wasn't coming until six, so I had—I checked my watch

—nine hours in which to hibernate. That seemed like a fantastic plan for the day.

I walked back towards the bedroom, but on the way, I made the mistake of glancing out of the terrace doors. And stopped.

As if of their own accord, my feet walked me outside into the open air. The view, quite literally, took my breath away. When I remembered to inhale again, I took in a big gulp of sea air tinged with the delicious aroma of freshly brewed coffee.

Stretched out in front of me was the sparkling azure sea with small, white-crested waves twinkling in the morning sun. Across the Gulf of Aqaba, through a thin shroud of mist, I could just make out the rocky shore of what was, if my rusty memories of GCSE Geography served me correctly, Saudi Arabia.

I looked to either side. Golden sand stretched out in both directions, gently curving around a sheltered lagoon. More hotels lay along the shore, and behind them, mottled reddish mountains rose to kiss the sky. On the beach, the first windsurfers were making their way out onto the water, their colourful sails bobbing gently in the breeze.

What. A. View.

All thoughts of going back to bed flew from my mind. I wanted to be outside! The sun's warming rays were intoxicating, and I couldn't wait to bask under them.

I sifted through my clothing until I found a one-piece swimsuit that covered my worst bits, teamed it with a pink cotton cover-up, and hopped into my flip-flops. I was out of the door without even a thought for breakfast.

What bliss... I whiled away the first couple of hours just lying on a sunlounger, watching the activities out on the lagoon. As well as the windsurfers, a few swimmers stroked lazily through the water, and half a dozen people holding onto small parachutes with boards strapped to their feet skimmed along the surface. From what Kat had told me, I guessed that was kitesurfing.

Occasionally, a powerful motorboat zipped up and down, towing someone on a wakeboard or water skis. When I squinted, I could make out a dark-skinned figure at the wheel. Was that Mo?

It was only when waiters appeared carrying the first of the lunchtime meals that I realised the entire morning had passed, and I hadn't thought about Bryce once. That of course made my eyes start leaking again, and I had to shoot back to the villa. Better to run than have to explain to a group of strangers that I had grit in my eyes.

Kat phoned to check up on me at just the right moment. Or the wrong moment, depending on how one looked at it.

"Just making sure you're not in your villa blubbing."

"No, of course not. I just stepped inside for...more sunscreen."

"Sunscreen?" She paused for a second. "Are you sure?"

I tried to inject some cheer I didn't feel into my voice. "Of course I'm sure. Oh, look, here's the bottle."

"Good. Now get back outside and find a nice man to rub it in for you."

"Kat, can we take this one step at a time?"

"Why? Life's too short for sitting around and moping over an asshole. Particularly one like Bryce."

"Look, I'm on my way out to the beach again. That'll do for now, right?"

I made a big show of slamming the door and slapping my feet on the ground as I trotted down the path.

"Fine, but you'd better still be out there when I come by later."

The sun had risen higher, so I switched to a shadier spot. No point in turning into a lobster on my first day. My new sunlounger was a stone's throw from the beach bar and came with an umbrella made from palm fronds. I'd only been there five minutes when an Egyptian man dressed in the white uniform of a hotel employee came over to me.

"Can I get you something to drink, Miss?"

How sweet of him to ask. Actually, I was quite thirsty. "Do you have fruit juice?"

"Certainly. We have mango, strawberry, kiwi, guava, orange and lemon. All fresh. We also have karkade."

"What's karkade?"

"Tea made from hibiscus flowers."

Karkade sounded interesting, but I wasn't feeling particularly adventurous that day.

"Can I have orange juice, please?"

"Of course. It would be my pleasure."

I thought he'd walk away, but instead he asked, "Are you Miss Callie?"

"Uh, yes?"

"I am very sorry to hear about your husband."

I was going to shoot my mother when I got back.

"The lady who phoned," he continued, "she say you look for new husband. We have many men here in Egypt. I can introduce you to some of my friends."

No, actually, shooting was too good for her. I was going to do something slower and more painful. At that moment, I couldn't think of exactly what, but it would come to me.

"No, really..." I squinted at his name badge. "... Islam. I don't need a husband. I'm absolutely fine."

His brow crinkled. "But every woman needs a husband."

"Nope, not me. I'm quite happy on my own, honestly. I'd just love some orange juice."

He shook his head, bemused, as he wandered off to get my drink. Damn my meddling mother. Was this what the whole holiday would be like?

Yes, appeared to be the answer.

A few hours later, after I'd eaten a delicious tuna sandwich for lunch and started a new book, a shadow darkened page thirty-seven. I looked up to find a blond-haired man in the teensiest swimming trunks I'd ever seen leaning over me. Good grief—if he made any sudden moves, he'd get arrested for indecent exposure.

"You are Callie?" he asked in a thick German accent.

"Uh, yes? Do I know you?"

He held out his hand, and I shook it automatically. Yeuch—it was all greasy, and worse, he hung on to it. Fingers crossed that was sunscreen and not something worse.

"I am Hans. I was told that you are looking for a man to talk to."

I tried not to groan as I tugged my hand free. "Who

told you that? The man at the beach bar?"

"No, the boy who cleaned my room this morning. The man at the beach bar just pointed out where you were."

The cleaner? Had they *all* been discussing me? What had my mother done?

And more to the point, how could I get rid of Hans without appearing rude? I racked my brain, but inspiration was taking a nap. Talking... He'd said it was just talking, right? Okay, I could do this.

I took a deep breath. "Right, er, Hans. Uh, have you visited Egypt before?"

"No."

"Are you enjoying it so far?"

"Not very much. It is too hot."

Hmm... I might not have known a lot about Egypt, but one thing that had immediately sprung to mind when Kat first mentioned it was that the whole country was flipping hot. It was famous for it. If Hans didn't like sunshine, why had he booked a holiday there?

"Oh dear. I guess that's a bit of a shame. Apart from it being too warm, what do you think of the place?"

"The food is terrible here in the hotel."

I'd only had one meal there, but it had seemed perfectly nice to me. "What's wrong with it?"

"This morning, at the breakfast buffet, there was no watermelon."

"No watermelon? Is that it?"

"That isn't bad enough?"

"I suppose if you really like watermelon then not having any might be a problem." Although there *were* a hundred other dishes to choose from. "How about the rest of the hotel? It's nice, huh?"

"It's okay," he admitted grudgingly. "Except the staff aren't very friendly."

"In what way?"

"When I had a cocktail last night, the barman forgot to put the little umbrella in it. And when I pointed out his mistake, he only apologised halfheartedly."

This guy obviously had more issues than Vogue. "Sounds shocking."

"I know! And this morning, when I got up at six to reserve my sunlounger, the towel boy was not yet awake. Laziness, that's what it is."

"That's awful!"

He didn't pick up on my sarcasm. *Please, just go away.*

"And there is nothing to do here. No museums, no concerts, no art galleries."

No, nothing to do whatsoever. All those people out on the lagoon were clearly not enjoying themselves.

"Sounds dull."

"And no theatre. Imagine not having a theatre."

At the mention of theatre, I thought of Bryce again. My heart plummeted. Without him, was this the sort of man I was destined to end up with?

Hans looked at his watch. "So, do you want to get dinner? I can spare exactly two hours."

Not even if he was the last man on earth and my sacrifice was mankind's only hope at salvation.

"I'm so sorry, but I can't. I'm meeting a friend in a little while."

He huffed, already turning away. "Suit yourself."

No doubt tomorrow he'd be telling some other poor lady about the ungrateful English woman and her flimsy excuses.

With the sun dropping, I gathered up my things and headed back to the villa. I had enough time for a shower before Kat was due to get there. She was fifteen minutes late, and when she arrived, she apologised for running on Egyptian time.

"Nobody around here ever does anything when they're supposed to. You're lucky if it gets done on the same day. I think it's part of the reason everybody's so laid back. Lateness is just accepted."

Bryce had been a stickler for timekeeping. His foot had started tapping if someone was so much as a second late. He insisted on being early for everything, sometimes ridiculously so. One particularly cringeworthy moment had come when we'd been invited for dinner at the home of a colleague. Bryce had got us there an hour early. *A whole freaking hour.* Alison had opened the door after he'd hammered on it for the third time, red in the face and flustered with her shirt buttons done up wrong. Her boyfriend was beside her, and he looked as if he wanted to take a swing at Bryce and possibly me as well. I hadn't been able to face Alison for weeks afterwards.

Egyptian time would suit me just fine.

"What are you thinking about?" Kat asked.

I told her, and she gave me a happy grin.

"Well, that's great! At least if you're feeling pissed at Bryce, you're not moping about him."

The aching pit in my chest told me otherwise. "I'll admit he wasn't perfect, but I still miss him so much."

"Then I'll have to distract you. Come on, find your party clothes. We're going out."

"Out where?" I asked suspiciously.

"Oh, only to a restaurant. I thought we'd go to The

Oasis. The food's great there." She adjusted the strap on her floaty red dress before adding quietly, "And maybe a bar afterwards."

Quiet or not, her suggestion didn't escape my attention. "No, no bar. Just dinner."

She smiled a little too sweetly. "Whatever you say."

We caught a taxi into the main part of town, which was a five-minute car ride away. The Oasis was beside the sea, with the front of the seating area overhanging the water itself. Due to the climate, the place didn't have a proper roof, just a series of umbrellas interspersed with the occasional palm tree, and the stars glittered overhead.

The maître d' greeted Kat by name and led us to a table where four comfortable looking seats adorned with colourful cushions awaited us.

Four seats.

"Kat, why is this table set up for four people?"

"Oh," she said, acting all innocent. "Mo's going to join us. Did I forget to mention it?"

She knew full well that she had. "That's three. And the fourth chair?"

"He might be bringing a friend."

"Kat! Why won't you and Mum stop meddling? I can't simply forget Bryce, you know. I'm not even sure I want to. I was in love with him for six years, and I can't simply turn that off."

"I'm sorry." She was contrite for about two seconds, and then she just couldn't help herself. "But he didn't deserve you. You can do so much better than him."

"Kat!"

She was already turning away from me. "Oh, look, here they are."

Two men walked through the doorway. While the one in front wasn't what I'd call classically good-looking, he was attractive in a swarthy sort of way. Was this my "date?"

He smiled, and it was clear that his happiness was genuine. I couldn't help grinning back. Then he walked right past me and gave Kat a sweet kiss on the cheek. She actually blushed, something I'd never seen her do before.

That must be Mo, then.

Which left me with his shorter friend. Five feet four at a guess, both high and wide. He stopped almost on my toes and looked up at me, then stuck out his hand and accidentally jabbed me in the ribs.

"I'm Eid."

"Oh, er, pleased to meet you, Eid. I'm Callie."

"I drive the banana."

Good thing I wasn't drinking anything fizzy. I turned my snort into a cough. "I'm sorry?"

"The banana."

Mo cut in. "He means he drives the boat that pulls the inflatable banana around the bay. The one people ride on."

"This is Mohammed. Mo." Kat got formalities out of the way. "Mo, this is Callie."

Mo leaned forward and gave me a kiss on the cheek too, European style. I knew at that moment why Kat blushed because he had that effect on me as well.

Eid then decided that he should do the same. He turned his head one way, I turned mine the same direction, and he got me on the lips by mistake. We both leapt back, him with a happy grin on his face and me wondering if I had any hand sanitiser in my bag so I could rub it all over my face.

Mo wiped a hand down his face. "Shall we sit?"

He pulled out Kat's chair before taking his own seat next to her. On the other side of the table, Eid leapt for the chair nearest the sea and plonked himself down on it. I shrugged and took the other one, surreptitiously inching it away from him as far as I dared.

Before we even got the menus open, Eid said, "I hear you're looking for a husband."

"Not exactly."

"But your boyfriend left you just before your wedding, no?"

"Well, yes. But I'm not in a hurry to get married."

A brief look of disappointment flitted across his face. "Maybe the right man can change your mind?"

"Well, I guess."

Eid grinned like the Cheshire Cat.

Over dinner, he didn't stop talking. Not once, even for a second. The rest of us ate our food, but Eid's remained almost untouched as he educated us on delights such as the history of Fidda Hilal, Egyptian traditions, and his favourite subject: himself.

"See, I could easily have got married already, but I thought it was important to finish my education first. I have a degree in communications, you know. From Cairo university. So anyway, now my mother is nagging me every day to find myself a wife. She wants grandchildren. Do you want kids, Callie?"

"I haven't really thought about it," I managed to get out.

Except I had, incessantly. Bryce and I would have had a boy and a girl. The boy first so he could do the "big brother" bit at school. I'd pictured them over and over in my daydreams, in between doodling my wedding dress and practising signing my name as "Callie Featherstone." Or sometimes "Callista Featherstone" because Bryce preferred the longer version.

Eid patted my hand, leaving his resting on top. "Don't worry, I'm sure there will still be time for you to pop a few out before your biological clock stops ticking."

"Excuse me, I just need to visit the ladies room."

I had to stop myself from sprinting across the restaurant.

In the restroom, I locked myself in a cubicle and sat down on the closed toilet, my head in my hands. What had I done to deserve this? Was losing Bryce not enough? Why did the universe have to carry on punishing me?

After a minute or two, I heard the door click.

"Callie?"

"I'm not speaking to you."

"I'm so, so sorry. Eid's our boss's son. Mo asked one of the other guys to come tonight, but he couldn't make it. Eid overheard the conversation and invited himself along instead."

"Why can't you just stop meddling? You and Mum are as bad as each other. Did you know she's asked the hotel to set me up with a man? I had to endure a serial complainer called Hans this afternoon, talking at me while I was trying to relax."

"I'm sorry. If that's what you want, then I promise I'll stop. I only want you to be happy the way I am with Mo."

I'd seen the glances they'd been giving each other

all evening, filled with love and longing. Kat had dated many men before, and over the years, I'd had to pick up the pieces after a waiter from Vietnam, a hairdresser from Thailand, and an Australian surfer among others. But Mo seemed different. Like his world revolved around my best friend.

Like he was everything Bryce wasn't.

I choked back tears, but Kat misinterpreted my strangled sobs.

"Don't worry, Eid's gone home. I told him you had a funny tummy."

"Great, so now he thinks I'm stuck on the toilet with the runs? What an impression I must have made."

"He was too busy bragging about the size of his wallet to pay much attention."

"Comforting."

"Look, I said I'm sorry. No more men. How about tomorrow we do girls' night?"

"Do you promise?"

"Cross my heart."

CHAPTER 4

THE NEXT MORNING, I decided to avoid the beach and lie by the pool instead. It nestled in amongst the villas in the middle of the hotel grounds, and my hope was that by hiding there, I'd be able to avoid Hans and Eid. Why did the watersports club have to be so near to the hotel? I'd be running from Eid for my entire holiday now.

I'd barely sat down when I was interrupted once again. What was that accent? Polish? Russian?

"Callie?"

"Yes?"

A portly man with thinning hair loomed over me. What now?

"I hear you are looking for a man to show you a good time?"

"I beg your pardon?"

"You know, a bit of bedroom fun? How do you say, rumpy pumpy?"

"I understand what you mean, but who on earth told you I wanted that? Was it the waiter at the beach bar?"

"No, the bartender. He said to check on the sunloungers for the pretty lady with big, uh, how you say...?"

He mimed a huge pair of knockers, and I glanced

down. Surely he was exaggerating? Mine were only D-cups.

"I'm terribly sorry, but I'm just not that kind of woman."

Hang on… Why was *I* apologising to *him*?

"So I am wasting my time?"

"I'm afraid so, yes."

He gave me a disgusted look and stalked off, muttering, "Tease-prick."

I opened my mouth and shouted, "You mean prick-tease, you idiot."

Oh. My. Goodness. Had I really said that out loud? Judging by the stares I was getting, half incredulous, half amused, I very much suspected I must have. I wanted to crawl under my sunlounger and die.

What could I do but gather up my things and flee back to the villa? Maybe I could just spend the rest of my break on the terrace. Yes, that seemed to be the best idea.

Except when I got there, I found the door open and a young Egyptian man in there, cleaning.

"You come back later," he told me, then grinned happily and closed the door in my face.

Gah. Beach it was, then.

On the beach, I picked a sunlounger as far away from the bar as possible and spread out my towel. The light breeze was enough to leave me feeling refreshed without being unpleasant. The windsurfers on the lagoon certainly seemed to be enjoying themselves too. I watched them for a few minutes before I picked up my book. Would this be my lucky day?

No. No, it wouldn't. I'd only managed to get halfway through the tense thriller when the sun disappeared, and I glanced up to find a man standing in front of me, holding a piece of paper.

"Callie Shawcross?" he asked. His accent was British, but from somewhere up north. Manchester, perhaps?

Oh no. Not again. "Who sent you? The waiter? The bartender?"

He looked a little sheepish. "Actually it was the security guard at the gate." He waved the piece of paper. "He issued me with a copy of your passport photo."

I thunked my head back onto the towel.

He gave a nervous laugh. "It took me a while to find you, I must admit. This photo doesn't look very much like you."

No, it didn't. It had been taken after a particularly nasty bout of food poisoning, which had left me as basically a corpse with mascara. And now half of the male guests in the hotel had probably seen it.

What were the other hotels in the town like? I wasn't bothered about the facilities—anywhere without a population of horny males would be fine. As long as it didn't have cockroaches. Cockroaches were also a no.

"Callie? You seem worried." The guy held up his hands. "Promise I won't bite. I was just going to ask if you fancied joining me for lunch. I'm here on my own too."

I didn't answer.

"You know what? I can see you weren't expecting this. I'll just...leave."

He took a step back. And behind him, I saw Eid approaching.

"Actually, you know what? I'd love to join you for lunch. How about we try the Italian place in the main building?"

I threw my stuff into my beach bag. Sunscreen, book, sunglasses, ashtray... No, wait, that wasn't mine.

"Really? Okay, great. That'd be great."

We walked along the winding path, leaving the beach and—more importantly, Eid—behind. Decorative turquoise pools bordered the way on either side, glimmering in the sun. Mum really had found a lovely hotel, even if some of its inhabitants left a bit to be desired. We turned a corner, and as a building loomed alongside us, I got a good look at the man walking beside me without having to squint into the sun.

I saw now that he was the same height as me—five feet eight—and that was good. Bryce had been a little shorter, and he'd always complained when I wore heels. Brown hair, a day's worth of stubble... My new friend's eyes were brown too, and they had a kindness about them. Maybe this wouldn't be as bad as I feared?

He held the door open when we got to the restaurant. One point in his favour. Not that I was keeping score or anything, but politeness never hurt. Then he pulled out a chair for me to sit down and earned another point.

The waiter came by and draped a napkin over my lap, then handed me a menu. "Can I get you a drink, ma'am?"

"Oh, yes, please. White wine would be lovely."

The waiter gave me a blank look.

"It's a dry country," my dining companion reminded me. "Well, mostly. Only the bar serves alcohol, or you can buy it at a couple of places in town."

Of course. No wine. And probably the man sitting opposite me thought I was a lush with the haste that I'd ordered it. Brilliant.

"Could I just get sparkling water?"

"Yes, Miss Callie."

"I'll have the same," the man said.

The waiter hurried off.

"You know my name. And also my date and place of birth too, but I know nothing about you," I prompted.

"How terribly rude of me. I do apologise. My name's Peter, and I'm twenty-seven and a Capricorn. My stars said I'd meet a beautiful lady this month."

He held out his hand. I moved to shake it, but when he took mine, he kissed it instead. What a gentleman!

Our drinks arrived quickly, as did several more waiters. Were they expecting an influx of guests? Peter ordered a salad, and so did I. After the wine comment, I figured pretending to be healthy wouldn't be a bad idea.

"It's nice to meet you, Peter." I surprised myself by meaning it.

"So, what brings you to Egypt?"

I recalled the lecture on dating that Kat had attempted to give me on the plane. Rule number one: avoid discussing past relationships.

"Oh, I just came to visit a friend. She's living over here at the moment. How about you?"

"I like to meditate. Sometimes I go for long walks in

the desert. It cleanses my mind."

Mind cleansing sounded nice. Could that work for me? Goodness knows, my mind was filthy. No, not in that way! I meant my head was stuffed full of baggage from Bryce.

"Do you find it makes a big difference?"

"Yes, definitely. I go home refreshed and ready to dive into work again."

Our salads arrived. Gosh, that was quick. Maybe they had as many chefs as they did waiters? It took four of them to bring our food—one with each plate, one to carry the cutlery and another with condiments. When they'd put everything down, they retreated to the edges of the room and hovered.

Now I knew how a zoo animal must feel.

"So, Peter, what do you do for a living?" I asked brightly as the chef joined the line-up.

"I'm a taxidermist."

A what? I coughed in surprise. Or perhaps shock.

"Sorry, something went down the wrong way." I took a hasty glug of water and desperately tried to arrange my face into an expression of mild interest. "A taxidermist?"

"I prepare stuffed animals."

I was well aware of what a taxidermist did. My question was actually more *why*?

"Uh, sounds fascinating."

"Oh, it is. It's more of a calling than a job, really. There's something about preserving an animal's beauty for immortality that speaks to my soul."

When he put it that way, it sounded almost normal. "So you...preserve people's pets? Like dogs and cats?"

"Sometimes, but taxidermy has gone out of fashion

in recent years. It breaks my heart. So I have to find other avenues to express myself through my art. If I go out for a drive at dusk, I can usually find some great specimens. Fresh."

Roadkill? He spent his life stuffing roadkill? I started to eat my salad faster.

"What do you do, Callie?"

"I'm a schoolteacher. For the reception class. Four-to five-year-olds." I shovelled another forkful in.

"Really? Sounds great."

He had a gleam in his eye. Probably he was imagining what my kids would look like stuffed, sorry, "preserved" and arranged in a cabinet.

"Yes, it's really satisfying, seeing their progress through the year."

"And how about in your spare time? What do you do for leisure?"

Good question. What did I do? I racked my brains. Mostly I'd trailed around after Bryce, doing whatever he wanted to do. But I wasn't supposed to mention him.

"I like to read, and I go to a weekly yoga class."

"That's it?"

"I took a watercolour painting class last year."

He seemed disappointed. "The painting sounds all right. I mean, at least it's creative."

"Yeah, it's fun. I've got my own paints and everything."

I took my last bite of salad. Peter had already finished his, and immediately seven waiters dived on us and cleared the plates away.

"Are you having dessert?" I asked.

I wasn't looking forward to hearing more about his

job-slash-calling, but it would be rude to bolt off if he wanted another course.

He glanced at his watch. "Actually I've got a telephone appointment with my astrologer in half an hour. I'll have to dash."

Wait a minute, I was being abandoned by a guy who had a fetish for dead things? Was my company really that bad?

"How about tomorrow? We could meet up then?" I asked, desperation creeping into my voice. I didn't really want to see him again, but it was more a point of principle.

He got kind of twitchy. "Look, Callie—I'll be honest with you. I'm sure you're a lovely girl, but I'm hoping to find someone, well, a little more adventurous."

So that was a "yes." My company officially sucked. Peter signed the receipt, and I was left alone at the table. Well, as alone as I could be with nine waiters watching.

My shame knew no bounds.

What a difference a few hours could make. Come evening, I sat on a cushion while Kat and two of her girlfriends howled with laughter as I recounted my tales of the Russian freak and Peter the taxidermist. We were all in my villa, taking advantage of the hotel's room service.

"Maybe he should stuff himself a girlfriend?"

suggested Simone, who worked as a waitress at one of the beachfront restaurants in town. "That way, he could be as adventurous as he liked."

"Eew, now you've put that vision in my mind, I can't un-see it," squealed Elaine, who worked at the local riding stables in the day and as a masseuse in the evenings.

"It doesn't matter. I'm off men for good. Wine is officially my new best friend." I held up one of the bottles that Kat had sourced from somewhere. "Anyone want a top-up?"

"I'll have one," Elaine said, holding out her empty glass. "And I'm with you on the man thing."

"Did you have another bad experience with one of your clients?" Kat asked.

She nodded and grimaced. "Yup. Tonight's was an Egyptian guy. He kept insisting he wanted a happy ending, and when I told him it wasn't that kind of massage, he grabbed my hand and tried to make me touch it."

"You didn't, did you?" Simone asked.

"What, touch his dick? It was so small I could barely see it."

"Did you tell the hotel?"

"Yes, and they called security, but he insisted it was all just a misunderstanding. Of course they believed him."

Poor Elaine. Seemed as if Bryce wasn't the only man to treat women like dirt.

"That's gross," I said. "Can't you specify female clients only?"

"I wish I could, but there aren't enough tourists around at the moment. I have to take what I can get."

She swallowed a mouthful of her wine. "But we're not here to talk about me tonight. We're supposed to be getting you drunk. So you forget Bryce-the-bastard."

"Kat's filled you in, then?"

"She might have given us an outline of the basics."

Was there anyone in Fidda Hilal who didn't know the sorry state of my love life? Probably not, if the guilty look on Kat's face was anything to go by.

Simone tried to help out by changing the subject. "So, girls' night. Let's do something fun. Do you have a movie channel here?

"I think so, but it's in Arabic. The only two English channels are CNN and BBC World. So unless you want to watch over-dramatised news or a documentary about child labour in the Far East, we're out of luck." I had a thought and turned to Kat. "How do you feed your movie obsession?"

Ever since we were kids, Kat had harboured a fascination for all things Hollywood. She knew who was hot, who was not, and could name the upcoming premieres for each month in chronological order.

"Netflix and celebgossip.com, mainly. If I didn't have those, I wouldn't be here. Mo would have to find himself a new girlfriend, and I'd go and live someplace where I could get my daily fix of Scott Lowes and Zac Kennedy."

"Is there a good internet connection here, then?" I was a little surprised considering the town was ages from anywhere, surrounded by miles and miles of the golden mountains that formed the backdrop to the resort.

"Wi-fi's actually pretty good. It has to be, seeing as the internet's the main connection to the outside world.

Without that, we'd be incredibly isolated."

"That's a relief."

At least I could check my emails when I felt brave enough. I'd been putting it off in case there was one from Bryce. Or in case there wasn't. I wasn't sure which would be worse.

"Have you got your laptop handy?" Kat asked. "We could pick out a film."

I dragged the bag from the bottom of the wardrobe and fired up my laptop, studiously ignoring the email icon that was taunting me. Kat logged into her Netflix account.

"Any requests?"

I shook my head. It had been ages since I'd seen a movie. Even then, I just used to watch what Bryce chose, which was usually either something obscure with subtitles or a movie with a plot so convoluted that only the person who wrote it understood what was going on.

"How about we watch something with Scott in it? *Forever Black*? *Out of the Blue*?"

Kat's crush on the Hollywood actor she referred to as "Scott," as if she knew him personally had been rolling on for years, ever since he rose to fame playing Jed Harker in *Forever Black*. I'd never seen either of those movies, but I felt as if I had due to the extraordinary amount of detail she always recounted them in.

Simone stretched out on the bed and groaned. "No way. You've made us watch them all ten times each. How about the latest *Mission: Impossible* film?"

"Seen it," chorused Kat and Linda.

"Or that romcom that just came out? The one with

Velvet Jones."

"No way. She's such a bitch," Kat said.

"Are you basing that assessment on anything other than the fact that she's rumoured to be dating Scott?" Simone asked, rolling her eyes.

"It's more than a rumour. She confirmed it in an interview last week."

I put my hands in the air. "Guys, guys, stop arguing. Can we please avoid anything with romance? And any actors that might remind me of Bryce? Also anything gory, since we've just eaten."

"That doesn't leave a lot," Kat said, flicking through the menu.

"There must be something."

In the end, we settled on *Despicable Me*. The minions were adorable, and we all loved a happy ending of the right kind.

Me especially, even if I was never destined to have one myself.

CHAPTER 5

I WAS NODDING off on my sunlounger when I heard footsteps approaching from behind. Noooooo! *Please don't let this be another weirdo with a freaky fetish.*

I was feigning sleep when Kat shook my shoulder and screeched in my ear.

"Wake up!"

"Ouch."

"Sorry. Are you awake now?"

I glared at her. "What do you think?"

"Oh, good. Mo's had a cancellation, so we thought you might like to have a go at wakeboarding."

"I'm good right here. I think lying down's more my thing."

Kat put her hands on her hips. "Perhaps I should have made things clearer. It isn't optional. You came to Egypt to have a good time, and wakeboarding's the best fun you can have on the water."

"I think sunbathing on a yacht would be more enjoyable."

"Well, we don't have a yacht, so this is gonna have to do." She grabbed my arm and tried to pull me up.

A groan escaped my lips. I'd been watching people being towed around the lagoon, and the whole process looked a bit scary. One poor man had attempted a backflip and landed head first. I wasn't even athletic. At school, I'd barely managed a forward roll in gym class without embarrassing myself.

I tried again to get out of it. "What about Eid? Won't he be there? I don't fancy another interrogation."

"He's gone to Sharm el-Sheikh to buy accessories for his iPad. He only left half an hour ago so he won't be back for ages."

With no excuses left, I let Kat tug me to my feet and shuffled along behind her in the direction of the watersports centre. Deep down, I still wasn't sure about this, but I also knew Kat was right. I should try new things. Peter's comment about me being boring replayed as well. I'd show him.

Which was why, twenty minutes later, I had my feet stuffed into a pair of funky trainers that were attached to a worryingly small plank.

"Don't be nervous," Mo said, giving me a reassuring smile.

"I can't help it. I've never done anything like this before." Unless you counted trying to ride on our next-door neighbour's skateboard when I was seven, which had resulted in two scraped knees and mum having to pick grit out of my hands with a pair of tweezers.

"You'll be fine, I promise. We won't try anything fancy today. The worst thing that can happen is that you'll fall into the water."

Or drown. He forgot to mention drowning.

"Hold onto my hand," he said, and I squeezed it so tightly that he winced.

Pivoting the board on the edge of the platform at the back of the boat, he lowered me slowly into the water. It may have been thirty degrees on the beach, but the water was freezing as it seeped under my buoyancy vest. I couldn't help squealing as my body sank under the surface.

"Are you okay?" Mo asked, concern radiating from his eyes.

I tried to stop my teeth from chattering. "N-n-never better."

Kat leaned over and took a picture of me with her phone. "That'll be a good one for Facebook."

"Don't you dare! You know I don't do social media."

She pouted at me. "Come on, loosen up."

"Hey, at least I'm having a go at this."

Before we could start bickering, Mo turned around from his seat in front of the wheel. "Okay, you remember what I taught you? Stay in a crouching position until the momentum of the boat pulls you upright."

I nodded. That was what I planned to do.

Only it didn't quite work out that way. The instant the boat pulled away, I got pulled over forwards, let go of the rope and did a face plant. I came to the surface spluttering as Mo drew the boat up alongside me.

"Just relax more on the next try. I can see the stress in your shoulders."

No kidding. I had more tension than a tightrope.

He passed the handle back to me and we tried again. This time, I tipped over sideways but swallowed marginally less water. That was an improvement, right? At least Mo was kind enough not to laugh, unlike Kat. I could see her snapping away on her phone while she giggled. Tell me again, why did I agree to this? If I survived, I'd be revoking our friendship as soon as I set foot back on the beach.

"Try keeping your knees bent for longer," Mo

suggested. "That way you won't be so unbalanced."

Well, that time I didn't tip over forwards. I did, however, give myself a saltwater enema and came fairly close to drowning before I accepted defeat and let go.

Mo stopped beside me again. I must have been frustrating him to no end, but he was still smiling.

"I know you're tired, but we'll have one more go today—this time point your toes more."

I tried that, not expecting much, but suddenly I ended up on my feet, being pulled along by the boat at what felt like a hundred miles an hour. I managed a good twenty yards before a wave unbalanced me and the board shot out to the side.

Still, I'd done it! I couldn't help grinning as Mo helped me back on board. I was knackered and dripping wet, but for those few seconds... What a rush!

"That was good," he said, smiling his shy smile and handing me a towel. "Soon you will be a pro."

That was a little generous of him, but I appreciated the sentiment.

"I got it all on film," Kat announced.

"I don't suppose I could convince you to erase everything but the last ten seconds?"

"No chance! When you're old and grey, you'll look back fondly on these moments."

Ah yes, the day I inhaled the Red Sea. What a great memory to treasure.

When the boat returned to shore, Kat scurried off to assist a customer while Mo helped me onto the jetty. It was a relief to be on dry land again.

"Thanks for taking me out," I said.

"You're welcome. You did well for a first lesson."

"I'm not sure about that. I think I'd prefer to be

where Kat was sitting—that way, I could just admire the scenery without swallowing salty water."

My throat still stung from it, and I made a face.

"Would you like a drink to take the taste away? We have mint tea and karkade."

"Yes, please. Mint tea would be lovely."

Mo made my drink, pouring out a third mug for Kat as well. Hers was the one with three sugars. She always said she could never be sweet enough.

"Have you always lived in Fidda Hilal?" I asked.

"No, I come from Cairo. I moved here six years ago."

"I can see why—it's beautiful." Sun, sea, a few palm trees—what could be prettier?

"It's not just the scenery. Life is slower, more relaxed. In Cairo, it's always so busy."

He handed me my tea and I blew the steam away, savouring the refreshing aroma.

"Will you ever move back there, do you think?"

His shy smile reappeared. "Not as long as Kat is here. I'll live wherever she lives."

Aw, he was as smitten with her as she was with him. I was so glad they'd found each other.

When Kat and Mo returned to work, I headed to my terrace. I'd cricked my neck in one of my tumbles, and when I worked it back and forth, pain shot up one side. Despite my moment of triumph at the end, I wasn't sure I was cut out for wakeboarding. Maybe I could try a different kind of activity? Something a little less strenuous, like working my way through the alcohol-free cocktail menu? I picked up the room-service booklet. No time like the present, eh? Ooh, was that chocolate gateau?

Perhaps this day wouldn't be so bad after all...

CHAPTER 6

THE NEXT MORNING, I braved the beach again, this time wearing sunglasses and a big floppy sun hat I'd borrowed from Kat. Which sunlounger seemed the safest? In the end, I picked one close to the water that gave me a good view of anybody approaching, meaning I could dash into the sea at a moment's notice to escape.

At least that was the theory. It went to pot when I fell asleep.

"Excuse me, Miss?"

This time, the voice that interrupted me was French, and I'm afraid to say I snapped. Why couldn't everyone just leave me alone? This was meant to be a holiday. A break. I wasn't paying good money to get bothered every five bloody minutes.

"Yes, I'm Callie. Yes, my fiancé left me three days before our wedding. No, I'm not looking for a new husband and, no, I don't want to go to lunch with you. Or dinner."

The man started to back away, hands raised as though they'd protect him from the obviously crazy woman sitting in front of him.

"I'm sorry to have disturbed you. I was only going to ask whether you'd be interested in making an introductory scuba dive. We're offering them free today."

I put my head in my hands. Once again, I'd made a complete fool of myself. The story of my life.

"No, *I'm* sorry. I shouldn't have yelled at you. It's just, well, my mother seems to have been encouraging the hotel staff to play matchmaker, and I can't get any peace."

He gave me a wry grin. "Yes, now I recall. I did get the memo. I didn't recognise you under the hat and glasses, though."

Oh heck, there was an actual memo? Next thing I knew, my face was going to be plastered around town on lamp posts, like some bizarre take on a missing cat poster. I had visions of boys handing my flyer out on the street, nightclub-style.

The man must have seen the horror on my face because he tried to reassure me.

"I swear that's not why I'm here. Between you and me, you're not my type."

A couple of tears leaked out—I couldn't help it—and the man took a rapid step backwards.

"No, no, it's not you," I told him, trying to suppress a sniffle. "I just can't seem to attract the right sort of men. Yesterday, a man who stuffs animals for a living told me I was boring. What else is wrong? Am I too tall? Too fat? Is my hair the wrong colour? Come on, you can tell me. Please?"

He offered a look of sympathy and crouched down beside the sunlounger. "If you must know, it's none of that. For me, you're too female."

Oh. "Oh."

"You might want to ease up on the attitude a bit, but I can assure you, you're not lacking in the looks department. I may not be attracted to women, but I can still appreciate beauty when I see it."

That was the sweetest thing anybody had said to me in a long time. Why did all the good ones have to be gay?

"So you don't think I should cut my hair?" I asked, just to clarify.

"It's perfect as it is. Most women would kill to have hair that thick and shiny." He blushed a little. "I dated a hairdresser once."

I sighed. "So it must just be my personality. Peter said I should be more adventurous."

"Peter?"

"The taxidermist."

"Right." His lips twitched at the corners. "The taxidermist. In that case, why don't you come with me and have a try at diving? That'd be an adventure. There's a whole other world down there, just waiting for you to discover it. And now that I recognise you, I also know your mother paid for the deluxe activities package."

Even though I hadn't enjoyed my wakeboarding lesson, I'd felt a sense of accomplishment when I stood up at the end. Maybe diving would give me the same buzz but without the choking?

"You know what? I think I will. This is going to be the new me. I'm going to try as many different things as I can on this trip."

"That's the spirit." He reached a hand down to help me up. "You never know, you might fall in love with one of them."

"I should think that's highly unlikely."

But as my mother always said, I wouldn't know

unless I gave it a go.

"I'm Gabriel by the way. Gabe."

"Gabe. What part of France are you from?"

"I'm from Switzerland. They speak a mixture of French, English and German there, and my mother was French, hence the accent."

"Your English is excellent."

"I went to boarding school in England for a few years. The first thing I learned was all the bad words, and then I worked on improving the rest."

"So why did you come to Fidda Hilal? Why not go back to Switzerland?"

"Switzerland is known for its snow, cuckoo clocks, and diplomacy," Gabe told me. "I rebelled as a teenager, and what better way to do it than to come to a region where it rarely rains, there's no concept of timekeeping, and the main export is dictators?"

I couldn't argue with that. If you were going to rebel, you might as well do it in style. I only wished I had the guts.

Diving wasn't quite as straightforward as I'd thought. Instead of heading for the water as I'd expected, I found myself in a classroom, watching as my would-be instructor inserted an old-fashioned VHS tape into an ancient video player.

"We need to go through the basics so you stay safe in the water," Gabe explained. "This stuff might be boring, but it's necessary."

"Safety is my middle name."

Half an hour later, and I was trying to squeeze myself into a wetsuit. Trying and failing. I nearly overbalanced as I hopped around.

"I don't think this one's the right size."

"It's supposed to be tight. Wetsuits work by trapping a thin layer of water next to your skin. If it's loose, the water washes around and you get cold."

"It'll be even colder if I can't get it on."

"Here, I'll give you a hand."

Between the two of us, we managed to get me into the wetsuit. That felt like an achievement in itself. Where was my trophy? But the suit was absolutely skintight, and I peered down in horror at my bulges. Everything showed.

"I can't go out like this."

"Nonsense. You're perfect. And remember, most people here will be either wearing a wetsuit or a swimsuit. You'd look more out of place in a kaftan."

I took a deep breath and remembered my pledge to be more adventurous. *I can do this.*

"So what's next?"

"You learned from the film that scuba stands for Self-Contained Underwater Breathing Apparatus. So we need to get you a BCD and regulator, plus boots, fins, and a mask."

I stood, feeling like an idiot as Gabe first shoved my feet into a pair of neoprene boots, and then screwed together the parts that would help me breathe. He put the waistcoat thingy with an air tank strapped to it, the BCD, onto a bench and motioned for me to sit in front of it.

"Just lean forward and put your arms through the holes. That's it." He fastened me in and smiled. "All done. You can stand up now."

Alrighty then. I tried to stand up. "I can't."

"Why not?"

"Do you have any idea how much this stuff

weighs?"

"Twenty kilos, give or take. We've still got to put the weight belt on you."

"There's more?"

By the time he'd helped me to my feet and strapped seven kilos of lead around my waist, I was stuck to the spot. If I leaned one way or the other, I was going to overbalance and fall over.

"Don't worry, you'll get used to it," he said cheerfully.

"Is it too late to back out? I could go snorkelling instead. That doesn't involve turning yourself into a pack pony, right?"

"No, but it's too late to change your mind now. You've got all the kit on. Tough luck."

I sighed. Or at least I tried to. I was struggling to breathe in the wetsuit. "In that case, is there a trolley or something that you can wheel me to the sea on? How about one of those things that they use for the suitcases?"

"You can walk, trust me. I'll help you."

He put his kit on effortlessly in thirty seconds flat, lifting his contraption onto his back as if it weighed the same as a bag of crisps. Then he beckoned me to follow him. I shuffled over.

"Do we need to put the flippers on?" I pointed at the two pairs he was carrying.

"Fins. We don't call them flippers. Flipper is a dolphin. And no, we'll do that once we're in the water."

He made it sound so easy. I wasn't sure I'd even make it to the water. It seemed an awfully long way. We set off, trudging slowly.

"So, judging from the way you bit my head off this

morning, I take it you've had a few man-related disasters?" Gabe asked.

"Three so far at the hotel, plus one that my so-called best friend arranged for me."

"Which has been the worst?"

"They were all so different. The German was bitter, the Egyptian was weird, the Russian was rude, and the English guy just left me feeling depressed."

"And the Swiss guy? How are you finding him so far?"

I gave Gabe a thumbs up. "Better."

And then we were at the water. How on earth did we get there? "You tried to distract me."

Gabe glanced over his shoulder as he waded into the sea. "It worked, didn't it?"

I stumbled in after him, and he put his breathing thing, the regulator, into his mouth for a moment, then dipped under the water to slide my feet into the fins.

"Now, put the regulator in and just breathe normally. I'll do everything else. You remember what I said earlier about clearing your ears?"

Equalising, he'd called it. As I descended in the water, I had to hold my nose and breathe out until my ears popped, otherwise the pressure would damage them.

I nodded. "Got it."

He spat into my mask, then rinsed it in the sea.

"Eew, what was that for?"

"It stops the mask from fogging up. Don't worry, I haven't got cooties."

I suppose he had at least rinsed it. He slipped it over my head and gave me the "OK" sign, forming an "O" with his thumb and forefinger. I repeated it back to him.

He put his own regulator in again, then used a button to deflate my jacket, and slowly, slowly, we sank beneath the surface.

The water was cold on my face, and my fears about not being able to breathe proved unfounded. It was just like breathing above the surface, except noisier as the air bubbles gurgled around my head.

And it was magical. Just feet from my head, a school of silvery fish darted back and forth, responding to our movements. A long, thin fish swam among them. As I watched, it changed colour, going from stripy grey to pearly white.

The sun shimmered down on the water, and shadows and patterns danced on the sandy slope that led out to the blue. Yellow, black, and white fish swam past regally, daring me to follow.

As we went deeper, Gabe supported me, changing the amount of air in my jacket to ensure I floated beside him. I wanted to smile, to let him know how much I was enjoying myself, but the regulator in my mouth made it impossible. I tried to tell him with my eyes instead.

Did he get it? I think he got it. At least, he took his regulator out and grinned at me. Show off. *I* wouldn't be attempting that trick.

The bottom changed from sand to coral: blues, yellows, and pinks. Small fish darted in and out of anemones. I pointed at a pair of yellow fish in front of me. *Nemo.* The little asshole flew at my finger, trying to bitc it, and I hastily withdrew my hand. Next to me, Gabe's eyes crinkled in laughter.

It was over all too soon. Gabe turned us around and

lazily kicked us back to shore. As we walked up the beach, two waiters and the towel boy gave us a small round of applause.

"Well done, Miss Callie."

"Was it beautiful?"

"Thanks, and yes, it was," I replied, a little breathless.

Somehow, the equipment didn't seem so heavy on the way back. I wasn't sure whether it was because I'd used up most of the air or because I just felt lighter inside.

Gabe helped me to take off the kit, then showed me how to rinse it in the freshwater tanks and hang it up to dry. I felt a pang of sadness as I glanced back at my gear. It had been the gateway to something special.

"So?" Gabe asked.

"So what?"

"I saw that look. Do you want to have another go?"

"Yes. Yes, I think I do."

Even if it *had* left my hair sticking out in a thousand different directions. I tried to flatten it down by combing it with my fingers, but the saltwater left it tangled.

"I have a course starting tomorrow if you'd be interested in joining? There's only one other person on it so far. It'll be nice and quiet. And I promise not to try setting you up with every man that walks past."

"What's involved?"

"It's a PADI open water course. You need to make nine dives, and after that, you'll be a certified diver."

I thought it over. Underwater, there were no rude Germans, Russians, or Egyptians, just peace, pretty colours, and fish. Even if Nemo had been a bit grumpy, it wasn't a hard decision.

"Okay, I'll do it. Am I being adventurous now?"

Gabe gave me a high five. "Nine o'clock tomorrow morning. You'd better get some sleep tonight."

It was only once I'd got back to my villa that I realised I hadn't thought about Bryce for the entire afternoon.

Yes, I was going to like this diving lark.

CHAPTER 7

GABE MAY HAVE been able to distract me yesterday while I was awake, but his touch didn't extend to my sleeping hours. Or rather, my tossing, turning, getting up and down and pacing around the room hours.

In the end, I resorted to watching BBC World until a documentary about the trials and tribulations of Mongolian basket weavers sent me off. Unfortunately, the tale of colourful woven wares and cheerful peasants worked a little too well, and I didn't wake up until eight thirty the next day.

Eating breakfast was clearly an impossibility, but could I get away without a shower? I sniffed my armpits. They'd do. And I could put my hair up into a ponytail. It was only going to get wet anyway.

I threw on an old T-shirt and a ratty pair of shorts. Gabe had seen me at my worst already, and if I could do anything to put off the men that the hotel staff kept dredging up, then I was going to try it.

I speed-walked as fast as I could in a pair of flip-flops, falling through the dive centre door in a flurry of apologies for being late. Then I realised that Gabe must be running on Egyptian time because there was no sign of him.

Dammit, I would have had time for breakfast, after all. I considered making a quick run to pick up coffee and some fruit. Okay, a croissant. And perhaps one of those little pastries that they had yesterday.

Alas, I knew that if I decided to go to the restaurant, then it guaranteed Gabe would turn up the instant I left. I headed instead towards the small seating area by the front door, intending to grab a magazine and relax until Mr. Tardy arrived.

Except when I turned, I realised there was already someone sitting there.

"Hi," he said.

Too late, I recalled that Gabe had mentioned I'd be getting a diving buddy today. Was this him?

The man sitting down was dressed almost as scruffily as me, wearing a faded T-shirt and shorts that rode low on his hips. He pushed back his floppy fringe and regarded me suspiciously with eyes that were just a shade lighter than the sea outside.

"Hi." *Say something else, idiot.* "I'm Callie."

Wow, that was imaginative.

He looked me up and down, a slow perusal that left me wishing I'd worn a different T-shirt. Anything but the one Kat had given me, which proclaimed I was "Hotter than Mr. Rancho's chilli sauce." The maraca-waving chilli pepper plastered across my chest suddenly seemed so juvenile.

"I know. I was issued with your picture and a brief fact sheet as part of my check-in package. Is it true you studied art history before you became a teacher?"

The only way the hotel staff could have possibly known that was through my Mum or Kat. I was going to find out which of them had spilled the beans and do something very nasty. But in the meantime, I had to deal with a complete stranger who knew more about me than some of my friends.

"Yes, but it's quite hard to get a job in that field. That's why I decided to take up teaching."

"A noble profession."

Was he mocking me? I wasn't sure.

"I find it very satisfying."

The stranger smiled through his unkempt beard, displaying a perfect row of white teeth. People would pay a fortune for those.

"I'm glad you're being satisfied in at least one way."

Oh yes, he was definitely taking the mickey now.

I was saved from saying something I probably would have regretted by Gabe, who strolled in looking delicious. Honestly, how could he look that good so early in the morning? And why couldn't he be straight? It's not as if I'd have stood a chance or anything, but a girl's got to dream, hasn't she?

He gave me a kiss on each cheek, then turned to the newcomer. "You must be Adam?"

The jackass nodded. "And I take it you're Gabe?"

"Indeed I am. Welcome to this fine and sunny establishment. Have you two already met each other?"

"He knows my whole life history," I blurted. "He has a flyer. Did you know about this?"

Gabe shifted uncomfortably. "Someone did hand me a copy when I was out in a restaurant last night."

"Is there anybody left in this town, anybody at all, who doesn't know that my love life is a complete mess?"

"Probably not," Gabe admitted.

The way I saw it, I had two choices: Run back home with my tail between my legs or stay and fight. Two weeks ago, I'd have been on the first plane out of Egypt, no question, but just being in this beautiful place had changed me. Despite the meddling by my friends and family, I somehow felt more relaxed. Perhaps they were putting something in the water in Fidda Hilal?

Whatever it was, I decided to take the second option.

Gabe regarded me nervously. "Do I need to get tissues?"

"No. I'm going to deal with this."

I clenched my fists by my sides. I could do this. *I could.* Both men breathed sighs of relief.

"So..." Gabe said. "Shall we start the course?"

"We?" Adam asked. "I thought it was only me on the course?"

"Callie decided yesterday that she wanted to learn to dive, and I decided that I was going to teach her. It'll be good for you to learn with a buddy. It's how you'll dive in the wild, so to speak."

Darkness clouded Adam's eyes, and he opened his mount to protest, but Gabe got in first.

"Look, if you want to learn on your own, I can give you a refund and you're welcome to find another dive school. But Callie's learning to dive, and she's learning with me."

Oh my gosh. I felt like leaping over and hugging him, but I managed to refrain. Not only would it have embellished my reputation as a crazy woman, but it would have involved exposing my armpits to the open air.

After a long moment, Adam sighed. "Fine. I'm here now, aren't I? I guess we'd better get started."

Gabe sat down, motioning to me to do the same, and went through the format of the course with us. We were to have homework. Homework! It really was like being back at school.

Today, Gabe explained, we'd be making two dives, both in the bay in front of the hotel. We'd have a set of skills to learn and practice, involving everything from taking out our regulator to flooding our mask. But before that, we'd have another video and a short test.

That all sounded so much more complicated than my effort yesterday. Couldn't I just float around with the fishes again? And Gabe, of course.

Once he was finished with the intro, Gabe herded us both into a classroom. As Adam stood up, I found he was taller than me, a smidgen over six feet at a guess, and when he sat on the wobbly wooden chair, he dwarfed it. I perched next to him, eyes forward. It was years since I'd been the student rather than the teacher. I felt as though it should be me at the front explaining how the lesson was going to progress.

Adam opened his textbook and started reading. I did the same, but I couldn't help glancing in his direction a couple of times out of curiosity. As well as the tatty clothing, his dark brown hair was weeks—if not months—past needing a cut, and his beard was crying out for attention too. His skin had a grey pallor, as if he hadn't been outside much recently.

As we jotted down our test answers, I peered over to see what Adam was writing. Bad idea. Not only was his handwriting so awful I couldn't make any of the words out, but he caught me looking. Damn.

Once we were done, Gabe came over and explained the bits we got wrong. Or rather, the bits *I* got wrong. It was clear I had some bedtime reading to do, but hopefully it would work out better than the basket weavers. After I'd been re-educated, it was time for the first of our training dives. I felt a bit better for having worn the equipment once already. At least I knew what I was letting myself in for.

"Have you ever dived before, Adam?" I asked as we walked through to the locker room. He hadn't uttered a word to me since we went into the classroom.

"No."

"What made you want to learn?"

He shrugged. "I thought it sounded like fun."

For someone who'd flown—judging by his American accent—halfway around the world to take the course, he didn't seem very enthusiastic about it. Or maybe it was just me he wasn't enamoured with. If so, I couldn't really blame him. Even I didn't like myself much at that moment. If it hadn't been for Gabe's constant encouragement, I'd have gone back to my room and cried.

At least, that was the case until I discovered that my course had a hidden benefit. I found this out when Adam took his shirt off. And his baggy board shorts. The Lycra boxer-style shorts he wore underneath didn't leave much to the imagination, and out of the corner of my eye, I caught Gabe looking too. He shrugged and mouthed, "Straight," then made an exaggerated sad face.

As Adam stood in front of me, wearing a tight pair of swim shorts, I didn't know where to look. Heat rose up my cheeks. Gabe started laughing but turned it into a cough.

Adam turned away, and now I was free to stare openly. The back view was almost as good as the front, and in my head, I christened him "The Ass." Gabe raised his eyebrows at me and licked his lips.

"Stop it," I whispered.

"What was that?" Adam asked.

"Nothing."

The men both climbed into their wetsuits, while I only managed to squash one leg into mine.

"Adam, please can you help Callie?" Gabe asked. "I want to see you working as a buddy team."

I gave him a glare that would have made a kitten keel over dead in its tracks, but Adam saw it too and regarded me warily.

"Gabe, *you* could help me. You managed to get me into the suit yesterday."

Please.

"I just need to, uh, go and check the battery in my dive computer. I'll be back in a few minutes."

He practically ran out of the door, and I could quite cheerfully have murdered him. He'd pretended to help me in my quest to avoid men, but in reality, he was as bad as the rest of the staff. Suddenly, Peter's idea of going for a walk up in the hills didn't seem so bad. I could do that. In a burka.

Meanwhile, I had to put up with Adam.

"Why don't you try leaning on me?" he suggested somewhat hesitantly. "If you can get your other foot in, I could pull it up."

Probably it wasn't every day he tried to squeeze a hippo into a condom.

I gingerly stepped forward, then reached out to support myself on his shoulder. Thank goodness there was a layer of neoprene between us. Between him tugging and me jumping up and down, I finally got into the wetsuit, and Adam pulled the zipper up the back.

Just in time for Gabe to saunter nonchalantly back in.

"Ready to go, guys?"

"Yes," I grated out through gritted teeth, giving him the dirtiest look I could muster.

Gabe must have felt a bit guilty for abandoning me because he helped me into the BCD. I fastened my weight belt, and we traipsed off to the sea again. This time, I think because I knew I could do it, it seemed easier. Or perhaps it was because I was once again distracted, this time by Adam walking in front of me.

How did he manage to look that good in something so unflattering? It really wasn't fair.

As we submerged, with me deflating my own BCD this time rather than Gabe doing it for me, I saw the expression of wonder that came over Adam's face, and it made me smile. Maybe he *was* part-human after all?

I could quite happily have watched the fish and Adam's ass the whole day, but Gabe's hand waving in front of my eyes reminded me we had a long list of skills to practise. Back to work.

First, we took a little swim, learning to control our direction and depth. The actual swimming part was easy. Even though I hadn't swum much since I did my badges at school, it all came flooding back. Controlling my depth was more difficult. I had to let air in and out of the BCD.

Several times I accidentally headed for the surface, and once Gabe had to grab me and hold me down. Adam was having no such problems. He paddled around lazily like a pro. Of course he did. He seemed to be one of those people who found everything easy. You know the kind. They have a PhD in rocket science, work ridiculous hours in the city, and yet still find the time to go on a skiing holiday every other weekend.

Although he hadn't had time to get a haircut. A tiny chink in his superhumanity?

After ten minutes or so, we let the air out of our BCDs and settled on the bottom. Even just kneeling was difficult. With the current, I kept keeling over to the side. Eventually I jammed one fin into the sand and propped myself up most inelegantly.

Then it was time for the bits that had been making me really nervous. First, we had to take out our regulator and put it back in again. What if water got into my mouth? What if I started drowning? I had visions of being airlifted to hospital. Except, I reminded myself, this was the wilds of Egypt. They probably didn't have a helicopter. And I wasn't sure I wanted to end up in their hospital either.

Next to me, Adam calmly spat out his regulator, waited a few seconds, then put it back in. Ten out of ten. He was pretty good with the regulator, too. All eyes were on me now. A weight of expectation settled on my shoulders, along with the air tank and eleventy million tons of seawater.

I took a deep breath and released the regulator, breathing out a stream of small bubbles the way I'd been taught. Then I put it back in. Just like that. I'd done it!

Gabe gave my hand an encouraging squeeze, letting me know I'd performed okay. My breath came in ragged pants as I tried to get my pulse under control.

And it still wasn't over. We had to do it again, except this time, instead of retaking our own regulators, we had to breathe from our buddy's spare. For that, Adam and I had to hang on to each other's arms at the elbow so we didn't drift apart. I took another deep breath and went for it, grabbing the yellow hose and tugging Adam's alternate air source free from his BCD. He gripped my arm, and this time it was him rather than Gabe who squeezed me for reassurance, making me gasp in surprise.

Seawater flowed into my mouth, and I started choking. Until that moment, I hadn't realised it was possible to cough underwater. Adam and Gabe remained calm while I was anything but. Finally, I got my own regulator back into my mouth and found Adam still holding my arm, concern rather than his usual grumpiness in his eyes.

He asked me, "OK?" with his fingers.

I signalled back that I was, although I was shaking inside. *Calm down, Callie.* My heart thumped against my ribcage, and I nearly started ascending, but I realised that if I gave up, I'd look like an idiot yet again and this time in front of two hot men.

No, I'd damn well stick out the final joyous task.

That one consisted of flooding our masks and then clearing them. I'd been dreading it, and I was right to. As the cold water trickled in, fear did the same. A feeling of claustrophobia washed over me. My eyes were screwed shut, and all I could see was blackness. Then an arm snaked around my waist, and I drew strength from it. I pushed on the top of my mask and tipped my head back, blowing out as hard as I could through my nose to clear the water.

Finally, I managed to open my eyes again.

As my vision returned, I expected to see Gabe kneeling next to me, but to my surprise it was Adam. He was the one who'd been holding me. Thank goodness I hadn't realised that before. If I'd known it was The Ass holding me, I'd have drowned for sure.

The last few bits were easy, just practising our hand signals, and after what seemed like forever but was actually only thirty-five minutes, we ascended. As my head popped out into the air, a rush of feelings welled up inside me. Yes, I'd managed to complete the tasks, but I'd made a fool out of myself twice. Not an utter idiot, but still a fool. What must the other two think of me?

The question weighed heavy on my mind as I walked up the beach behind them, exhausted. When we got back to the dive centre, I barely had the energy to take off my gear.

Gabe noticed and caught me before I collapsed back onto a bench.

"You okay? You look white."

Great, so all those hours sunning myself on the beach had been wasted.

"I'm okay, I just feel a bit..."

I swayed a little on my feet, and Gabe lowered me onto the seat before stripping off my gear. Once the weight was gone, I breathed more easily.

"What have you eaten today?" he asked me.

"I ran out of time for breakfast."

"You should always eat breakfast," he scolded. "No wonder you can hardly stand."

"I couldn't sleep. Then suddenly I did, and I couldn't wake up."

He put his arm around my shoulders and squeezed. "It'll get better, I promise. But in the meantime, we need to find you some food. What do you want to eat?"

"Can we just order something and eat it on my

terrace?"

"Sure thing. Adam, you okay on your own?"

"I'll be fine."

Gabe bundled me up in a towel and half carried me to my room. Thankfully most of the hotel staff seemed to be busy, and I didn't have to face a barrage of stares. Having to explain why I was stumbling around like I was drunk wasn't something I felt up to doing that day.

I made myself presentable in the bathroom, and when I came out, Gabe already had a platter of assorted fruit, cakes, and sandwiches set out on the table. I picked up a piece of chocolate cake. Just to get my blood sugar levels up, you understand.

"Feeling better now?" he asked.

"Mmm-hmm. I can't believe I have to do it all again this afternoon, though. I didn't realise the course would be so much work."

"It's not easy, but it'll be worth it, I promise. Plus we have a delicious piece of man candy to amuse us now."

I almost spat out my drink. "You can't say that!"

"Why not? I'm right, aren't I?"

"I guess Adam's okay to look at," I admitted. "But he seems really grouchy."

"I thought that too. I don't understand it. When he emailed to book the course a couple of days ago, he seemed keen to come as soon as possible."

"Maybe that's just his personality? I think there's some sort of law that says a guy can't have the whole package. Like if he's handsome, he can't be friendly as well."

"Or gay."

"That too. Although you seem to have managed all

three."

Gabe gave me a cheeky grin. "I guess I'm an anomaly."

Chapter 8

AFTER LUNCH, I struggled back into my wetsuit. My energy had returned, and to a small extent, so had my enthusiasm.

Which was a good thing because the afternoon's session was even tougher. We had to remove our masks completely and keep them off for over a minute. It stung to open my eyes, so I kept them closed, though that meant I was totally reliant on Adam to guide me.

On the bright side, I was so worried about the exercise that I completely forgot to go gaga when I touched him. Thank goodness for the small mercies, eh?

I'd almost jacked the whole lot in after this morning's dive, but I felt a lot better when I finally emerged from the water for the day. I was glad I'd kept going.

Kat called as I was packing up my kit. I'd spoken to her last night to let her know I'd be taking a diving course and not to worry if I didn't answer the phone in the daytime.

"Callie, I'm so sorry, but I'm going to have to bail on you tonight. You remember the other windsurfing instructor? The one that I told you didn't turn up last week? Well, she still hasn't, and a bunch of us are heading out to hunt for her."

"Do you need any help?"

"We have enough people, I think, and you don't know the area. Stay at the hotel and enjoy yourself. Have any better men turned up today?"

I glanced across the room at Adam. The jury was still out on him. He'd been a gentleman during the underwater tests, but he'd barely said a word to me since.

"No. Just Gabe." I'd told Kat all about him too.

"Oh, well, enjoy yourself with him."

She sounded distracted, but that was understandable if her colleague was missing. And I couldn't say I was disappointed at the prospect of spending a quiet evening alone.

"Yes, ma'am."

I gave her a mock salute before I hung up, which of course she couldn't see. But Adam could, which earned me a bemused look.

"Been stood up?" Gabe asked, sounding far happier about it than I felt.

I nodded. "But it's fine. I don't mind."

"In that case, you've got no excuses. You're coming out with us tonight."

"Who's 'us?'"

I wasn't going to agree to something without knowing the facts. Not again.

"Only me and a few friends."

"Do you promise you won't try to set me up with anyone?"

"Cross my heart."

"Okay, what time?" I asked, trying to stifle a yawn. It didn't work, and I slapped my hand over my mouth to hide it.

"Pick you up at eight?"

"That late? We're not going to stay for ages, are we? I'm exhausted."

"Of course not."

Why wouldn't he look me in the eye? I gave him a sharp glance.

"Don't worry, I'll keep you awake," Gabe promised. "And I'll save you some energy now."

With that, he swooped in and flung me over his shoulder. My ass bobbed in the air, and I was shrieking as he turned to face Adam.

"You're welcome to join us."

"Thanks, but I'll skip it," he said, as he tried, and failed to keep a straight face. He was laughing as Gabe strode out of the room.

Yes, definitely part-human.

The next morning, I woke up as sunlight glinted through the gap in the curtains.

I had a guy with a jackhammer chiselling away at my brain, and my face was damp from where I'd drooled on the pillow. I lifted the cover and found that I was still wearing the dress I'd put on last night.

The clock said eight thirty-five. I attempted to drag myself out of bed, but my body refused to cooperate, and who was I to argue? I slumped back down again and closed my eyes.

What had happened last night? I remembered Gabe

picking me up, then going to some club that was shaped like a giant boat. There was music and dancing and...alcohol. Yes, there'd definitely been alcohol.

I had a vague recollection of Gabe holding my wine while I tried—and failed—to do the splits, but everything after that was a blur. *What had I done?* Callie Shawcross didn't behave like that. If I'd ever acted that way when I was with Bryce, he'd have had me committed.

I was in the process of passing out again when somebody hammered at the door. If that was Gabe, he could take his early morning and shove it somewhere uncomfortable.

I stomped up to the door and threw it open, ready to give him a piece of my mind, only to find a waiter. With breakfast.

"I didn't order this."

"No, Miss Callie. A man called and ordered it for you." He beamed as he emphasised the word "man."

Okay, so maybe Gabe was partially forgiven. He still had a way to go, though. A *long* way.

I was only ten minutes late to the dive centre, but Adam looked pointedly at his watch as I stumbled through the door.

"I'm sorry, okay? *Somebody* decided it would be a good idea to stay out late last night."

"Yeah, I know. I've just been looking through the photos. You want to straighten your legs a little more when you try a handstand," he suggested.

Oh. My. Goodness.

"There are photos?" I asked dumbly. Of course there were photos. Didn't everyone have a smartphone nowadays? I sank onto a chair, head in my hands. "I'm never going out again."

Gabe sat down beside me. "Don't worry, I've deleted the worst of them. And the one of you getting a piggyback from the hunky Dutch barman is cute."

I might as well give up, I decided. While some women swanned around elegantly, had their gorgeous boyfriends wrapped around their little fingers, and spent their spare time lunching with their equally fashionable friends, I was destined to be a klutz.

Why fight against fate?

Rather than ask to see the photos, which were undoubtedly worse than I could ever imagine, I spoke through gritted teeth.

"Shall we get on with the diving?"

"We've actually got another fun-filled, action-packed video first."

Adam and I both groaned.

"Has anybody got an aspirin before we start?" I asked.

Gabe tossed me a packet. It was the least he could do.

The video and pre-dive briefing told me that today's dives would be even more challenging than yesterday's. If I could have turned back the clock, I'd have stayed in bed with a nice cup of cocoa yesterday evening.

At least I was getting the hang of putting my wetsuit on. I hopped around like a pro, grabbed a door handle just before I overbalanced, then turned around for Gabe to zip me up. I did of course spoil the effect by screwing my regulator onto my air tank upside down, but you live and learn, don't you?

Gabe helped me rectify things while The Ass stood by, looking bored. Then we were off to the bay again. I managed to quell my disgust at having to spit in my mask, mainly by imagining it was Bryce's face. *Take that, you twit.* See? I was learning.

"Right, guys. Instead of me putting your fins on for you today, you're going to do it yourselves with your buddy helping. Breathe through your snorkel while you look down to see what you're doing, and your buddy can support you by holding onto your air tank."

"Do you want to go first, or shall I?" Adam asked me.

"You go."

I wanted to see how the heck I was supposed to do this.

Well, I got ahold of the strap on his air cylinder, blinked, and missed it. Good going. Next it was my turn.

I leaned back, put my face under the water, realised I'd forgotten to put my snorkel in my mouth, came back up, went back down again, fiddled around a lot, and finally got my feet jammed into my flippers. Fins.

Hurrah.

Then Gabe dove under to check I'd done it properly, and it was good to know he had every confidence in me.

"Okay, first exercise," he said when he bobbed back up to the surface. "Switching between our regulator and snorkel. We're going to lie face down on the surface, and practise taking one out and putting the other in."

Now, this one I could do. It was almost like yesterday, when we'd had to take the regulator out and put it back in again. I completed the exercise and started watching the fish. There was a really pretty one with a checkerboard pattern on its side that kept staring at me.

Gabe made me jump by tapping me on the shoulder. Through his mask, I saw him roll his eyes.

Slave driver.

He motioned us both deeper into the sea. The view got bluer and the water colder as we swam down the sandy slope to a point where a rope was anchored. It was time for the Controlled Emergency Swimming Ascent. One at a time, we took out our regulators and swam in line with the rope up to the surface, breathing out tiny bubbles as we did so. Gabe had comfortingly told us that if we forgot to breathe out, our lungs would explode. That was a pretty important health and safety point.

Once we were on the surface, we inflated our BCDs and bobbed around like corks in the ocean. Except slightly bigger. It was the part I'd been dreading, the tired-diver tow. I wasn't looking forward to it for two reasons. Firstly, because I'd have to tow Adam and he was much bigger than me, and secondly, because I'd have to get up close and personal with him.

For some reason, my heart sped up the nearer I got, and I didn't even understand why. A primordial reaction to a tight ass, perhaps? It certainly wasn't because he'd gone out of his way to be nice to me.

Adam went first. I lay back in the water, although I didn't relax. In fact, every nerve ending felt as if it was on fire as his arm hooked around my chest, just below, well, you know. He pulled me along without even breathing hard. It was me who had to stop myself from panting.

Then it was my turn. I gingerly held onto him and kicked my legs. Nothing happened. It was like a shrimp trying to tow an oil tanker. He was at least four inches taller than me and a heck of a lot wider.

Gabe swam up alongside us, took out his regulator, and shouted encouragement.

"Come on, kick your legs."

What did he think I was doing?

Slowly, slowly, we started to move, but by the time we neared the shore, it was me who needed another tow. When we got out, I staggered up the beach with one man gripping each of my arms.

Gabe sat me down on the bench. The Ass crouched in front of me, seemingly oblivious to the amount of weight he was carrying on his back.

"Are you okay?" he asked.

I managed a weak nod.

He dumped off his equipment and returned to give me a hand with mine. It was the first time he'd done anything to help. Shame it took me nearly dying to get him to assist. He pulled my wetsuit off, hung it up for me, then stripped out of his. I was too knackered to even ogle his backside. A second later, he disappeared into the locker room and came back with my towel.

"Here." He draped it over my shoulders. "Better?"

Much to my surprise, I was. "A little."

He held out a hand and I took it, trying to ignore the zing that came from his fingertips as we walked into the office.

Straight away, Gabe glanced down at our joined hands. I hurriedly let go and backed away a few paces until I tripped over a plant pot and nearly hit the deck. I say nearly, because The Ass leapt forward and caught me.

He set me on my feet, and I stepped back again, more carefully this time, mumbling, "Thanks."

"You're welcome."

"She's like Calamity Jane, isn't she?" Gabe put in cheerfully.

Thanks, Gabe.

He carried on, oblivious, "We'll take lunch, then we've got a fun dive in the afternoon."

Really? Gabe's idea of fun and mine had already proven to be wildly different.

"Fun in what way?" I asked suspiciously.

"We're going to make our first open-water dive. We'll take the truck out to a different dive site, and yes, Callie, we can look at the fish."

It was only my second time in a vehicle in Egypt, and in daylight when I could see all the stuff we almost hit, it was even more terrifying. When the driver screeched to a halt just centimetres from a dog that was having a snooze in the middle of the road, I grabbed at Adam's hand and squeezed it hard.

"Easy, I want to have some bones left intact."

I looked around and realised he was wincing.

"Sorry!" I quickly transferred my grip to the edge of the seat.

When the pickup pulled up next to the pile of rocks on the beach that Gabe informed us marked the Turtle Cove dive site, I was amazed I had any teeth left. If I'd had fillings, they would have rattled out for sure.

"Is there a real turtle here?" I asked.

"Yes. We might see her if we're lucky."

We got dressed on a plastic mat by the side of the truck. It was there that I discovered there was something worse than putting on a dry wetsuit in the shade of the dive centre, and that was attempting to put on a damp wetsuit in the hot sun. I was again reliant on the efforts of Adam and Gabe.

The fact that I was sweating buckets under the thick neoprene did provide me with a certain impetus to get the rest of my kit on quickly though, and by the time I lowered myself gratefully into the sea, I was certain I must be suffering from heatstroke. I almost relished the chill of the water seeping in.

If I'd been impressed by the reef at the hotel, this one took my breath away. Well, not literally, because that would have led to several impressive manoeuvres from Adam and Gabe and a lot of panic from me.

We kicked through a narrow channel as coral pinnacles rose skyward on either side of us, each one surrounded by more colourful fish than the last. I saw more Nemos, which Gabe had explained were actually clownfish. They always lived together in a pair, each claiming their own anemone.

To my left, a huge, multicoloured fish scraped at the coral with a beak-like mouth. If I stopped breathing for a second, I could hear the scraping noise as it chipped away. Everything was so breathtaking, it was a wonder I managed to inhale any air at all. And then, on the way back, the turtle swam right across in front of me, slowly, not a care in the world.

Wow.

Back in the truck, I couldn't stop babbling. "Did you see the turtle? And that huge shoal of tiny orange fish?

What was the long thin one that swam in front of us at the beginning? Do those big coloured fish hurt if they bite?"

Gabe started laughing at me, and even Adam didn't look totally pissed off.

"This is where I try to encourage you to take the follow-on course. There's a fish identification module you can do where you'll learn all that."

"Okay, yeah, that sounds great. Will we see more turtles?"

"If we're lucky."

Tiredness came back in waves as the thrill of the sea life wore off and I realised I still had to clean my kit. I was weaving from side to side when Adam guided me back into the dive centre.

"I'll see you tomorrow?" Adam asked.

"Bright and early. And thanks for helping me this morning."

He gave me a smile as he walked out of the door. It was the first genuine one I'd seen from him, and it started a butterfly dance-off in my stomach. Or maybe the nausea was just the after-effects of the boat-bar party, coming back to get me?

Even though I wanted my bed, I waited around until Gabe got off the phone. Mum had brought me up to be polite, so I couldn't leave without thanking him for breakfast.

"Breakfast?" he said.

"You sent it to my room?"

"Wasn't me, sweetie. Seems as if you've picked up another admirer."

Huh? Who could it be? I racked my brains as I walked back to the villa. Eid? I'd seen him from a distance on the beach today, watching me.

I shivered even though it was thirty degrees.

If it *was* Eid, I wasn't going to seek him out and show my gratitude, no matter what my mother might think.

CHAPTER 9

THAT EVENING, I finally got around to visiting Kat's home. She lived with Mo in a second-floor apartment two streets away from my hotel. We met at Coral Cove and walked there together.

"Mo's making dinner," she said. "He finished work earlier than me, and besides, he's the better cook. I think we're having pasta."

Carb overload. My absolute favourite. Well, except for dessert. Dessert trumped carbs every time. It was in a class of its own.

"You had to work late again?" I asked.

Kat made a face. "Yeah. Irina, the other instructor? Well, there's no sign of her. We went to her apartment, and one of the guys climbed in through an open window. There was nobody home, but it looked as if all of her belongings were still there."

"What if she took a trip? Or went home for a while? If she did that, she wouldn't have to take much with her."

"That's what the police said."

"You spoke to them?"

"Yes. Well, not personally. A couple of her other friends went to the station. They said the cops were spectacularly unhelpful, which is par for the course around here, unfortunately."

"I suppose there's not much for them to go on."

"No, I guess not, but it still doesn't help Irina. Maybe she really did go home. It's odd, though. A similar thing happened a few months back as well, with a waitress Simone knew. She just vanished one day. The police said she must have flown home to Indonesia, but she never got there. The odd thing was, she had a flight out booked for the following week, but she didn't take it."

Another shiver ran through me. I was going to be looking over my shoulder from now on.

Kat must have noticed my worried expression. "I'm so sorry—here I am, supposed to be cheering you up, and I'm worrying you. No more depressing talk. Let's have dinner and then we can watch a movie."

Dinner was amazing. I'd been expecting something average, but the pasta was homemade, and the carbonara sauce—sans bacon of course, since we were in Egypt—was so delicious I troughed down the whole lot, calories be damned.

"Where on earth did you learn to cook?" I asked Mo. "Are you secretly Italian?"

He shifted in his seat and blushed. "Before I learned to wakeboard, I worked in the kitchen at an Italian restaurant."

"Well, if the watersports thing doesn't work out, you can always open your own."

He gave me a shy smile, and when I moved to take my plates to the kitchen, he waved me away.

"No, no, I'll do that. You sit with Kat."

I wasn't about to argue. It was movie time. Kat already had her laptop out, and as she flicked through the menu, I leaned in close.

"You really need to keep him."

She turned to me with a look in her eyes that I'd never seen before. It took me a few seconds before it clicked. It was love.

"I know," she whispered. "He's different from all the others. I know now what I've been searching for."

I gave her a hug as a tear rolled down her cheek.

"I'm so happy here. But sometimes it just feels a bit overwhelming."

Aw, sappy Kat was cute. But the gaping hole in my chest taunted me, and I swallowed back tears of my own.

"Can we just put the movie on?" I asked.

She sprang back. "Of course. I'm so sorry! I should have remembered, you know... Right, enough relationship stuff. Let's do Hollywood. Hot men and explosions."

I appreciated her understanding. "What are we watching?"

"Ben Sharp's new movie. He's so dreamy."

"What happened to Scott?"

"Scott's so last week. It's all about Ben now. I hear he takes his shirt off in this one."

That was the Kat I knew and loved. The movie wasn't bad, either.

Mo and Kat both walked me back to the hotel at ten so I could catch up on some sleep. After all the talk of disappearances earlier, I'd gratefully accepted the company when they'd offered.

I slept better than I expected, happily with a semi-naked Ben Sharp flitting through my dreams rather than Bryce. Except at one point, he looked at me, and he had Adam's face. What was that all about?

It was the wine. It must have been.

I was up and dressed before a waiter knocked on the door at eight thirty bearing a tray. Breakfast again.

"Who sent this?" I asked him.

He shrugged and shook his head. "I do not know, Miss Callie. The kitchen just told me to bring it. Is there something you don't like?"

"No, no, I'm sure it's delicious. Thank you." Later, I'd have to try to find the person who took the order.

I ate a few pastries and had a cup of coffee, then kept a wary eye out for Eid as I walked to the dive centre. Just in case. As usual, Adam was there before me. How did he get up so early? Didn't he understand he was supposed to be on holiday?

"Sleep well?" he asked.

Heat spread across my cheeks as I remembered his face in my dreams. "Y-y-yes, thank you." Where were my manners? "How about you?"

"Very well. This place is growing on me."

"I know what you mean. It's like time slows. Things that were problems before you arrived suddenly don't seem so bad anymore, do they?"

"No, they don't. I was talking to the barman last night, and he told me there's an old legend that says the mountains here can heal your soul."

"I could do with that."

"The town's name, Fidda Hilal, means 'silver

crescent moon.' They say that if you go up into the mountains as the moon rises through a gap in the peaks, when its light hits you, all your worries will disappear."

"Where do I sign up?" I asked in complete seriousness.

He laughed. "I'll try to find out for you."

I heard footsteps behind us, and then Gabe's voice.

"You're up early this morning, princess."

"I had an early night. And yes, I've eaten breakfast. My mystery admirer sent it again."

"Well, good. Every girl should have one."

I wasn't so sure. I'd much rather know who it was.

"So, where are we diving this morning?"

"Nowhere. We've got a nice, challenging, classroom session."

Adam and I both groaned. That was one thing we agreed on.

"I know, I know, but we have to get it out of the way. Then we'll go out somewhere nice this afternoon. We might even see another turtle."

He wasn't kidding when he said "challenging." We were supposed to be using tables to work out how long we could safely dive for without getting the bends. Or decompression sickness, as the textbook called it. The safe amount of time varied with depth, and we had to understand how to calculate it.

I was okay with the first bit, but when Gabe introduced the added complication of making two dives in one day with a surface interval in between them, I wanted to cry in frustration. It didn't help that Adam seemed to comprehend it perfectly.

"But why is it forty-seven minutes? I have thirty-six

minutes. I don't get it."

Gabe sat with me and patiently went through the little charts and lines and boxes yet again. Nope, I still didn't understand. It was like being back at secondary school all over again. Maths had never been my strongest subject. *C-minus, must do better*. I'd have found it easier to represent England at gymnastics than solve a quadratic equation, and I couldn't even do a handstand properly.

"I might as well quit right now. I'm never going to pass this. It's like you're speaking in Swahili."

"Shall I explain it again?"

I glanced over at The Ass, who was staring out the window. He must be bored out of his mind, waiting for me to finish.

"I think you'll have to. I'm sorry this is taking so long, Adam."

He drew his gaze away from the beach outside—where six shirtless guys were playing volleyball—and faced me.

"How about we give this a break? We'll go diving, and I can help you with it later on. Sometimes if you focus on something else for a while, when you go back to the thing that had you scratching your head, it all suddenly makes sense."

That sounded like a good plan. But hang on...*he* would help me? What about Gabe?

Gabe cut in. "Excellent idea. We can stop for lunch on the way. I'll fetch the car."

"Maybe we should just go over it again now?" I suggested.

I'd much rather Gabe help me. The thought of being alone with Adam made me nervous.

"Nah, I'm hungry," Gabe shot back over his shoulder as he walked out.

We stopped for lunch at a little café right next to the sea. Gabe pointed to a tattered flag flapping on a stick about thirty yards away. "That's the dive site. See, isn't this convenient?"

After we'd unloaded the gear, we settled down on cushions in front of a low table. An Egyptian wearing the traditional flowing white robes of the Bedouin came to take our order, but the butterflies in my stomach decided they weren't hungry. They were too busy flapping around, trying to find an excuse to skip Adam's explanations later.

"I'll just have fruit juice, thanks."

Except when Gabe's burger and fries arrived, I couldn't resist stealing one. Handful.

"You should have got your own," he said with his mouth full.

"I didn't think I wanted any at the time."

He rolled his eyes. "Women!"

Adam slid his plate over to me. "Here, have some of mine. I won't eat them all."

Suddenly I lost my appetite again. The Ass confused me when he was nice. It was far easier to be around him when he acted moody with a touch of grouchiness.

I tried to change the subject. "Did you hear about those missing girls?" I asked Gabe.

"What girls?"

"One of the windsurfing instructors Kat works with disappeared, and a few months ago, a waitress vanished as well."

"I heard about the waitress, but everyone assumed she'd gone travelling. From what I heard, she was backpacking around the world."

"Kat said she was supposed to fly home and she didn't. And the police won't even look for Irina, the windsurfer."

"That doesn't surprise me."

"Really? Why won't they do anything? I mean, there's a girl missing."

Gabe shrugged. "I'm not sure whether they're lazy, incompetent, or just corrupt."

"Can't somebody put in a complaint?"

He gave a wry laugh. "That's not how it works around here. It's not like England. In Fidda Hilal, the police have all the power, and they like to abuse it. One time, they inspected a friend's dive boat, and as they boarded, the deckhand asked them to remove their shoes the same as everybody else. They took offence and refused to let the boat out of the harbour all day."

"How can they get away with that? What happens if there's an actual crime?"

"Usually whoever did it gets away scot-free. Or sometimes, they arrest any old person to look as if they're doing something. People tend to sort out their own problems, especially the Bedouins."

I shuddered. "That actually sounds a bit scary."

"The majority of people around here are friendly. They just avoid the police and things work okay."

"Really? But what about kidnappings and stuff? I overheard someone in the hotel restaurant talking about those. They take tourists."

Gabe laughed again, but this time in humour.

"What?" I asked.

"Most of the kidnappings aren't really kidnappings, per se. They're more like compulsory hospitality. The

Bedouins do it to make a political point. They round up a busload of holidaymakers and announce that they've abducted them. The media gets excited, but in reality, the Bedouins take them out to the camel races and then feed them dinner. Most of them quite enjoy it."

"Seriously? That really happens?"

"Yeah. They had a bunch of bemused Portuguese people presenting the winning owners with their prizes a couple of months ago."

"That doesn't sound so bad, I suppose."

"Just another facet of life here in Egypt. You get used to it."

I guess I'd have to. I'd be staying there for five more weeks.

"So, what are we doing on this dive?" Adam asked. "Is it another easy one like yesterday?"

Gabe gave me a look of sympathy. "Sorry, but no. We're going to work on the same skills we did at the house reef yesterday, but deeper. And if you don't waste time getting distracted by pretty things, we can have a swim around at the end."

Why did Gabe stare at me when he said that? Adam looked in my direction too.

In the end, I found the dive much easier than yesterday morning's. Not only the exercises, but being close to Adam. I no longer jumped every time he touched me. And it showed in my air consumption. Since I was no longer huffing away like an out-of-shape marathon runner, my tank lasted longer.

That meant we could spend more time underwater, the consequence being that I was freezing when I got out. Despite the blazing sun, the chill in my core meant my teeth chattered as I stripped off my wetsuit.

"Are you okay?" Adam asked.

"Y-y-yes. J-j-just a bit cold."

"Where's your towel?"

He didn't wait for me to answer, just rummaged through the stuff in the back of the pickup until he found it, and then he bundled me up in it the way my mum used to when I was small.

"Better?" he asked.

I nodded, resisting the temptation to sag back into his arms. "Yes, thank you."

By the time the truck rumbled back into the dive centre, I'd warmed up and stopped shivering.

"Do you want to try a thicker wetsuit tomorrow?" Gabe asked. "It'll be warmer."

"Will it be easier to get on?"

"No. Perhaps a fraction more difficult."

Great.

"Don't worry, we'll manage," Adam said. "It's better than getting hypothermia."

We'll manage? He wasn't the one who'd lost three fingernails trying to get into the other one.

"I'll think about it," I said.

He gave me a look that said I'd be stupid not to. "Are you ready to study?"

Ah yes, the moment I'd been dreading, for more reasons than one. I nodded reluctantly.

"Great—your place or mine?"

Sorry, what? What was wrong with this place?

"I thought we'd use the classroom here."

"Sorry, no can do," Gabe said. "I need to lock up before I go."

Oh gosh, what to do? I didn't want to be alone with The Ass. Maybe we could go to the bar? No, because that would look as if we were on a date. And this most definitely wasn't a date. No, siree.

I wasn't sure I wanted to visit his man-cave. A small element of not trusting myself, perhaps? But if he came to my room, how would I get rid of him? Hey, what if we just sat on a bench somewhere?

Stop being ridiculous, Callie. It was only studying. And maybe dinner. And a few drinks. No! Definitely not drinks.

"I'll come to you." My mouth made the decision rather than my brain.

Adam beamed at me, and I blinked in the glare of the lights on his teeth.

"See you in ten?"

I nodded. My mouth had gone too dry to speak.

CHAPTER 10

I WALKED NERVOUSLY up the path to Adam's villa. Was my hair all right? I'd avoided wearing any makeup because that would look as if I was trying too hard for our study-date. Session. Study-session. I breathed into my hand and sniffed. Good, I wasn't going to knock him out.

I tapped on the door.

"It's open," he callcd.

I pushed against it, holding my textbook in front of my chest like a shield. As I stepped inside, Adam was walking out of the bathroom, tugging a T-shirt down over his head.

I caught a glimpse of his six—no, wait a minute—eight-pack and felt a rush of heat somewhere I really shouldn't.

Think of boring things, Callie. Like grocery shopping and housework and, oh yeah, dive time calculations.

And don't freaking pant!

I perched on the edge of the sofa, ready to do a runner at a moment's notice. The seat dipped as he sat down beside me, and I tipped towards him. No, no, no. I pushed myself upright and made a show of opening my book. My pen... Where was my pen?

"Shall we start?" I asked.

What was that little smile? Why did I amuse him? "Yeah, sure."

After half an hour of him patiently explaining, drawing diagrams, and walking me through calculations, it finally clicked. I leapt up and did a happy dance, and then I lost my freaking mind and flung my arms around him. Then I realised what I'd done, released my grip, and stumbled backwards over my own damn feet. My backside hit the floor, but was my moment of mortification complete? No, of course it wasn't. The tinny sound of Celine Dion's "My Heart Will Go On" sounded from my pocket, and I felt the colour drain from my face. Drip, drip, drip. All the blood seeped down to my feet.

"What's up?" Adam's voice sounded like it was coming from a distance. "You've gone white."

I fished around for my phone, holding it as if it was a piece of dog turd. *Bryce calling* flashed up on the screen.

Then it stopped. I breathed again.

Two seconds later, Celine was back, because Bryce never had known how to take a hint. I snatched it up and answered, stalking to the other side of the room. Without thinking, I sat on the edge of Adam's bed.

"Bryce?"

"Of course it's Bryce. Who else would it be?" he snapped.

Why was he being so snippy? "What do you want?"

"Oh, don't play dumb. I can't get into your apartment."

"Why not?"

"Because you've changed the locks, or do you not remember? Really, Callista, I didn't expect such barefaced hostility from you. I'm extremely perturbed."

"I didn't change the locks. Are you sure you're using the right key?"

"Of course I am. We were together for a considerable length of time, if you recall? I believe I can remember which key operates your lock."

"I don't know what to suggest."

"Well, I do. I strongly recommend you return immediately from wherever you're residing and assist me with my entrance."

"Bryce, I'm not even in the country." Tendrils of comprehension filtered into my brain, and I clenched my teeth. "Wait a minute. Why are you trying to get into *my* apartment?"

We'd never lived together. Bryce had always been reluctant to commit to that without having formal paperwork in place. A marriage certificate. Apparently, a signed lease agreement didn't count.

"Because, Callista, I accidentally left some terribly important paperwork there when I last visited. It is vital that I retrieve it."

"What paperwork?"

"The script for my upcoming theatre role. It had all my notes in the margins."

"Well, maybe you could get another copy and make new notes?"

"Don't you know anything about an actor's craft, Callista? We can't simply improvise on the spot. Every move, every action, every snippet of dialogue has to be carefully considered in advance in order to bring the greatest joy to our audience."

"Look, I can't just hop on a plane and fly back. I've got more important things to do."

And I'd had enough. I was sick of being told how to live my life.

"What could possibly be more important than doing justice to the works of Shakespeare? The Bard's works are not something you can trifle with. Any great thespian..."

I felt a warm body press up against me. Adam's breath whispered across my ear as he said, in an extraordinarily posh English accent, "Babe, whoever that is, you're going to have to wrap it up. I'm not waiting any longer to take you to bed."

Bryce went silent. Although that might've just been because I dropped my phone.

My heart couldn't make up its mind whether to pound like a jackhammer or stop altogether, but as The Ass sauntered back across the room with a satisfied smile on his face, it settled for an erratic rhythm that made me feel faint. My phone... Where the heck was my phone?

By the time I snatched it up. Bryce had recovered.

"Who the hell was that?"

Wow, a whole sentence of one-syllable words. I guess he must have been really flustered. But the part of me that still ached from his "it's not you, it's me" speech couldn't resist going in for the kill.

"Your replacement."

My finger shook as I jabbed at the "off" button, and when the screen had gone dark, I stuffed the phone back into my pocket. Freaking heck. Had I truly just done that? I looked up to find Adam appraising me from where he sat, feet propped up on the coffee table.

"Seemed as if you needed a hand."

"Thanks. I think that's the first time he's ever been

speechless."

"The ex, I take it?"

"The one and only. He wanted me to fly back to England because he can't manage to open the door to my apartment. *My* apartment. Can you believe that? And all because he left his stupid script there. He's an actor, *dahling*, and he's so up himself. Cocky, and self-centred, and arrogant... They all are. Constantly flouncing around, self-aggrandising... I swear I'm never, ever dating another actor again as long as I live. No, even longer. I'm going to have 'no actors' written on my tombstone."

"That's quite a sweeping statement. Are all actors really that bad?"

"All the ones that I've met are. I don't think Bryce had a single friend from the profession who wasn't a complete prick. So that's my new rule. No actors." I pouted and marched over to the tiny kitchenette. "Do you have any wine?"

I opened a cupboard and found plates and mugs. No good. A glass overbalanced, and I only just caught it, juggling it between hands before it hit the floor. Adam got up and joined me before I could destroy his entire collection of crockery.

"In here," he said, reaching over my head to open a cupboard.

He poured us each a generous glass of red and led me back to the seating area.

"Come on, relax. I don't like to see you uptight."

I deflated. "I'm sorry. Bryce just has that effect on me. It's odd—now that we're not together, I can see how he was suffocating me, but at the same time, I still miss him. It's so confusing."

Adam sat down and patted the seat beside him. "Sometimes it's good to talk about things. Get them off your chest. Why don't you tell me about it?"

As the alcohol took effect, I found myself doing exactly that. And Adam didn't judge. Didn't look at me like I was a complete idiot. No, he merely topped up my glass and listened as I rambled on until I ran out of things to say.

"So, that's my story. Basically, I'm an idiot."

"You're not an idiot. You just cared about the wrong person. You can't change the past, but you can control your future. From now on, do whatever makes you happy."

And it struck me that at that moment, I actually was happy. After his initial surliness, Adam had turned out to be a nice guy. Perhaps even a friend. And I had Gabe, and Kat, and Mo, and then there was the diving... Adam reached out and traced my cheek with a finger, his aqua eyes fixed on mine. Wow. *Maybe I shouldn't call you The Ass anymore.* The trail of heat sizzled, and I wondered what I'd see if I looked in the mirror. Third-degree burns?

"You call me The Ass?"

Oh, hell. Had I said that out loud?

"Uh... I meant it in a purely complimentary way. You know, like 'The Rock.'"

"Sure you did."

Dammit, why did I always have to screw up? "Okay, so I'll admit I didn't like you all that much at first."

"And now?"

"Now?"

"Do you like me now?"

"Uh..."

"It's not a trick question, Callie."

What was I meant to say to that? Things had been so much easier with Bryce. He'd said all the hard stuff, and I'd just nodded in the right places.

"I guess I don't *not* like you."

"Okay, I can work with that." Adam broke into a grin. "What do you want for dinner?"

"Dinner?"

"It's the meal at the end of the day. Pizza?"

"Yes, pizza. Pizza's good."

With food, the conversation got lighter. Although it helped that we were both buzzed from the wine. Adam seemed to have a good stash hidden away. When I asked him about it, he said the bottle shop had a "buy twelve get one free" offer and he'd never been able to pass up a deal.

"So that English accent earlier, what was with that?" I asked. "Did you used to live there or something?"

"No, I've just always been good at mimicking people. I used to watch old movies as a kid and copy the voices. My grandma used to tell me I should become an impressionist."

"But you didn't?"

He shook his head.

"So what do you do?"

"At the moment, nothing. I'm between jobs."

Unemployed? Well, at least he was upfront about it. Even though Bryce worked for his father's company in between acting jobs, he'd sponged off me all the time. On the rare occasions I'd mentioned his finances, he reminded me he was a serious actor and was therefore meant to suffer for his art.

Adam seemed to mistake my silence for judgement because he started to explain further. "I had some money saved up and thought I'd go travelling. Try my hand at being a beach bum. I suppose I'll have to go back and join the rat race sooner or later, but at the moment, I'm having a good time here."

"In spite of the company."

"Because of the company. More wine?"

I held out my glass. More wine was always a good thing, right?

Wrong.

I woke up in the morning to a marching band holding a rehearsal in my head, except all their instruments were out of tune. I used my fingers to peel an eyelid open and found I was back in my room. How did I get there? The last thing I remembered was Adam taking the mickey out of my ringtone and us both attempting a terrible rendition of Ms. Dion. Beyond that, totally blank. I lifted the covers. Phew. I was still fully clothed.

A knock at the door sounded, and the waiter was there with my breakfast. Oh, goody. I took one look at the omelette and ran to the bathroom.

Once I'd put on my darkest sunglasses to stop the sunlight burning out my retinas, I picked up a banana to eat later and walked outside. The fact that I was only fifteen minutes late was a minor miracle.

Adam came along his path at the same time and

looked me up and down.

"She lives," he said.

"Barely. How's your head?"

"I don't think I've felt this bad since college."

We were propping each other up in the seating area when Gabe arrived.

"Boy, that must have been some party. Where was it? Come on, I want the juicy details."

We glanced at each other, then quickly looked away. Adam answered for both of us.

"No party, buddy. And no details."

That was all he needed to say for Gabe to put two and two together and make sixty-nine. A big grin came over his face as he walked over and clapped Adam on the back.

"Congratulations! About time. We've all been rooting for you."

I jumped up, then regretted it because my head swam. "It wasn't like that! Nothing happened. No clothes were shed. I just got a bit upset over Bryce and drank one too many glasses of wine."

"Bottles," Adam muttered under his breath.

"Fine. Bottles. Can we stop talking about it? I hate being the centre of attention. Everywhere I go, people stare at me. Do either of you know what it's like to have people constantly following you, assuming things that aren't true? Well, do you?"

I was staring at Gabe, but from the corner of my eye, I saw Adam shift uncomfortably.

"Sorry," Gabe said softly. "I was out of line."

The steam left me, and I sagged back into my seat. "Apology accepted. Can we go diving now?"

"Of course, of course. We're back in the bay out

front today. The first session will be partly scuba and partly skin diving."

"Skin diving? Like, in just our skin?"

I must have looked horrified because both men started laughing at me.

"No," Gabe said through his guffaws, "It means you don't wear a scuba tank. You can keep your wetsuit on."

"Oh. Good. Then let's get started."

The scuba session came first. We had to take our masks off, swim fifteen metres without them on, then replace and clear them. I was getting good at it, both the mask part and at holding Adam's hand as he guided me safely along the bottom of the bay. In fact, I was even starting to enjoy it. So much that I was almost tempted to muck it up so I could have another go.

Then we moved on to buoyancy control, or "hovering around, watching the fish" as Gabe put it. Except while Adam was watching our finned friends, I used the time to slyly watch Adam out the corner of my mask. Especially *The Ass*.

Hmm. I was starting to get a little worried about myself.

Skin diving was a different story, though. While Adam and Gabe elegantly soared down several metres, my attempts were more of an inelegant lurch with much kicking of feet. Much like my whole life, really.

When Gabe declared I'd passed that section, I grabbed my scuba tank and hugged it.

"Oh, tank, I'm so sorry I dumped you. I'll never be without you again."

More laughter.

"Your relationship's improved a tad since the first day," Gabe said. "That's good to see."

The afternoon's dive involved much putting on and taking off of gear, both on the bottom and at the surface. I was surprisingly good at it. Probably because every time I'd gone out somewhere with Bryce, I'd taken off and put on at least five different outfits in an attempt to make him happy. He rarely was.

And looking back, neither was I.

At the end of the day, Gabe gave us the bad news.

"You guys have got a couple of videos to catch up on, plus a test to do. I'd suggest we spend tomorrow morning doing that, then take the rest of the day off. We'll finish off the day after with our final two dives of the open water course."

"Sounds fine to me," Adam said.

I nodded my agreement. Much as I was starting to love diving, I wasn't going to say no to a day of R&R.

When we reached our two villas, Adam coughed nervously as we were about to part ways.

"I was wondering if you wanted to do something with me tomorrow? I mean, after the classroom session?"

Was he asking me on a date? I wasn't sure, and I was too nervous to ask. If I did and he wasn't, I'd probably scare him off. And if he was...

Was it too soon after Bryce? Would I just be using Adam as a rebound guy?

I heard Kat's voice in the back of my head. *Have a*

little fun, Callie. Everybody needs to get some.

And what else would I do tomorrow afternoon? Sit alone in my room? Go to the beach and hide from Eid? Get propositioned by some new arrival?

"Okay, I will. I'd like that."

I got another of his dazzling smiles, the ones that were rarely seen but which made me melt inside.

"Great. I'll organise something for us to do. Goodnight, Callie."

He dipped down and gave me a lingering peck on the cheek before walking to his villa without looking back. I couldn't move until his door closed behind him. My legs had stopped working. I reached up and touched the spot where my face still burned.

He'd kissed me. Not with tongues, but it was still a freaking kiss.

The question was, should I be ecstatic or terrified?

CHAPTER 11

I MET KAT in town for dinner that evening. She had a pass out as Mo was going to watch the Egypt versus Tunisia football match at a bar down the road. We found a quirky Thai place above a jewellery store and snagged a table where we could look out over the bay.

"Still no sign of Irina?" I asked, nibbling on a spring roll.

Kat had dark grey smudges under her eyes. The additional workload was clearly taking its toll.

"No, nothing. It's as if everyone's starting to forget her. This town has such a transient population, people are always coming and going. The newcomers have no idea she ever existed and the older residents... Well, if they don't think about a problem, it doesn't exist, right?"

"What else can you do?"

"Nothing. That's what's so frustrating. And even if there *was* something, I wouldn't have time because I'm teaching from dawn till dusk."

"Are they going to hire a replacement for her?"

"Eid's father already has. But she's coming from Slovakia, and she won't get here until next week." Kat sighed. "I'm sorry, I'm being an awful friend. I've barely seen you since you arrived."

"Don't worry, I've been busy too."

"With the diving course?"

"Yup. Tomorrow afternoon will be the first bit of free time I've had in ages."

She brightened. "Why don't you come to the sports club? You could join in one of my lessons."

I put down my fork. Picked it up again. Should I tell her or not? I had to, didn't I?

"Don't read anything into this, but I already have plans. With a guy."

Who was I kidding? This was Kat. Of course she'd read something into it. She squealed in delight, and half the diners in the restaurant swung their heads in our direction.

"Ooh Callie, you didn't hang around, did you? That's great! Your mum'll be so pleased our efforts weren't in vain." Kat clapped a hand over her mouth. "Could you forget I said that last bit?"

"You knew about her meddling?" I gave her a sharp look. "You were in on it, weren't you?"

"I just want you to be happy. To help you forget Bryce."

I should have been mad at Kat, but I couldn't be. She only wanted what was best for me, even if she'd gone about it in a way that set my teeth on edge.

"I'm trying to forget Bryce. He called me late last night, though."

"Seriously? I wouldn't have thought he'd have the nerve, the little rat-bag."

"He wanted to know why he couldn't get into my flat."

Kat snorted. "Because your mother changed the locks, that's why."

"What? Why didn't she tell me?"

"She did. Once when you were crying on the couch, and again in the car on the way to the airport."

I rifled through my thoughts. I didn't even recall riding to the airport, although logically I must have.

"I don't remember that."

"Your expression was kind of glazed. I hope you didn't try to help him."

"I don't know what I could have done. He wanted me to fly home and open the door for him. I told him I couldn't."

Kat cracked up. "The guy's so selfish it's unreal. He thinks the world revolves around him. What did he say when you refused?"

"Not a lot. He heard Adam in the background and got all cross, and then I hung up."

"Hang on... Adam was there? Last night?"

"We were studying together. In his room."

"Studying? Oh, that old chestnut."

The look on her face showed exactly what she thought had gone on.

"No, honestly, we really were studying."

"What, and at eight o'clock you just trotted off back to your room?"

"I'm not totally sure. I was drunk."

"Oh, this gets better and better."

"Kat! Nothing happened."

"Okay, okay. Fine, nothing happened. But you want it to, right? He could be your rebound guy. Is he hot?"

"Kind of, in a scruffy sort of way. I'm not keen on beards though. But even if he was interested, which is a massive 'if,' I'm not sure I want a fling. I've never had one before."

"All the more reason to go for it. Just have some

wild, uncomplicated sex and enjoy yourself."

"You make it sound so easy."

"It is, Callie. It is."

To Kat, maybe, but this was me. I wasn't sure I could set my emotions aside that easily.

It weighed on my mind the whole way back to the hotel, and as I lay there, trying to sleep, I still didn't know what to do. Was Adam even interested? I was terrible at reading people—I'd proved that with Bryce. I'd just have to see what the next day brought.

The morning dawned bright and clear. Not a cloud in the sky. No surprises there, then.

I'd been dreading the classroom session, and most especially the exam. But after a couple of cheesy videos starring people with bad hair and considerably more scuba ability than me, plus a bit of help from Adam, I managed to pass the test. I breathed a sigh of relief.

"We'll celebrate tonight," Adam told me.

"Not with wine, though. I'm never drinking again."

"Not even champagne?"

Champagne was different, wasn't it? It was fizzy. Practically a soft drink.

"I'll think about it. What are we doing after this, anyway?"

"This afternoon, we're chilling on the beach. I've got something planned for later, but it's a surprise."

I'd always loved surprises. At least until Bryce had

sprung that last horrible one on me. It began as such an innocuous conversation—he'd started by saying he wasn't able to take my car for its service the following month and finished by telling me our wedding was off.

I had hope that Adam's surprise would be a little nicer than that.

A few hours on the beach would be good too. I'd spent so much time in a wetsuit that I was only a shade or two past pasty white, and at this rate, I'd have to plaster myself with fake tan in the toilet at Luton airport before I caught a taxi home.

"Ace! I'll just scoot off and change. Meet you down there?"

He smiled and nodded, and I ran out of the dive centre. Well, walked quickly. Flip-flops and running weren't really compatible.

I was within spitting distance of my door when Eid popped out of nowhere.

"Callie, I'm so glad I found you. I've told my mother all about you, and she's invited you over for dinner tonight so you can meet the family."

Meet the family? What? I'd barely even met *him*.

"I'm going to have to take a rain check on that."

"A rain what? We do not have rain here. It's very dry."

"A rain check. A pass. I have other plans tonight."

"But my mother is cooking stew. It's delicious."

"Maybe another time. I really am busy."

"Another night is not possible. My cousins are coming as well. There are so many of them that it's difficult to get them all together in one place."

How many times did I have to say no?

"It's kind of you to think of me, but..." I gasped as

an arm wrapped around my waist and pulled me tight up against a hard body.

"Babe, there you are. Did you find the sunscreen?"

Adam reached past me and stuck out his hand. Eid shook it, but with the reluctance of a man forced to touch rotting meat.

"Adam. Nice to meet you. I see you've met Callie. She's a doll, isn't she?"

"I am Eid." He turned to me. "Is this what your plans are tonight?"

I nodded, not daring to speak. Five fingers were sending shivers through me, and my stomach clenched.

"Well, if that's the kind of woman you are, I can see that my mother would not like you. She wants me to marry somebody with class."

He stalked off, nose in the air.

For a second, I was speechless, then Adam and I looked at each other and fell about laughing.

He touched his finger to the end of my nose in a gesture I wasn't quite sure how to interpret. It wasn't exactly intimate, but my body sure reacted that way. Heat rushed south.

"Don't worry, I'll take you and your lack of class any day."

I swallowed hard. The implications of that made me very nervous.

Thankfully, I made it into the villa without further incident, and while I changed in the bathroom, Adam stood guard at the door just in case Eid decided to make a reappearance. I'd never had a man get protective of me before, and twice now he'd helped me to get rid of unwanted suitors. Whatever the future held, I had to be grateful for his presence

Bikini or one-piece? Bikini or one-piece? I stared at the array of beachwear I'd laid out on the bathroom vanity. How brave was I feeling? Oh, screw it—I threw caution to the wind, and before I could change my mind, I put on a bikini and strode outside.

With a cover-up over the top, of course. I mean there's brave and there's stupid, and I wasn't about to parade through the resort half-naked. The waiters would probably have photos of me on match.com within twenty minutes.

We picked two sunloungers at the edge of the beach and draped our towels on them. Adam strode off to get some drinks while I whipped off my cover-up and slathered on sunscreen.

I'd asked for fruit juice, but when he returned, he was holding two multicoloured concoctions decorated with umbrellas and sliced melon, orange, and grapes.

"This was what they gave me. I was almost embarrassed to be seen carrying them." Then, more quietly, "Do you want me to do your back?"

Did I want him to touch me? Have his strong, smooth, hands rubbing over me? My brain screamed no, but the parts of me that hadn't seen any action in weeks overrode it.

"Yes, please." I handed him the bottle.

He squirted some of the lotion out, warming it in his hands before he gently rubbed it into my back. When he got to my shoulders, his thumbs dug in and he started massaging. A low moan escaped before I could stop it.

Oops.

It was answered by a groan from him. "I'd better stop now."

What? Why?

He handed me the bottle. "Would you mind returning the favour?"

Oh, okay. That seemed fair.

His skin was silky under my fingers, and the lotion was long soaked in before I was able to tear my hands away. My nether regions were hotter than the sun. I flopped back onto my lounger to try and compose myself while Adam lay back on his and picked up a book. I recognised the cover of a story I'd read a couple of months ago. It was a great thriller.

I fished my own novel out of my bag. The title was *Confessions of a Wedding Planner*—secretly, I still hadn't given up on the dream.

I snuck a glance over at Adam. What would he look like in a tux?

Good grief, Callie! I gave myself a mental slap. I'd barely touched the guy, and I was already imagining what it would be like to take his surname. Whatever it was.

Beside me, he put down his book, stretched, and rolled over. Now I had a view of his perfect ass instead of his abs. *The* Ass. I couldn't complain.

But I could daydream. I imagined we were on a secluded island, just the two of us and the waves crashing on the shore. The quiet chatter of the other holidaymakers and the occasional hum of Mo's boat as it pulled wakeboarders around the bay all faded away. Adam picked up the bottle of sunscreen again, but this time, he straddled me and tugged off my bikini top before he ran those hands over my back again. Neither of us said a word. We didn't need to. We both knew exactly what we wanted.

Didn't we?

Back in the real world, I snuck a glance at Adam, but he was still reading. What would he say if he could read my thoughts?

And more worrying, why was the waiter from the beach bar gesticulating between me and a guy at least twenty years older? Ouch. Those Donald Duck Bermuda shorts weren't flattering in the slightest.

Donald appeared to win the argument and marched over to me, waving a piece of paper.

I sat up as he approached, squinting into the sun.

"I'm putting in a complaint," he announced.

"I'm sorry?"

"This pamphlet distinctly says you are single and unattached, but now I've wasted my time finding you. You're clearly with another man. I don't do threesomes."

I opened my mouth, but no words came out.

They didn't have to. Adam was on his feet beside me in an instant, staring the man down. For an unemployed beach bum, he sure possessed an air of authority. Helped, no doubt, by him being a head taller than Donald, who had to tilt his neck to look up at him.

"Apologise and leave."

"W-w-what?"

"You don't walk up to a beautiful lady on the beach and start yelling at her."

Adam thought I was beautiful? I melted back onto the sunlounger.

For a moment, Donald looked as if he was about to argue, but Adam took another step forward and he thought the better of it.

"Sorry," he bit out before marching back from

whence he came.

Adam sat beside me and took my hand in his. "I'm sorry too. That was a shitty thing to happen. I'll have a word with the hotel manager. They shouldn't still be giving out those leaflets."

"They shouldn't have been giving them out in the first place."

The corners of his eyes crinkled as he grinned at me. "I don't know. How else would I know that your chocolate fudge cake won first prize in a bake-off last year? That's a very valuable piece of information."

"I'll make you a cake one day," I blurted. "You know, as a thank you for saving me from all these unsuitable suitors. You're my knight in shining... swimming trunks?"

Adam chuckled, then leaned over and kissed me on the forehead.

"I've got an ulterior motive," he whispered.

I was frozen to the spot as he got to his feet.

"But I wouldn't say no to a cake." He held out his hand, and I took it and let him help me to my feet. "We may as well leave. It's almost time for your surprise, and we need to get changed first."

As I pulled on a pair of jeans and a sweater, as per Adam's instructions, my mind was in a spin. The bottom of my belly fluttered. The butterflies were back. At this rate, I could take up lepidoptery.

What had he meant by having an ulterior motive?

And was it what I found myself hoping it would be?

Chapter 12

IN THE LOBBY, I found Adam standing beside a small Egyptian man with half a dozen gold chains around his neck. His eyes gleamed when he saw me. The Egyptian man's, not Adam's. Adam was too busy looking out the door at the...

"Quad bikes? We're riding on quad bikes?"

"Sure seems that way."

"Where are we going?"

"Up to the mountains to watch the moon rise. We'll see if it really does have the power to heal a broken soul."

"Oh my gosh, you remembered! We talked about that ages ago."

He tapped his head. "An elephant never forgets."

Or, it would seem, a hot diving student.

The greasy Egyptian addressed my chest. Which, granted, was about at his eye level, but he could at least have made the effort to look up.

"Visiting Jebel Hilal can change your life."

"Let's hope so."

Adam filled in the paperwork before we set out, and I peered over as he wrote.

Name: Adam Lowestein

Age: 25

Address: Oakside House, Vale Road, Ashbury

Heights, San Francisco.

Wow—in ten seconds, I'd doubled the amount I knew about him. He was only three years older than me, which was roughly in line with my guess. And San Francisco! What an amazing place to live.

The man gave us each a scarf to wrap over our face. What was he planning to have us do? Rob a bank?

"It will keep out the dust," he explained. Then he handed us helmets and got us to sit on the bikes while he went through the controls.

I leaned over to Adam and whispered, "Would this be a bad time to mention I've failed my driving test four times?"

"You passed eventually, right?"

"No, but I know the bus timetable by heart."

"Uh, okay." Now he looked as nervous as I felt. "I'll make sure we keep it slow."

The Egyptian guy set off in front, and I gingerly twisted the throttle. The bike lurched forward and stalled. Good start. On my second attempt, I managed to keep the engine going, and we moved off cautiously along the road.

True to his word, Adam crawled along at a speed I was happy with, and despite the pace, we made it up the mountain in time to see the moon peeking through the gap between two peaks.

I stood motionless, glued to the spot. Mesmerised.

"Isn't it awesome?" Adam murmured.

It was, but what took my breath away was his arms wrapping around my waist. His fingers twined through mine, and his beard tickled my cheek.

I stiffened on instinct, but after a minute or so, I gave in to the moment and relaxed against him. His heart thudded against my back, although it was still beating far more slowly than mine.

We stood there for the time it took for the moon to clear the mountains and start its journey overhead. I didn't dare to move a muscle. The only sound was our synchronised breathing.

At least, it was until our guide broke the spell by clearing his throat.

"We go back now."

Adam stirred, running his fingernail lightly up the length of my arm. I shivered as a ripple of pleasure ran through me. Who knew that could feel so good?

His lips brushed my ear, as he asked, "Are you okay?"

Was I? I had no idea. Two weeks ago, I'd been preparing for my wedding in England, and now I was on top of a freaking mountain with a whole other guy. Feelings I didn't understand tumbled around inside me. Where was this going? Adam lived on a different continent, for crying out loud.

But now wasn't the time to start analysing every move, and Adam was waiting for an answer.

"Super, never better. Thanks for asking."

That was met with a hoot of laughter. "Fuck, you're so adorable."

Adorable? Was that good or bad? Other women were sleek, sophisticated, and elegant. I was *adorable*.

Slowly, I made my way back to my quad bike, tripping over a rock in the darkness. Adam played the hero once again and kept me from falling, then helped me onto the bike and showed me how to turn the headlight on.

Two minutes later, we were off, with me going even

more slowly because I had terrible night vision. If we were lucky, we might make it back before breakfast.

Or perhaps dinner, because my bike suddenly sputtered and ground to a halt.

"Uh, guys? I think mine's broken."

The guide backed up the track to where I'd stopped and swore under his breath.

"No matter, someone can fetch it tomorrow. You can ride back with me."

He turned and patted the seat behind him.

Uh, help?

Thankfully, Adam came to the rescue. Again. He really needed to start wearing his underpants on the outside. Or possibly not at all. That would work too.

"You're coming with me," he said, leaving no room for argument.

Thank goodness! I hopped up behind him, and with nothing else to hold on to, I was forced to wrap my arms around his waist. I say forced—it wasn't exactly a hardship.

We set off down the mountain again at a much faster pace than before. I began to hope we might actually make dinner tonight rather than tomorrow. The only problem was, I might not have any teeth left to eat it with because they'd most likely have been rattled loose.

It was a wild ride down the wadi, and I clung on tight, feeling Adam's abs working beneath my arms as the rocky vista flashed by in the gloom.

Woohoo!

All too soon, we were back at the hotel. I unpeeled my arms, but my legs refused to cooperate.

"Give me a few seconds, would you?"

Instead of waiting, Adam bent to lift me from the seat.

"Hey, stop! I'm far too heavy."

"I managed just fine the other day when I carried you back to your room. You weren't too heavy then."

He'd *carried* me? So that was how I'd got back. I hadn't really thought about the logistics before, but it wouldn't have surprised me if he'd borrowed the luggage trolley from the porter.

I still wasn't sure what I'd done to deserve the attention of such a gentleman, but I sure wished I was able to find out so I could keep doing it.

A quick taxi ride later, and I found myself at an Italian restaurant, seated in a comfortable chair at a table on the beach. I slipped off my sandals and scrunched the sand beneath my toes. Adam sat opposite, watching me in the light of a flickering candle. It struck me that this was my first ever candlelit dinner. Bryce had always preferred to see exactly what he was eating so he could pick out the bits he didn't like and leave them on the side of his plate.

The food was excellent, and so was the company. Adam was knowledgeable about every topic under the sun, or so it seemed, and we spoke about everything from the war in Iraq to our favourite animals. He loved dogs, the same as me, but he didn't have one of his own.

"I'd love to get a dog one day," he confided. "From a shelter. There are so many needing homes."

I'd always wanted a dog too. Bryce had claimed to be allergic to pet hair, but in reality, he was just terrified of it sticking to his clothes. But now that he was gone, I could get one if I wanted to. I felt a sudden rush of freedom.

When I got back home, that's what I'd do. I'd get a companion who would love me even if I did occasionally forget to vacuum.

I ordered a dessert not because I was hungry, but simply because I didn't want the evening to end. Adam sipped his espresso as I picked at my tiramisu.

"Thank you for a lovely time," I said.

"It's me who should be thanking you. It's been a long while since I've spent such a relaxed evening with a woman."

That was the first time he'd mentioned his dating history, and I got a sudden bout of nerves. *Adorable.* Was that good enough?

"Are you seeing anybody back home?"

"Do you think I'd be here with you if I was?"

"Sorry, I shouldn't have asked."

"It's fine. I mean, I know all about Bryce. Did he really take you to watch him in a play as a date?"

"When did I tell you that?"

He mimed drinking out of a wine bottle.

"Oh. Right." Me and my big drunk mouth. "Yes, he did. I sat on my own all night. Even afterwards, he stayed backstage for drinks before he took me home."

Adam shook his head in disbelief before gifting me another of those smiles.

"So... How does your soul feel now? Better?"

Yes, and it wasn't just my soul. From the rubble of my broken heart, a foundation was being built, and Adam was the one stacking up the bricks and mortar.

I nodded. "It was magical. I forgot to take any photos, though."

"Then we'll have to go back there again one day,

won't we?"

"I'd like that."

After dinner, which Adam insisted on paying for—now there was a novelty—he took my hand. Rather than catching a taxi, we walked back to the hotel along the coastal path.

Just the two of us and the moonlight, all the way back to my villa.

On the doorstep, Adam paused, and my stomach clenched in delicious anticipation. Would he try to kiss me?

The answer was yes, but barely. With an arm around my waist, he dipped his head and pressed his lips chastely to mine. They lingered for a second, and then he pulled back a fraction and murmured, "I'll see you tomorrow. Enjoy your breakfast."

Once I'd staggered inside, I sat down on the edge of the bed, my eyes vacant, my mind empty of everything except the feel of Adam's soft lips on mine. The faint trace of coffee on his breath. The press of his hand on the small of my back.

Oh boy, was I in trouble.

For once, I got to the dive centre early the next morning. I wanted to see Adam. And thank him for breakfast. After his comment last night, I'd done the math and realised that he was my mystery benefactor.

Yet another thing to be grateful to him for.

Except today he was late. Even Gabe got there before him.

"Last day of the open water course, Callie—you've almost made it."

Gosh, how time had flown. "Don't tempt fate. I still have two more dives to go, right?"

Things had been going far too well. In Callie-land, that meant I was due for a fall soon.

"You need to have more confidence in yourself, kiddo. That ex of yours really did a number on your head, didn't he?"

That was something Kat had said too, but I didn't want to think about it. Bryce was just, well, Bryce. And I'd been happy with him for six years. At least, I thought I had. I wasn't sure if I trusted my own judgement anymore.

Luckily, Gabe didn't seem to be expecting an answer to his question.

"Shall we start getting the equipment ready? I'm sure Sleeping Beauty will turn up eventually."

Sure enough, fifteen minutes later, he did.

"Apologies—I couldn't sleep for hours, and then I overslept. It won't happen again."

"Delhi belly?" Gabe asked.

Adam shook his head. "Just got a few things on my mind."

Was I one of them? I couldn't help but hope.

"Are we going somewhere in the truck today? Or diving out front?" Adam asked.

"House reef today. We'll swim a bit deeper, and we have to learn how to navigate with a compass."

Oh, great. I couldn't even find my way with SatNav and a map.

But Gabe wasn't to be deterred. First, we practised on dry land, walking through the hotel gardens. Around the swimming pool, across the beach... Every time we went past the restaurant, I noticed two girls staring at Adam.

After much whispering, one of the pair finally approached us.

"Excuse me, but I'm sure I know you from somewhere. Have we met before?"

He laughed and surprised me by switching to an incredibly sexy French accent. "I get that all the time. I must have one of those faces. Besides, I'm sure I would remember *une fille* as pretty as you."

She went pink and giggled. "Sorry to have disturbed you."

Adam was so sweet. If it had been Bryce she'd asked, he'd have given her a chronological list of his TV and stage appearances, then insisted on signing autographs. And it would probably turn out the girl had confused him with her milkman.

Had I turned into a bitter old shrew?

Possibly.

I kept finding myself comparing the two, and Bryce always came up lacking. Had our entire relationship been terrible? Or was I just twisting things in my mind based on how he last treated me? Confused didn't even begin to cover it.

What was Bryce doing now? Did he think about me the way I was thinking of him? Or had I slipped from his mind, an inconsequential memory that would fade away in time to nothing?

"You just went south when you should have gone east," Adam said from beside me.

Aaaand back to the real world. "Sorry, my mind wandered."

Navigating was even harder in the water. First we swam on the surface, and I'll admit I cheated a little and simply swam parallel to the shore. Underwater, I copied Adam. We were supposed to be buddies, right? Buddies stuck together.

The two dives were over before I knew it, and we both passed. Thank heavens. My first attempt at adventure, and I'd not only survived but enjoyed myself doing it. Score one to Callie.

"Now what? I don't want to stop."

Gabe chuckled. "I seem to remember you volunteering yourself for the advanced course the other day."

"What? Did I?"

"You did," Adam put in. "I heard you say it too."

Really? "Are you doing it?"

"Sure am."

"In that case, sign me up." Anything to spend more time with Adam. "Erm, what's in it?"

Gabe reached into a cupboard behind him and fished out a couple of manuals. Great, more studying. I might have groaned.

"Don't be like that. It's not as bad as the open water course. There are a bunch of modules to pick from, and you need to do five of them. The deep dive and underwater navigation are compulsory."

More navigation? Was it too late to change my mind?

"Read through the book tonight," he continued, "and let me know tomorrow which ones you'd like to do."

As we headed back to our villas, the new, brave version of me plucked up the courage to ask Adam a question.

"Do you want to go out tonight? To celebrate passing the course? My treat this time."

"I can't tonight."

My heart plummeted like a dead elevator. Was he giving me the brush-off? Had I totally misread things last night?

"Okay, no problem then."

"I'd love to, but I have to do something."

A vague excuse was almost as bad as an outright no.

"I have to call my brother. I speak to him at this time every week." He frowned as if he was struggling to come to a decision. "He's in rehab," he confided. "I can only phone him once a week at the moment. And after that, I have to give my mother an update on how he is."

The way he spoke, quietly and hesitantly, told me how difficult it had been for Adam to share his secret. And it was the first moment I sensed that whatever was building between us might go deeper than a holiday fling.

I put my hand on his. "Don't worry, I totally understand. Of course your brother has to come first."

"We could go out tomorrow instead? If you don't have other plans, that is."

"Tomorrow's perfect."

We reached my door. This time, in the late afternoon shadow of a bougainvillaea tree, Adam kissed me properly. A little tongue, a lot of heat, and a long groan when he finally pulled away.

"Tomorrow," he whispered before he left me gripping the door jamb in a stupor.

CHAPTER 13

I STOOD OUTSIDE my door until I heard Adam's close, my toes curled in my flip-flops. Holy hell, the man could kiss. I could still taste him in my mouth, feel the sting on my chin from his beard.

Adam hadn't kissed me; he'd devoured me.

Dazed, I slotted the key into the lock on my fourth attempt, and when I got inside, I collapsed back on my bed, reliving the moment in my head. Over and over again for at least an hour. The man had magic lips.

And a kind heart, and he cared about his family too.

Speaking of family, perhaps I should give my own mother a ring. And a piece of my mind too.

"Mum, I can't believe you did that!" I screeched as soon as the pleasantries were over. "Everyone in town knows my life history."

"Somebody had to be proactive, dear."

"I could have gone out and met people on my own. I'm not a complete hermit."

"Yes, I know, but I wanted to hurry things along a bit. I'm not getting any younger, and I'd like some grandchildren."

"You have a granddaughter."

"All right—I'd like some *more* grandchildren."

Sometimes, she could be impossible. "I'm never going to live up to Persephone's standards, Mum."

"You don't have to. You just need to live up to your own. And maybe set your bar a little higher. So tell me, have the men been beating down your door?"

"Stalking me around the hotel grounds, more like." I told her about the problems I'd had in graphic, excruciating detail. I still cringed when I thought of Peter the taxidermist.

"Oh, Callie. I'm so sorry, sweetheart. I didn't realise it would all go so wrong."

Great. Now I felt guilty for quashing her hopes.

"There is one guy I like," I said in an attempt to cheer her up. "But I didn't meet him through your meddling."

Dammit, Adam probably heard her shriek through the wall.

"Tell me everything, dear. Have you done it yet?"

Did my own mother really just ask me that? I wanted to wash out my ears.

"I'm not giving you any more details. I've only just met him."

Usually, a vague response didn't satisfy Brenda Shawcross, and I braced for further questioning. When it didn't come, my spidey-sense tingled.

"Don't worry, that's fine." Why did she sound so chipper? "All in good time. You just go out and enjoy yourself."

After the past few days, I knew exactly what she was up to. The moment she put down the phone, I threw on a clean T-shirt, dashed through the hotel, and hopped into the nearest taxi. Five minutes later, I was hammering on Kat's door.

She opened it, phone in hand. I snatched it from her and hung up.

"Don't you dare tell my mother anything. If you do, she'll gossip to everyone at the Women's Institute, and by the time I get home, everyone in town will know I've had a holiday fling."

"That was Mo on the phone. He was just telling me he was on his way home for dinner."

"Oh. Sorry."

The phone rang in my hand, and I glanced at the display. *Now* it was my mother. I answered it.

"Mum, Kat's not going to tell you anything either. Go and watch *EastEnders*."

"Darn, foiled again."

Yes, and I was proud of myself. For once in my life, I'd gotten the upper hand.

"Here." I held out the phone, then changed my mind and moved it beyond Kat's reach. "I'm not sure if I should give this back."

"Okay, point taken. Now that you're here, do you want to stay and eat? I'm cooking, so it won't be as good as last time."

"I'd love to."

"Not out with your mystery man tonight?"

"He had some things to do."

"As long as it was 'things' and not other women. I don't want you getting hurt again."

"It's definitely just things. He's not like that, Kat."

At least, I didn't think so.

Despite Kat's claims, dinner was excellent, and afterwards—in customary Kat tradition—it was time for a movie.

"We have to watch something with Trent in it," she announced.

"Trent?"

"Trent Baxter, Hollywood's new hottest property. I'll get you educated one day."

"What happened to Ben?"

"He's still on my list, along with Scott and Brett and Zac and Carl."

"It's getting to be quite a long list now, isn't it?"

"You say that like it's a bad thing. You should try it. That way, you'd get a different gorgeous man visiting you in your sleep every night."

Back in my hotel room, as night fell, Adam's face was the only thing I saw. Okay, his body was there too. In glorious technicolour.

My list only had one man on it.

Morning arrived, and with it came my regular order of breakfast. Then I was off to find Gabe and—quite literally—the man of my dreams.

Adam was waiting for me in the dive centre, and I got another of his sexy smiles as I walked through the door. Honestly, he could get a million dollars for that grin. Possibly two million if he shaved off his beard so people could see it better.

Although I'd grown quite fond of the beard. It was growing on me. Well, on him. It made him look rugged and laid back at the same time, like a sexy lumberjack. And I couldn't imagine him without it now. What if he had a weak chin?

"Morning, beautiful," he said.

I glanced behind me, just to check there wasn't a prettier girl following.

"Yes, I'm talking to you. Callista, Greek for 'most beautiful.'"

I'd always thought my dad was having a joke with that. Although he'd been spot on with Persephone's name. Queen of the Underworld suited her perfectly.

"What does Adam mean?"

"Nothing so exotic. It means 'from the earth.'"

It should have meant 'sexiest man on earth.' Because in my eyes, he was. Heat pooled between my legs as I walked over to kiss him on the cheek, except he must have been talking to Eid because he turned his head so I got his lips instead.

Just as Gabe walked in.

"Put him down, Callie. We have work to do."

What was redder? Me or a beetroot? Probably me if Gabe's laughter was any indication.

Adam squeezed my leg and got up. "What's the plan for today, boss?" he asked Gabe.

"Two dives. Which ones did you want to do?"

Oh, crap. I hadn't even opened my book.

"I like the idea of a night dive. And a boat dive, if that's possible?"

"There's a boat we can hire. We could do that tomorrow if you want? Callie, what are your thoughts?"

"Uh, what he said."

More laughter.

"Busy night, was it?"

"I went to Kat's. We watched a movie."

"Which one?" Adam asked.

"I forget the name. Something with Trent Baxter in it. A romcom."

"*Stars over Memphis*?"

"That sounds familiar. Have you seen it?"

"A while back."

It couldn't have been that long ago. Kat said it was new out. And why was Adam watching a romcom anyway? Were sexy lumberjacks into that sort of thing? And more importantly, who had he watched it with? It was hardly the kind of thing a man sat down to enjoy by himself.

Stop, stop, stop. Why had the green-eyed monster come to pay a visit?

"That still leaves one dive to pick." Gabe brought me back to the task at hand.

"How about fish identification?" Adam suggested. "We could learn more about what we're looking at down there."

"Perfect—that's our five. We can do navigation now and a night dive this evening. Then a trip on the boat tomorrow, which includes the deep dive, and finish up with fish identification the day after. How does that sound?"

We both nodded our agreement, then suited up to go and get lost in the bay. Once Adam had stopped me from swimming out to the open sea and we'd managed to find our way back to the dive centre again, we got our gear ready for the evening's trip. I was a bit nervous about diving in the dark, but Gabe assured me we'd have torches.

"We'll go into the water just as the sun disappears. Some of the creatures—lobsters, for example—only come out at night, and the corals open up. If we're lucky, we'll also see some bioluminescence."

"Some bio-what?"

"Things that glow in the dark. Corals, jellyfish, things like that."

"Sea monsters?"

"Hopefully none of those."

My nervousness didn't vanish entirely, but the thought of seeing the reef at night was exciting. Perhaps this newfound sense of adventure wasn't so bad after all.

"What do you want for lunch?" Adam asked.

"How about we just eat on your terrace? That way, we can avoid anyone who might still have one of those leaflets."

"Good plan."

His terrace was bigger than mine, a secret slice of paradise surrounded by fragrant bushes and shady palms. And it had a hammock. I'd always wanted a hammock, ever since I was a little girl, but I'd never had anywhere to tie one.

"Can I try it?" I asked, pointing.

"Be my guest."

Easier said than done. I tried to climb into it, but that damn thing kept moving.

"Is there a knack to this? Because I don't have it."

"Sure." Adam hopped up into it in one smooth movement.

"You've done that before."

"I've got one at home. Come on."

He offered me a hand, and I tried to hide the shiver that ran through me. What if I made us both fall out?

"Callie?"

Okay, okay. The hammock wobbled as Adam dragged me on top of him, skin on skin. Holy hotness. How much was I sweating? Inside, I was on freaking fire. My head was resting on Adam's chest, and my right arm had nowhere to go but around him. He was hard *everywhere.*

Did I say I was in paradise before? Because I was wrong. This, right here, this was paradise.

I lay there for what seemed like hours, listening to the twitter of birds and the steady beat of Adam's heart, my fingers entwined in his smattering of chest hair. Lunch was forgotten. In fact, everything was forgotten because I fell asleep.

"Hey, don't."

I wriggled away from the tickle on my back. What *was* that? Heck—was it a creepy-crawly?

"Wake up, sleepyhead."

Oh, it was just Adam's finger, stroking up my spine. Mmm. That was nice.

"What time is it?"

"Four o'clock."

I hadn't drooled on him, had I? I cracked an eyelid open to check. No, thank goodness.

He kissed the top of my head. "I can't think of a nicer way to spend an afternoon, but it's time we got up. Are you hungry?"

My grumbling stomach told me I was. Adam ordered a fruit platter and pastries while I used the bathroom. *His* bathroom. I picked up his aftershave from the counter and sniffed it. Hugo Boss Orange.

Maybe I could buy myself some when I got home?

Or maybe I could just turn into a complete fangirl. What had come over me?

I lined the bottle back up with the one next to it—it seemed Adam had a touch of OCD—and headed back out to the terrace where Adam was on a sunlounger tapping away at his phone. He shoved it into his pocket as I sat next to him.

"Gabe's confirmed we've got the boat for tomorrow. We're going to head south down the coast."

"Sounds great."

I wasn't thinking about the diving. Just a whole day on the boat with Adam.

"It does. I can't think of anything I'd rather do. Or anyone I'd rather do it with."

I gripped his biceps as he pulled me onto his lap. When he kissed me, it felt as if my heart was balancing on a knife-edge. One wrong move and it would be lost forever.

Was I ready for that?

I still hadn't come to a definite conclusion when I heard a knock at the door.

"Lunch is here. Well, afternoon tea."

He stood, and I could hardly fail to notice the impressive tent in his shorts seeing as it was at eye-level. I coughed nervously. The size was slightly daunting.

"It's my turn for a quick trip to the bathroom. Would you mind getting the door?"

"No, no, of course not."

The hotel kitchen had thoughtfully included knives, forks, spoons, and even a pair of chopsticks, but I didn't need to use any of them. Adam fed me slivers of fresh pineapple and mango, and when he kissed me again afterwards, he tasted like a fruit cocktail. And fruit was good for me, right? One of my five a day. Before, I'd always counted red wine, apple-flavoured gummies, orange Fanta, strawberry shortcake, and ketchup—tomatoes were *technically* a fruit. But I could be turned on to this new way of thinking.

No way was I going to attempt getting into the hammock again, so we just squashed onto one of the sunloungers, side by side. We lay there, soaking up the last few dying rays until Adam's phone started beeping.

He groaned. "We need to go now. I set the alarm because I knew we'd lose track of time."

"I'd rather stay here."

"Me too, but Gabe might be disappointed if we didn't turn up."

"Or worse, he might come and find us."

I straightened my bikini, which had come remarkably close to being indecent, and threw a T-shirt and shorts over the top. Adam only needed a T-shirt. I glanced down. And a cold shower.

He saw where I was looking and rolled his eyes. "I'll catch up."

If I'd thought getting my dive kit ready in the daytime was difficult, it was twice as hard at night when I couldn't see properly. I put my regulator on the wrong way around, and it took me four tries to attach the inflator hose to my BCD.

But obviously that was just me. Gabe and Adam had no such problems.

Lowering myself into the murky blackness was like entering another universe. Before I flicked on my torch, I took a look around, and in the distance, I saw dim blue and pink lights moving around. Biolumi... Glowing in the dark.

Adam took my hand for a spellbinding swim along the reef wall. Anemones waved in our light beams, and the glowing eyes of fish stared back at us. It was like being an intruder in someone else's dream.

Except it was my own. I even pinched myself to check.

All too soon, it was over. It was only when I stepped onto the beach that I realised how cold I was. For the most part, I'd gotten used to the temperature of the water, but I was accustomed to climbing out into the beating sun, which warmed me up. At least I had Adam now. In the truck on the way back, I snuggled up next to him, wrapped in a towel. His beard tickled my forehead as I rested my head on his shoulder.

"Fun?" he asked.

"Which part? The diving?"

He chuckled. "What else would I be talking about?"

Of course. "It was amazing. How about you? Did you enjoy yourself too?"

"I did. Who knew there was such beauty underwater? The fish were okay as well."

CHAPTER 14

I STIFLED A yawn as I walked into the dive centre the following morning. My body clock had reset to Egyptian time, and it didn't like me getting up an hour early to go out on the boat.

"Didn't you sleep well?" asked Adam.

"I slept well, just not for long enough."

"You can sleep on the boat if you're still tired," said Gabe, walking in with a pile of wetsuits. "There'll be plenty of time to rest between dives. Just try not to get sunburned. The lobster look wouldn't suit you."

"Don't worry," Adam told me as Gabe walked outside. "I've got sunscreen and the hands to put it on with."

Yes, I was looking forward to today's trip.

We all piled into the truck for the five-minute ride to the jetty, and wow, that was some boat. The Fidda Nijmah, according to the black letters on the stern. An Egyptian flag fluttered in the breeze above the name.

"How many people are going?" I asked Gabe.

"Just us."

Really? But the boat was huge. "How many people can the boat fit?"

"Twenty-six fully equipped divers, plus crew."

"Isn't that a lot of space for three people?"

"I guess nobody else wanted to come today."

Who wouldn't want to go out on the water on such a beautiful day? Still, I wasn't going to complain about some alone time with a hot American.

"So does it only get used for diving?"

"Yes. That's what it was designed for. It was one of the support boats for Ahmed Gabr's world record dive a while back. He got to 332 metres."

"That's insane. We've gone to what? Eighteen?" Adam asked.

"It took him fifteen hours, and he had to make a *lot* of decompression stops. We all breathed a sigh of relief when he got out, I tell you. Everyone was worried he'd pop, even the doctors. And yes, you've done eighteen metres so far, but today you'll go to thirty."

Nerves almost got the better of me as Gabe gave us a briefing, diagrams and all. Those butterflies were back, and this time, they'd brought their friends.

Our first stop would be Dahab's famous Blue Hole, a sinkhole that plunged one hundred and twelve metres into the depths just yards from land. We'd be picked up in a dinghy and taken to shore, where we'd start our dive at El Bells.

"It's like a narrow chimney you descend down, feet first. It's called the Bells because everyone clangs their tank on the side," Gabe told us. "After we come out at twenty-six metres, we'll swim along the reef wall, then over a small saddle into the Blue Hole itself. Don't get too excited, though—the hole itself isn't that exciting. It's just deep. But we can watch the free divers going down. Those guys are crazy."

Thinking back to my own attempt at diving sans tank, I certainly agreed with that sentiment.

"Where are we going in the afternoon?" I asked.

"Farther south, to Gabr el Bint. It translates as 'grave of the girl.' Legend says that once upon a time, a Bedouin girl eloped with her lover, but she was caught and killed there by her family."

"Isn't that a bit morbid?" Adam asked.

"The site isn't as grim as the name suggests. It's actually one of the most beautiful spots in Sinai. And because it can only be reached by boat or camel, the coral stays relatively undamaged. You'll both love it, trust me."

Adam gave me one of *those* smiles. "I know we will."

According to Gabe, we had over an hour to go until we reached the dive site, so Adam and I headed up to the top deck to take advantage of the morning sun.

As promised, Adam applied my sunscreen for me. And boy, did he do a thorough job of it. It took him at least twenty minutes. Only once he'd finished kissing his way across my shoulders did I lie down and pick up my novel. But I didn't read. My heart was still beating erratically, a staccato played by a musician with no sense of rhythm. It took me a couple of minutes to realise I was holding the fricking book upside down.

The boat swayed gently from side to side as it chugged through the clear blue waters of the Gulf of Aqaba, keeping a heading parallel to the shore. I soon gave up on the book completely and instead got distracted by the desolate beauty of Ras Mohammed national park.

I was used to England where you couldn't go six yards without seeing a shop or a housing estate, or at the very least a field with some horses or a few cows. But out here, there was nothing. No buildings, no roads. Just the occasional Bedouin and a handful of camels, travelling to or from some unknown destination. Miles and miles and miles of empty coastline.

After what seemed like forever, I spotted a cluster of buildings, and the boat started to slow.

Gabe poked his head up the stairwell. "We've arrived. The Blue Hole is just over there."

He pointed at a patch of sea darker than the rest, a stain that spread out in the blue. Half a dozen snorkelers bobbed around in the middle.

"Adam!" I nudged him and he sat up, rubbing sleep from his eyes. He looked adorable. *Adorable?* Oh, crap —now I was at it.

"We're here," I told him. "The Blue Hole."

He gave me a quick peck on the lips before he leaned over to look.

"I know Gabe said it was near to the shore, but if you stepped out of one of the restaurants, you'd practically fall into it."

"Well, *I* would."

Queen of the klutzes, reporting for duty.

"Let's go take a closer look."

On the main deck, we donned everything except our masks and fins, and then climbed down the ladder at the back into a bobbing dinghy.

Miracle of miracles—I didn't fall in. We perched on the edge as the boat puttered towards the shore, taking all the time in the world and giving me plenty of opportunity to sweat to death in my wetsuit. Egyptian time, once again.

Adam and Gabe hauled me onto dry land, and we set off along a sandy track that ran in front of the cafés.

As it started to climb uphill, I pointed at a rough-hewn wall filled with decorative plaques.

"What are those?" I asked Gabe.

"Each person who dies here gets a memorial. It's so we remember what a dangerous diving spot this is."

"I wish you'd told me that before we came here. Is it too late to go somewhere else?"

"You'll be fine as long as you don't do anything stupid. Some people say they hear the depths of the Blue Hole calling to them, and they feel compelled to head down. There's also a tunnel out to the open sea at fifty-six metres, and some idiots come to a nasty end when they attempt to go through it without the proper equipment. Just remember—don't go deeper than thirty metres, and if you're feeling suicidal, look up and keep looking up."

A nervous giggle bubbled out of me. "Look up. Got it."

My legs were on the verge of quitting when we finally got to the rocky ledge at the top of El Bells. One at a time, we lowered ourselves into the water and put on our masks and fins.

Gabe went first, then Adam, then me, and we squeezed through the chimney. *Clang, clang, clang.* The Bells was certainly living up to its name, although we weren't very tuneful. Good thing I wasn't claustrophobic.

At the bottom, we faced a wall of blue with nothing below or in front of us, only the reef wall to the sides. The sheer expanse of nothingness made me feel tiny and inconsequential, a mere speck in the universe, which was all I was in reality.

Every time I went somewhere new in Egypt, I found

a fresh perspective on life. Even though Fidda Hilal was in the middle of nowhere and the conditions could be a little primitive outside the hotels, I saw why Kat had stayed there. The town changed you. Whether it was the air, the water, or the mountains, I couldn't say, but I felt like a new person. And then, of course, there was Adam.

Hey, where did everyone go? I realised I'd spent too much time contemplating the meaning of life and kicked my feet to catch up with the others, swimming past coral shaped like elephant ears and thousands of tiny orange anthias fish. What was that frilly thing hiding under a rock? A lionfish?

All too soon, we swam over a coral saddle and arrived in the Blue Hole itself, its depths stretching away to darkness beneath us. A streamlined figure in a wetsuit whizzed past me headfirst, kicking with a single large fin. How deep were we? Fifteen metres. Gabe was right—the free divers were nuts.

As our air ran low, we surfaced, and Gabe hauled me back into the dinghy. Soon we were tootling back to the mothership.

"A fish kept biting me," Adam said as we changed over our air tanks. "My ears must taste good."

"It was a cleaner wrasse," Gabe told him. "They pick off bits of dead skin and stuff."

What a lovely visual. "You must be dirty."

"You don't know the half of it, babe."

My loins begged to disagree. And they told me they wanted to know the whole of it.

There was a throaty roar as the Fidda Nijmah's engines started, and the captain adjusted our heading for Gabr el Bint. The Grave of the Girl. The name made me shiver. In all this space, this vast blue ocean, how many other graves could there be? What lurked under the smooth blue sea?

Above the water, Gabr el Bint was nothing special. On the shore, there were just more of the ubiquitous mountains and a narrow camel track. But Gabe hadn't been lying—beneath the surface, it was something else. We descended into the most beautiful underwater garden I'd seen so far. In a huge sandy bowl, schools of fish circled clumps of coral, colours flashing in the sunlight that rippled through the water.

Pufferfish hid under giant table corals, and we found a blue-spotted stingray too, although that sped off as soon as it saw us. A turtle put on a show as it dove in front of us before heading off into the blue.

Gabe pointed upwards, and I saw the shadow of Fidda Nijmah above us. Time to go back already? I could have stayed down there exploring forever.

Adam was my consolation prize, and I curled against him on our private deck for the return journey. I'd always thought my favourite day, the one I'd remember for the rest of my life, would be my wedding day, but the trip to Gabr el Bint trumped every dream I'd had of walking down the aisle.

The stars were twinkling when we arrived back in Fidda Hilal, and the moon hung low over the mountains on the Saudi Arabian coast. By rights, I should have been exhausted as I helped to load the equipment onto a handcart on the jetty, but instead I felt energised.

"How about getting dinner in town?" I asked Adam.

"A date? Why not?"

We found a quiet table, tucked away at the back of a tiny restaurant next to the sea. Fish was our choice that evening, and Adam checked it had been ethically caught before we ordered.

"Do you fancy dessert?" I asked Adam,

I'd already loosened the drawstring on my shorts, and I wasn't sure I could eat another thing, but I might have been willing to try if there was cake.

"Let's have dessert back at the hotel."

"Do they still do room service this late?

"Dessert's sitting in front of me."

Oh. Oh!

"Babe! Are you okay?"

"Er, yes, uh, just a bit..." Shocked? Surprised? "Uh, a bit giddy."

I wasn't sure why. I mean, we'd surely been leading up to this. The thing was, I'd only ever slept with Bryce. We'd done it reasonably often, once a fortnight at least, but even so, my experience was limited. Most of what I knew came from reading romance novels, and I'd hardly tried any of it out in practice.

Adam walked around the table and crouched by my side, one hand on my thigh. "We don't have to if you don't want to. I thought you were into this as much as I am."

I didn't want to back out. "I am. Really, I am. Yes, I want to. I do. Really."

Come on, sense of adventure, don't desert me now.

We fell through the door to my villa, our hands everywhere. Muscles rippled under Adam's skin as he pressed against me, and heat zapped through my veins as he caressed my arms, my face, my stomach and then... His hands moved upwards.

"Are you okay with this?"

"Yes," I whispered. At least, I thought I was. I was more apprehensive than anything.

He peeled off my top, and I lifted my arms over my head to help him remove it. IIe sucked in a breath as he stood back and took me in. I sucked in a breath too, but mostly because I was afraid of muffin top.

"Beautiful," he whispered.

Good thing the lighting was dim, wasn't it?

My bra was the next thing to go as Adam expertly flicked open the catch. The flimsy scrap of pink lace that Kat had insisted I pack sailed through the air and caught on a light fitting. At least Adam was tall—there was no way I'd be getting that down by myself.

Lingerie wasn't Adam's only area of expertise—he knew what to do with the stuff underneath too. His fingers fluttered over my breasts, and my stomach clenched in a delicious promise of things to come. Then his mouth replaced his fingers, and my legs forgot what they were for.

Hold me up, dammit.

"I won't let you go, baby," Adam said as he nuzzled

my neck.

Oh, crap. I had to stop vomiting words out loud.

Finally, finally, Adam lifted the edge of my skirt, and a single stroke of his finger in exactly the right spot was all it took to send a rush of pleasure through me. My legs gave way completely, but I was saved by Adam's arms, holding me tight against him as I moaned something that was no doubt incoherent. Then my world went black.

As I regained my senses, I was aware that a courgette had somehow found its way into the mix. No, strike that. Not a courgette. A cucumber. I touched it tentatively, and Adam let out a low groan.

"Baby, the things you do to me."

With sudden clarity, it struck me that I had no idea what to do with a cucumber other than chop it up and put it into a salad, and I didn't think Adam would appreciate that.

Bryce had only had a gherkin, and in the six years we'd been together, I'd barely gotten any practice at this type of food preparation.

As Adam hooked his thumbs into my underwear, it was Bryce's face that popped into my mind, and it wasn't a face that said I was chef of the year. No, his vaguely disappointed expression suggested I was better at sticking a TV dinner into the microwave than attempting something gourmet.

That I was just "okay."

Average.

Mediocre.

Adam needed spectacular, amazing, fantastic.

Adam needed supercalifragilisticexpialidocious.

That wasn't me.

"What's wrong, beautiful?"

I wasn't going to be good enough. I was going to let him down. How would I be able to manage a marrow when I couldn't even keep a cornichon?

"I can't do this. I just can't do it."

Panic overcame me, and I ran to the door. Except once again, my sense of direction failed me, and instead of legging it into the night, I found myself in the bathroom.

Dammit, dammit, dammit!

"Callie?"

"I just need a minute."

The tears came as I sank onto the floor behind the door, floods of them. Rivers.

I'd ruined what we had.

Wrecked it.

By being me.

CHAPTER 15

FOR FOUR HOURS, I stayed in the bathroom, sitting on a towel with the fluffy white hotel bathrobe wrapped around me. I'd only spoken once—to ask Adam to leave —but I hadn't heard the door. Mind you, I'd been sobbing so hard a volcano could have erupted without me noticing.

This was worse than after Bryce. When Bryce left me, my heart had been shattered. Right now, it had been torn out of my chest, stomped on by an elephant, barbecued for a couple of hours, and then frozen into a block of ice.

Eventually, when I'd run out of both tears and toilet paper to blot them with, I struggled to my feet. Pins and needles stabbed at my legs. Had Adam gone? I peeped through the tiny gap, and the light on the bedside table cast a dim glow over the room. Everything was still.

Of course he'd gone.

I climbed into bed and pulled the covers over my head, which might have insulated me from the world outside, but it couldn't save me from my thoughts.

Over and over again, the mess I'd made ran through my head. Why couldn't I have gone along with things? It might have been okay. *Might, might, might.* The devil on my shoulder spoke in Persephone's voice.

Because you're just not good enough.

Of course I wasn't. I couldn't even manage to have a rebound fling properly.

At eight thirty, a knock on the door disturbed my misery. Oh, hurrah. Breakfast was here. Sent by Adam. More tears formed from somewhere and leaked out onto the pillow, leaving a streak of black as they mixed with what was left of my mascara.

The waiter didn't knock again for a whole hour. Were the catering team on Egyptian time too?

"I don't want any breakfast, thank you." My voice cracked on every word.

What was that metallic scraping sound? And how did Gabe get into my room?

He held up a bunch of keys, answering my unasked question. "I have a friend who works in hotel security, and I told him I was concerned about your welfare. Now, what's going on?"

"Nothing. I'm fine."

He burst out laughing. "Missy, you're crying in bed wearing yesterday's clothes when you should be at the dive centre. Adam's turned up, but he looks as pissed as a cobra in a frying pan. 'Nothing'…" Gabe made little air quotes. "Is not the answer I'm looking for."

I didn't know Gabe well enough to go into the sorry details of my sex life, or rather my lack of one. I'd save that for Kat later. Mental note: ask her to bring more tissues.

"Adam and I had a difference of opinion last night."

"That sounds like the understatement of the year."

"Well, it's as much as you're getting, so if you wouldn't mind leaving, I need to get some rest."

Why was I so much braver when I was upset and

sleep-deprived?

"No can do. You've paid for the course, and you're damn well going to finish it. You've got thirty seconds to get out of bed and into the bathroom before I carry you to the dive centre as you are."

He stared down at me, biceps flexing as he folded his arms. I didn't doubt he could make good on his threat.

Or that he would.

Fine. Fine, fine, fine. I got up and stomped over to the bathroom.

"And don't even think about locking the door," he shouted through the wood. "I've got a screwdriver, and I'll take the hinge pins out."

Dammit! How did he know that was my plan?

I showered and brushed my teeth as slowly as I possibly could. Flossing was very important, so my dentist always told me. She'd have been proud of me that morning. I got dressed in the plainest one-piece I owned and covered it up with a shapeless black kaftan, then went back out to Gabe.

"Well, lookee at you, trying to blend in with the locals. Come on, the driver's been waiting for an hour."

"You should have gone without me."

"Not happening."

He took me by the arm and half carried me all the way to the dive centre, depositing me in front of Adam, who was sitting down with his head slumped over his knees.

He looked up at the noise, and the anger Gabe had mentioned morphed into concern.

"Thanks, buddy. Give us a minute, would you?" he asked.

I didn't know where to look. Adam stood up and gently turned my chin so I faced him.

"I've been so worried about you, sweetheart. I don't know what went wrong, but I'll do anything to fix it."

"You left."

"I thought that was what you wanted."

"I don't really know what I wanted."

"What happened? Why did you get upset?"

How could I tell him that Bryce had popped into my head at the most inopportune moment? I shouldn't have been thinking of one man while I was with another.

"I just... I just wasn't ready, I think."

"We can wait as long as you want. In case you haven't noticed, I'm crazy about you."

"But what if I'm never ready? Or worse, what if we try and I'm not good enough?"

Adam took my hands in his. "Baby, one day you will be ready. And I know, I absolutely know, that you'll be everything I've ever dreamed of." He pulled me closer, and his lips brushed my ear as he whispered into it. "I'm not him."

Didn't I know it? I burst into tears again.

"Sweetheart, baby, don't cry. Please."

Salty rivulets streamed down my face. What an attractive sight I must be. But Adam leaned his forehead on mine and used his thumbs to wipe my tears away.

"Can we try again?"

I tried to nod and ended up bumping his head with mine. *Klutz.*

"Leaving you there by yourself destroyed me."

"You promise we can take things slowly?"

"Anything you want, I swear. You can take the lead."

"That's part of the problem. I don't know *how* to take the lead."

"Then I'll help you. We'll do this together, okay?"

I nodded again, and he gave me a gentle kiss on my cheek.

"What do you want to do today? Do you want to dive? If you don't, I'll tell Gabe, and he'll have to live with it."

"I'm here now. I do want to complete the course."

"Let's learn about fish."

Adam fetched Gabe back, and he provided each of us with a copy of the *Red Sea Reef Guide*, which he assured us was the definitive reference for marine life in the area.

"We'll stop for drinks in the café before we dive, and we'll take a look at what we can expect to see. I've picked a great site for us to dive today: Shark Cave."

My eyes widened. "Does it really have sharks?"

"No, and it doesn't have a cave either. I have no idea why it's called that. What it does have is a great reef, a coral garden, and the best selection of fish in Fidda Hilal."

The café was close to the shore, and we set up the gear before we sat down for drinks. I wasn't hungry, so I settled for a smoothie that would give me some energy.

Gabe launched into his descriptions of the marine life we would see, finishing with, "Look out for the trunk boxfish. I'll point them out. If you wiggle your finger in the sand, they'll come and play with you. I've brought the camera so we can take photos."

He'd certainly picked the right place to bring us. The first thing we saw was an eel garden on a sandy slope. The eels anchored themselves in the sand, and as we swam close to them, they retracted back into tubes in slow motion. Sort of like lipstick.

Gabe pointed out things we'd seen in the book, like a tiny, colourful nudibranch clinging to a rock and a moray eel hiding in a gloomy hollow. It saw us coming and snapped its jaws together. Persephone's spirit animal.

A school of bluefin trevallies swam past. Gabe had described them as the Porsches of the ocean because of their speed and sleek shape. He also spotted a scorpionfish, almost hidden against the rock it blended into.

The trunk boxfish were my favourite, though, and I had to remember to breathe as one cautiously approached me, looking for food disturbed by my finger in the sand. Oh my gosh! It came near enough to peck at my fingertip, and I withdrew the digit quickly. Not food. Not food!

Adam snuck up on me, and I looked up to see him next to me, his eyes crinkled in a smile. I tried to smile back around my regulator, but some water went into my mouth and I quickly thought the better of it.

Although I hadn't been too fond of Gabe this morning, I was glad he'd fetched me. Things were still a bit uncomfortable with Adam, but at least they were heading in the right direction again.

When we got back to the dive centre, I thanked Gabe profusely, both for his intervention and for the dive lessons.

"It's not over, you know. You may have completed both courses, but I'm still expecting you back here over the next few weeks."

"Definitely. I'm hooked now."

"Both of us are," Adam added as he walked in after rinsing his wetsuit.

"Glad to hear it." Gabe looked from me to Adam and back again. "Now go and enjoy the rest of your afternoon."

He gave me a wink.

I was still nervous as I slipped my hand into Adam's, but he gave it a little squeeze.

"What do you want to do this afternoon?" he asked.

"I haven't thought that far ahead. Could we just sit on the beach? Unless there's something else you'd prefer?"

"If that's what you want to do, then that's what we'll do."

We'd almost come full circle. Just a few days ago, we were lying on the beach like this, side by side, but so much had happened since then. I'd fallen for him, almost lost him, and then got him back.

I vowed not to screw things up again.

Which was exactly what Kat said too when I told her the whole sorry story later that evening. Mo was cooking again, which left us sitting on the sofa while he did the hard work.

"Are you crazy?" Kat asked. "He was offering it to you on a plate, and you knocked him back? I'd have been right in there." She paused for a second. "He's hot, right?"

I nodded.

"Yeah, I'd definitely have been right in there."

"I'm not you, though, Kat. I wish I could be so casual about the whole thing, but I really, really like him. More than I should. I want to go further, but what happens afterwards? I mean, he lives on a different continent."

"Just take each day as it comes. If things are meant to happen, they will."

"You sound like a philosopher."

"They do need school teachers in America, you know."

I threw a pink-tasselled cushion at her. Bullseye. "Kat! What happened to taking it slowly?"

"I can't believe I still haven't met this guy," she carried on, oblivious.

"I'll introduce you soon, I promise."

"Double date?"

"Maybe. If Adam agrees."

"He's smitten. He'll go anywhere you go."

She reached for the bottle of wine that was sitting on the table and topped up my glass. That would be my last drink. I was determined not to end up tipsy this evening, or worse, hungover in the morning.

"Mo and I are going diving tomorrow," Kat said. I'd forgotten she'd done her PADI course when she first came here. "We've got the day off. Why don't you join us?"

"I'll pass. My fingers are still wrinkled from being in the water so much. I'm looking forward to a few days chilling out on the beach before I get back into a wetsuit."

"How about dinner? Tomorrow evening? You can both come here and Mo can cook."

"He's cooking today."

"It's his hobby."

I wanted to spend more time with Adam, but having other people there would take some pressure off me. I was also curious as to what Kat thought of him. Hopefully, she'd have a higher opinion of him than she did of Bryce.

"I'd need to double-check with Adam, but I think that would be okay."

"Do you know what kind of food he likes?"

"He seems to eat everything. In quite large quantities."

"Got to keep his energy up, eh?" She winked at me.

"Shut up." I changed the subject. "Where are you going diving tomorrow? Anywhere I've been?"

"I don't think so. It's not a site the dive schools go to because the entry's difficult. You can only get in at high tide. It's just before Lionhouse Reef, but it doesn't have a name."

"I don't know where Lionhouse reef is."

"On the south side of town past the Happy Beach Hotel, about twenty minutes from here. It's one of the farthest sites you can drive to in that direction. The road ends, and you have to take camels after that, which is a bit out of our budget."

I'd never ridden a camel before. They always looked, well, slightly cheesed off. But I was supposed to be doing new things.

"Maybe we could do the camel thing before I go home? My treat."

"You don't have to do that."

"I know, but I'd like to. As a thank you for putting up with me over the past few weeks. I don't know what I'd have done without you in my corner."

"You'd probably have been moping at home while Bryce begged you through the letterbox to give him his script back."

"Don't remind me."

Mo came in with homemade pizza, and talk turned to lighter subjects as we ate our meal. We just had time to watch a movie with Mason, Kat's latest celebrity crush, before I headed back to the hotel.

"Mason's better than Scott and Brett and Zac and Carl and Trent and Ben," Kat told me as the opening credits rolled.

My eyes rolled too. "In what way?"

"He's got a ten pack."

"Is that even possible?"

"See for yourself."

I did. In fact, I was so busy trying to count, I had no clue what the movie was about. And Kat? She was enraptured. I was thrilled to see her happy—with her movies, with Mo, with her new life in Egypt. I only hoped that one day, I would find that happiness too.

CHAPTER 16

WHEN I TOLD Adam about Kat's invitation the next day, for dinner and a movie, he was more nervous than I thought he'd be.

"Kat won't bite. Just be yourself."

"It's not that, it's just...never mind. Of course we can go. It's kind of her to invite us."

"Awesome. My two favourite people in Fidda Hilal at the same table."

"Kat and Mo?"

"Kat and you, you dope."

I was starting to get used to it now, but that smile still made my heart skip.

"Glad that was your answer. So, what do you want to do for the rest of the day? I picked up a brochure from the tour company in reception."

I flicked through it. Trips to Petra and St. Katherine's monastery, horse riding, camel trekking, dinner in the desert at a Bedouin village...

"These all look great, but we'd need to book them in advance. Why don't we choose something for tomorrow?"

"Sounds good. The Bedouin dinner?"

"Why not?"

"But that still leaves today," Adam pointed out.

"How about we pop into town? I need to pick up

some gifts, and I haven't had a chance to mooch around in the high street yet."

I may have got a tiny bit carried away with the shopping. For such a hot country, the shops sure sold a lot of scarves, and I bought a whole rainbow of them, plus every time a waif of a child asked me if I wanted to buy a bracelet made from colourful string, of course I said yes.

I got dried hibiscus flowers to make tea, a guidebook for the town, and a couple of necklaces. I fell in love with a painting of a dolphin and that found its way into my bag too, as did a selection of postcards and a miniature shisha pipe, just because it was twinkly.

Adam bought a T-shirt.

Although he'd agreed to come into town, he didn't seem to be having much fun. Shopping had actually been one of Bryce's strong points—although he used to gripe about the prices, he understood colour, and he didn't mind spending an afternoon on the high street. Adam moped around, waiting in the corner of each shop while I browsed.

"We can go if you want. I don't have to do this."

"If you want to shop, we'll shop," he insisted.

I wrapped it up early. I could always go back another day with Kat. She loved shopping too. I'd already seen at least ten of the scarves hanging on a hook in her apartment, and she kept her bracelets stuffed into a pot on a side table.

We were due at Kat's at six, which gave us plenty of time to shower and change. I decided on a jade green skirt with a sparkly white tank top. Even though it was just Kat's and she'd seen me in my pyjamas often enough, I was going with Adam so I still wanted to look nice. A pair of jewelled sandals, and I was ready to leave.

Adam had made an effort too. It was the first time I'd seen him in a button-down shirt, and he'd dug out a pair of tailored shorts. The combination made my heart flip.

Since we were running early, we decided to walk. Adam dragged his feet like a condemned man walking to his execution. What was wrong with him today?

"If you really don't want to go, we can still dip out," I offered.

"No, we're going."

Step by step, we walked up the single flight of stairs, and I knocked on the door. Adam stood behind me, suddenly interested in his feet. Why had he gone so shy all of a sudden?

Nobody answered the door. I knocked again. Nothing.

Kat's home was on the top floor of a two-storey building, accessed by a metal set of stairs screwed to the side. I leaned over the railing, trying to see through one of the windows.

Adam grabbed me. "Careful you don't fall."

"I don't know why she's not answering. She definitely said six o'clock. She wanted an early night because she's got a new group of windsurfing pupils arriving first thing tomorrow morning."

"Could she have gone somewhere else first? The grocery store? Or perhaps to buy more liquor?"

Stopping to buy alcohol was a definite possibility for Kat.

"I guess. She was going diving with Mo, but that was in the morning. I got the impression Mo was going to cook something special, so wouldn't he have had to start preparing the ingredients? Why isn't *he* here at least?"

Adam tried to see in the window himself. With his extra height, he could lean farther across.

"It's dark, and I can't see any movement. I don't think they're home." Adam looked out to the street. "What car do they drive?"

"Mo just borrows a truck off a friend when they need it."

"Try calling Kat."

I pulled out my phone and dialled, but it went straight to voicemail. *Had* Kat mentioned going anywhere else yesterday? I sifted through memories and came up blank.

"She's not answering. What if they had an accident? While they were diving? It was only the two of them. What if they got caught in a current or tangled in a net or something?" Now I felt sick. "What if they drowned?"

"If they were going diving, they'd have needed to borrow the truck. They couldn't have carried all the gear otherwise. So if they didn't come up, the truck will still be there."

"We need to go and check."

Adam laid a hand on my arm. "Steady, baby. We will. Do you know where they went?"

"Not exactly. I mean, Kat said the place didn't have a name. It's near Lionhouse reef, to the south."

"I'll call Gabe, see if he's familiar with it. Hopefully he'll know somebody with a vehicle we can use."

Gabe did better than that. He met us back at the hotel with the dive centre's truck.

"Before we drive all the way out to Lionhouse reef, are you sure your friend didn't mention any other plans? Going to a restaurant, maybe?" he asked me.

"I'm certain. Well, almost. Ninety percent."

"She's sure," Adam said.

After twenty minutes, we left the asphalt and continued on a sandy track. Good thing it didn't rain in Fidda Hilal, because that "road" would have been a mess.

Five minutes later, a uniformed policeman stopped us at a checkpoint. Adam and I kept quiet and let Gabe do the talking. He spoke Arabic? I hadn't realised that before. After a few minutes of back and forth, I saw a banknote change hands, and we were on our way.

"I told him we're going to visit some friends at the Happy Life Hotel. There's not much else out here. He was in a good mood so I got away with paying the local bribe rate rather than the one they charge to foreigners."

"That's common?" Adam asked. "Bribery?"

"Out here? It's a way of life. We've got one more checkpoint to go, but I bet there's nobody there. The guy who mans it usually sits in the hotel kitchen, watching the football."

Gabe was right. We got through unhindered. Another five minutes, and he pulled up by the rocky shore.

"Well, this is the place. It's the only place you can dive between Lionhouse Reef and the next dive site along. And that's only three hundred yards more in that direction." He pointed back the way we'd come.

There was no truck in sight. Just to be sure we hadn't missed an important clue, we set out on foot, searching with the torches Gabe had fetched from the equipment locker before we left.

We'd been walking back and forth for half an hour when something glinted in my torch beam. I stopped to pick it up. The sight of the slim silver bracelet with a couple of charms on it—an ice cream cone and a cat—sent a chill down my spine.

"This is Kat's. She was here today."

"Are you sure?" Adam asked.

"I gave it to her for her birthday the year before last. Her cat had died a month earlier, and she missed him."

"The ice cream?"

"She's a girl."

"You can't be sure she dropped it today," Gabe said. "It could have been lying there for weeks."

"She was wearing it when I saw her yesterday evening. I remember because I planned to get her another charm for her birthday."

I'd even looked for one on our shopping trip today.

"Well, even if she was here earlier, she's gone now."

"Unless she's still in the water."

"The truck's gone."

"What if somebody stole it?"

Gabe was silent.

"Buddy, that's possible," Adam said.

"I guess," Gabe conceded.

The three of us looked at each other, and it wasn't

hard to see that Adam and Gabe were thinking exactly the same as me: what now?

I spoke first. "We need to check down there. Can we go back for the diving stuff?"

Gabe took his time answering. "I suppose we could come tomorrow and take a look. Man, I hate dead bodies."

Adam glared at him. "Have some tact."

"Sorry."

"What about tonight?" I pushed. "We did a night dive before."

"I've only ever dived here once. The entry's tricky, and the site itself is difficult to navigate. There's a maze of coral pinnacles before the reef wall drops off into the blue. Even if you two weren't relatively inexperienced, we wouldn't stand a chance of finding anyone in the dark."

Adam put an arm around me. "Baby, he's right. And I hate to say it, but if they are down there, an extra couple of hours won't make much difference."

Nausea turned into dizziness, but Adam held me tight. In my head, I knew they were both right, but that didn't make it any easier to climb into the back of the truck beside Adam and drive away.

At the dive centre, Gabe checked the tides online. High tide at the site would be at ten the next morning, and we'd be there.

I was still shaking as Adam walked me back to my room. Kat was my best friend. She'd always been there for me, and now I'd be there for her, but the thought that tomorrow I might find her body terrified me.

"Let's order some food and then try to sleep," Adam said. "That way, we can be fresh in the morning."

"I don't think I can eat anything."

"You have to try. Please? You need to keep your strength up."

I managed half a slice of pizza and six fries. I couldn't stomach any more.

"How about dessert?" Adam suggested. "I could order something else."

I shook my head, a move I instantly regretted because it made my fledgling headache worse.

"No, I couldn't stomach it, but I'll try to eat breakfast."

"Do you want me to come over and eat with you in the morning?"

Now I went tongue-tied. I tried to speak, but no words came out. All I managed was a pathetic cough, and Adam handed me his glass of water.

"You okay?"

"Yes." No. Not even a tiny bit. I took a sip of water, which at least soothed my throat. "I was just hoping that you might… stay with me tonight. Just to sleep. Nothing else."

His expression softened. "Of course. I'll get my pillow from next door and take the couch."

"I meant in the bed. I just… I just want to be close to you."

"It'd be my pleasure, baby."

It felt strange having a man next to me at night again, kind of like having a hot water bottle when I'd been without one all summer. Plus Adam was different to Bryce. Bryce had had his side of the bed and I'd had mine, and any accidental invasion on my part had been met with either a nudge or a polite request to move back to my own domain.

Adam slept smack in the middle and held me so tight I could feel every muscle in his chest. I'd been convinced I'd never sleep, but cocooned in his arms, I managed to get a few hours' rest.

In the early hours of the morning, I woke ages before the alarm to find the quilt had fallen off and I'd draped myself over Adam like a contented cat. Heck, I'd probably been purring in my sleep.

I moved one leg and...wait. Oh boy, that was an impressive piece of kit. Adam's eyes were closed, and his breathing was steady. Surely it couldn't hurt to have a little peek?

Slowly, slowly, I lifted his waistband and peered in. Then gulped as something the size of one of the Petronas Towers stared back at me. How in hell was that even supposed to fit?

"Sweetheart, if you're curious, you only have to ask."

I jumped out of my skin and snatched my hand away and glared up at Adam, my cheeks heating. He was grinning, the sod.

"I, uh, I..."

"That belongs to you. I belong to you. Do whatever makes you happy."

Did I dare? Be adventurous, right? I reached down again, and this time, I pushed his shorts off his hips to get a better look.

"That's never going to fit."

"Believe me, it will. Once I've warmed you up, it'll slip in easily."

I wanted to believe him, but still... Logistically, it was ambitious.

I ran a fingertip across veiny skin, silk over steel,

and jumped when a shudder ran through him.

"Did I hurt you?"

"Quite the opposite. If you carry on like that, we're going to make a mess."

"I don't mind cleaning up," I said quickly, then sighed. "But as you've probably gathered, I don't really know what I'm doing."

"Want me to show you?"

I couldn't look him in the eye.

"Please," I whispered.

He took my hand and placed it on his hardness, with his hand over the top. It wasn't long before he let out a low groan.

"I'll grab a tissue."

I got halfway out of bed before he pulled me back.

"Just stay with me for a few minutes, would you? I want you in my arms."

I stayed. He slept, and I slept.

When the alarm finally played "Blurred Lines" at eight o'clock, we made even more mess.

Neither of us cared.

CHAPTER **17**

"WE HAVEN'T MISSED the tide, have we?"

"Relax," Gabe said from the front seat. "We've got plenty of time."

Relax? How could I relax? Kat was still missing. I'd tried calling her ten times this morning, and we'd stopped at her apartment on the way to Lionhouse Reef, but nothing had changed.

Today, Hamid was behind the wheel of the pickup—the same Bedouin who'd driven us on our previous excursions. I gripped Adam's hand in the back seat, and I had to keep reminding myself he wasn't a stress toy. He hadn't said anything, but I'd noticed him grimace a time or two when I squeezed too hard.

I stared out of the window, watching but not seeing the passing scenery. Two trains of thought warred for my headspace. Firstly, Kat and Mo—I was beyond scared for them, but at the same time, I couldn't bear to think about what might have happened.

Better to think about Adam, and in particular, what had happened last night. Although we hadn't gone all the way, we'd definitely taken a step forward. And I'd loved every second of it.

I glanced at him from under my eyelashes. That man made my insides turn cartwheels. He made me *feel* with every strand of my DNA.

And last night, he'd said he was mine.

Well, I was his. I just needed to find the courage to tell him.

But Kat and Mo took priority. We got through the first checkpoint by paying the requisite fee, no problems, but when we reached the second, we hit a snag. Four policemen were on duty there. None of them looked friendly, and they all had guns.

I clutched at Adam's fingers while Hamid fired off rapid streams of Arabic, only to be met with grunts and shrugs in response. Gabe tried as well, but eventually he too admitted defeat.

"They won't let us past. They say the dive sites are closed for maintenance."

"Maintenance?" What maintenance? "Seriously? It's just rocks and sand."

"Exactly what I said. It's bullshit. We even offered them extra money, but they wouldn't play ball. We can't go past."

"Why would they say that?"

"No idea. A lot of things that happen in Fidda Hilal have no logical explanation."

"Is there another way around?"

"Not unless you can abseil down a mountain."

"So what do we do now?"

"We go back. We don't have a choice."

I tried to protest, but Hamid swung the truck in a wide arc and headed back the way we came.

"Can we go to the police station, see if we can get them to grant us permission?" Adam asked.

Gabe let out a long sigh. "Sorry, but I can't. If you cross the police around here, they make your life a living hell. And I've got a small issue with my work permit."

"What kind of issue?"

"I don't have one. But don't worry, my PADI qualification is absolutely kosher."

"Dare I ask why not?" A note of exasperation tinged Adam's words.

"They're scarce as hens' teeth, and even if you *can* get one, they're expensive—about eight thousand Egyptian pounds. Most foreigners here just take a chance and pay the occasional bribe for the police to turn a blind eye to the problem."

"Fine." Adam's exasperation turned into full-blown annoyance. "In that case, can you at least drop *us* off at the police station and we'll go in on our own?"

"Sure, I guess."

I scurried along behind Adam as he marched up the steps to the police station and stopped in front of a rickety wooden desk. And when I say rickety, I mean it was practically firewood. One leg had been replaced by the bottom of a chair with a three-inch stack of dog-eared paper tied to the top to increase the height. What were all those sheets? Crime reports?

The young officer sitting behind the desk looked up, his face twitching.

"Do you speak English?" Adam asked.

"No."

So how come he'd answered in it?

"Spanish?"

A shake of the head followed by a shrug.

"You speak Spanish?" I asked Adam.

"A little."

Perhaps we could try Google Translate? I typed in the phrase, but I'd only got halfway through mangling the Arabic for "How do we report a missing person?" when an older man appeared from a back room.

"We can help you?"

"I want to report two people missing."

He shrugged. I could sense a theme here.

"People come, people go."

"They haven't gone anywhere. Their home and all of their belongings are still here."

"Then they go to visit friend."

"They were meant to meet us last night, and they didn't turn up."

He laughed and showed us his watch—made by Kalvin Clein, no less. "Egyptian time. Maybe they just running late."

"Can we at least file a missing persons report?"

"No reports, all up here." He tapped a finger on his head.

"In that case, I'd better give you their names."

"No bother, I forget."

This was hopeless. I wanted to scream in frustration and punch something. Preferably the village idiot standing in front of me.

Adam tried again. "We think they may have had an accident diving. We went to look for them by Lionhouse reef, but we couldn't get through."

"Yes, we are doing maintenance," he announced, pride evident in his voice.

"Could we go through if we promise not to disturb anything?"

"Maintenance. Very important."

Adam gritted his teeth. "How long will 'maintenance' take?"

"Maybe one month, maybe two month." Another

shrug. "Maybe three month."

Adam tensed up, and if he'd taken a swing at the irritating little man, I'd have gladly mortgaged my soul to pay his bail money. But that wouldn't have helped the hunt for Kat.

"Leave it," I whispered. "He's not worth getting in trouble over. We'll think of something else."

How difficult *was* abseiling?

Out in the street, Adam waved down a passing taxi. At least, the driver claimed it was a taxi. I had my doubts since it was a single cab pickup and I had to sit on Adam's lap. Despite the fact that at least four policemen loitering outside the station saw us like that, none of them moved to stop us—it seemed they didn't get too picky about seatbelts in Fidda Hilal. Not like bloody maintenance.

"Let's take another look at their apartment," Adam said. "Just in case they've come home."

As soon as we reached the bottom of the steps outside the apartment, we knew there was a problem. The door hung askew on its hinges, creaking back and forth in the gentle breeze.

"Shit," Adam muttered.

Inside, the place was trashed. And I mean trashed. Kat's beautiful scarves lay strewn on the floor, and someone had poured a bottle of cooking oil over them. The couch cushions had been slashed, as had most of Kat's and Mo's clothing, and shards of crockery littered the floor.

This was more than just a simple burglary.

"Why?" I gasped.

Adam was equally horrified. "Fuck me." Then under his breath, he added, "What did they get themselves into?"

"What do you mean? Kat wasn't 'into' anything."

"Easy, sweetheart. I didn't mean she was peddling drugs to kiddies or anything like that. But the fact is, the pair of them have disappeared, and from the look of this place, they did a good job of pissing somebody off."

"Kat would never have got into anything bad. She's not that kind of person."

"How well did you know Mo?"

"I've only met him a couple of times, but he seems really kind. And Kat's head over heels in love with him. More than anything, I trust her judgement."

Adam perched on the end of the couch, squashing down the remains of the spilled stuffing.

"So, where do we start?"

I was as clueless as him. "I have no idea."

"How about we try searching for the truck? That's a pretty big thing to hide. Any idea who Mo would have borrowed it from?"

"No, but we could try asking at the watersports club. Someone there might know."

We checked around the apartment before we left, just in case there were any clues. Not that either of us knew what we were looking for. A map with a big red X would've been handy, or a diary.

At least I managed to salvage Kat's jewellery and some cash. Thankfully, the burglars had missed the tin of chickpeas that wasn't really a tin of chickpeas at the back of a kitchen cupboard. Kat had used tins as hiding places ever since we'd shared a flat at university. I'd put the hoard into the hotel safe until we found her.

The front door no longer closed properly, but we used the remains of a paperback to wedge it shut as best we could. I wasn't worried about the place being broken into again. There really wasn't much more damage anyone could do.

Eid gave me a dirty look as we walked into the sports club.

"See who it is. The English slut and her new fiancé."

Adam balled his fists up.

"Leave it," I whispered. "Think of Kat."

I could quite cheerfully have socked the slimy git too, but I heeded my own words and smiled sweetly.

"Eid, I was wondering if you've seen Kat or Mo? I can't get hold of either of them."

"No, I have not. Neither of them turned up for work today. When you do find them, you can tell them they're both fired. My father is never employing an English person again. They are unreliable."

Oh, how I wanted to pound Eid into the colourful woven flooring.

"Would you happen to know who Mo borrows a truck from on occasion?" I asked through gritted teeth.

"I can't imagine anybody would be stupid enough to lend a vehicle to someone so untrustworthy."

Adam took hold of my hand. "Come on, we're wasting our time with this idiot."

Who else could we ask? I was scanning the windsurfers on the lagoon, searching for anyone proficient enough to be a colleague of Kat's, when a ginger-haired girl scurried up to us.

"I overheard you talking to Eid," she said. An Aussie—Fidda Hilal was a real melting pot of cultures. "I think I might be able to help, but I need to finish setting up the windsurf boards first or Eid will fire me next."

"We'll meet you afterwards," I quickly offered. Could this be the lead we were looking for? "Where and when?"

"In half an hour? By the beach bar?"

"We'll be there."

Adam and I snagged a table straight away, but I was so nervous that I barely touched my soft drink. Food was out of the question.

"Do you think she'll come?"

"It was her idea, sweetheart."

When she didn't arrive on time, I began to fear I'd been right to worry, but forty minutes after we met, she slipped furtively into the seat we'd left free for her.

"Hi. I was worried you might have left—setup took me longer than I thought. I'm Grace, by the way."

"I'm Callie, and this is Adam."

"Do I know you from somewhere?" she asked Adam, squinting against the sun. "Have you been here before?"

He shook his head. "A lot of people say that. I've just got one of those faces."

Maybe he really did—it was the second time I'd heard someone ask that.

"I guess. Anyhow, I heard you ask who Mo might have borrowed a truck from?"

"That's right."

"He has a friend in town. Samir. He works at the

Octopus dive shop, and he's got a big maroon truck with alloy wheels. I'm sure I saw Mo driving it once. Does this have anything to do with Kat and Mo not coming to work today? Eid's chucking a mental, and we're all working triple time under threat of being sacked if we don't."

"Eid's a treasure, isn't he?" I said. "As for Kat and Mo, we can't find either of them. They were supposed to meet us for dinner yesterday but they didn't show up, and when we went to their apartment, we found it'd been burgled."

Grace lifted her hands to her cheeks as she gasped. "That's terrible! They were both such lovely people." *Stop using the past tense. They still* are *lovely people.* "I talked to Kat every day at lunch, and she never mentioned any travel plans. We were planning to have a movie night next week. She told me about you. I'm sorry about the whole wedding thing, by the way. That was a shitty thing to happen."

"Thanks. It was quite a shock."

"I'd better get back." Grace tapped her watch. "Eid times us on our breaks because it beats doing proper work. I might see you around?"

"Yes, I hope so."

"Good luck with finding Kat and Mo." She pushed her chair back and got up to leave, but before she walked, away, she leaned down to whisper in my ear. "By the way, I think you lucked out on the replacement."

Even in a scruffy Harley Davidson T-shirt and a pair of Raybans, Adam looked like a model, but more importantly, he was beautiful on the inside too.

Yes, I definitely did luck out when I met him.

CHAPTER 18

ONLY ONCE WE were in a taxi on our way into town did we realise we had no idea where the Octopus dive shop actually was. Thankfully our taxi driver was able to help us out.

"Walk down the small street beside the supermarket. It is on the *yemeen*—the right. You can't miss it."

Well, he was right about that. You'd have to be blind not to see the giant fibreglass octopus outside. It was the size of a small car, each arm jauntily holding up one letter of the word "Octopus". Of course, there was an arm left over, so they'd used that for the exclamation mark.

Flashing lights on each arm pulsated in time to bawdy piped music, and on a normal day, that alone would have been enough to stop me from going near the place. I'd go insane if I had to listen to it for longer than ten minutes.

As promised, there was Samir, standing behind the counter. How did I know that? Because his name badge read *I am Sa ir. How may I hellp?*

"Samir?"

He paused for a second, then reached under his floppy hair and removed a pair of earplugs.

"Sorry?"

"You're Samir?"

He looked at me as if I was stupid, then pointed to his name badge. Okay, yes, he was definitely Samir.

"I'm searching for a couple of friends of mine. Kat and Mo?"

At the mention of Mo's name, Samir's face clouded over, and he slammed his cup of coffee down on the counter.

"When you find him, tell him he is never borrowing my truck again."

"Uh, okay. Can I ask why?"

"When he bring it back yesterday, he just leave it outside with the keys in it. Anyone could have steal it."

Oh? So the truck was back with its owner?

"That sounds most unlike him. What time did he bring it back?"

"In the evening, and he promise to bring it back by lunchtime."

"Did he say anything when he dropped it off?"

"I didn't see him. I just woke up this morning and the truck was there, lucky for him. It is expensive truck."

Adam came up behind me. "Can I buy these?" He put two diving torches down on the counter. "And could we take a look at the truck?"

When Adam forked out a pile of cash for two expensive flashlights, Samir became a little friendlier, if not slightly bemused as he led us through a door at the back of the shop. A gleaming Dodge Ram was parked in a dusty yard, most out of place among the palm trees.

Adam gave a low whistle. Samir was right—it was a very nice truck.

"My father is top camel breeder," he told us. "This

was birthday present."

He popped the locks, and I opened the doors. I had no idea what I was looking for, which was probably why I didn't find anything.

Meanwhile, Adam fished around in the bed of the truck. There were various bits and pieces kicking around in there, and he retrieved a diver's mask from under a grubby woven mat.

"Is this yours?" he asked Samir.

I scrambled ass-first out of the truck as Samir shook his head. Adam passed the mask to me, and I saw the initials KMR scratched on one edge.

"Katerina Marie Rawlins," I murmured.

"So this is Kat's?"

"Well, I can't say for certain, but those are her initials."

"Assuming it is, she must have come up from the dive. She wouldn't have gone down there without a mask."

"So where the heck is she?"

We left our phone numbers with Samir, who grudgingly agreed to ask around in case anyone saw Mo leaving the truck. He promised to call if he found anything.

Then we were back to square one.

"Do you have a recent photo of them?" Adam asked.

"I don't have any of Mo, but I have some of Kat."

I handed my phone over because I couldn't bear to look at them. The last pictures were from just before my aborted wedding. We'd been trying our outfits on the day before Bryce called everything off.

"Is this you in your wedding dress?" Adam asked quietly.

"Yes."

"You'd have made a beautiful bride."

A tear leaked out. Dammit! I thought I was past all this.

Adam kissed it away. "You still *will* be a beautiful bride. Just with a different man."

That was it. Another piece of my heart, lost.

I let Adam do the talking as we hit the high street to show Kat's photo to the shop and restaurant owners. What would I have done without him? It didn't bear thinking about. Nobody had seen her, and my shoes were pinching by the time we returned to the hotel. Even though Adam must have been exhausted himself, he insisted I rest on the sofa while he massaged my feet.

Was it too soon to fall in love again? I was beginning to think I might not have a choice in the matter.

Despite the dire situation, or perhaps because of it, I was so tired I almost fell asleep before the food arrived. I managed to force down a few morsels of pasta before I collapsed into bed. There was no question over whether Adam would stay. We didn't even discuss it. He just lay down beside me, then held me as we both drifted off.

In the morning, I woke up in the same position as I had the previous day. Adam too. The only difference? I was a bit braver as my hand slid downwards. When the alarm went off twenty minutes later, Adam's huge wotsit had been replaced by a huge grin, and I was feeling a sense of self-satisfaction because I'd learned a new skill.

One I intended to perfect with practice.

With little else to go on, we agreed over breakfast to canvass the shopkeepers we hadn't spoken to yesterday. Adam had the idea of getting flyers made up, so we also needed to find a printer.

"Maybe the hotel could help," I suggested.

"Good idea. I mean, they did a fairly professional job on the one for you. Someone even photoshopped your face into a little heart shape."

Was I ever going to live that one down?

Just as we were heading out the door, Gabe strolled up the path.

"We can't go diving today," Adam told him. "Or at all unless Kat and Mo turn up. They take priority."

"I wasn't expecting you to. Kat and Mo are the reason I'm here. Have you heard the rumours?"

"What rumours?"

"The rumours that Mo topped Kat and the other two missing girls and took off for parts unknown. There're a handful of variations—maybe he was involved in an operation to traffic people into Israel or possibly something drug-related—but those are hazy."

I'd received so much bad news lately that this time, I barely even felt giddy.

"Are you serious? Mo?"

I hadn't picked up any bad vibes from him. On the contrary, he'd seemed to be a gentle soul, and Kat would have told me if he'd done anything that concerned her. We spoke about things like that, Bryce excepted.

Gabe held his hands up. "Hey, I barely knew the guy. Don't shoot the messenger. I just thought you should know, that's all. People might not be too keen to help you."

"But why wouldn't they help us look for Kat?" I asked. *She* hadn't been accused of any wrongdoing. Surely people would show some compassion?

"The townsfolk don't like scandal. Fidda Hilal relies on tourists for its income, and if stories got out about foreigners coming to a nasty end, revenues would drop. It's far easier for people to pretend she decided to leave for some reason."

"So money's more important than a woman's life around here?"

"I didn't say it was right. But it's hard to make enough money to survive in this sandpit. Too many people scratch out a living on the breadline. If tourists don't come, families don't eat—it's as simple as that."

"Bad publicity or not, we have to keep looking," Adam said. "We can't sweep this under the carpet and go on with our vacation as if nothing happened."

"I'm not saying you should stop. Just be careful, that's all. And don't be surprised if you come up against a brick wall."

The nausea came back. Finding a needle in a haystack was hard enough without the haystack fighting against you. We went into town anyway, but by noon, we knew Gabe was right. Our search was fruitless. Yesterday, people had been non-committal but taken our details and promised to call if they heard anything, but today, they turned us away before we finished a sentence.

If it wasn't for Adam plodding along by my side, I'd have lost all hope. The man was a saint. He'd never even met Kat, but there he was, giving up his time and energy to search as hard as I was.

It was then that I realised I loved him, and it was

that love that kept my heart beating.

Midway through the afternoon, we bought sandwiches from a pavement café, but I ate two bites of my cheese one and threw it away. My stomach couldn't tolerate even the blandest of foods. We'd just been to the only print shop in town, and they refused to help with leaflets. That left us with the hotel to try.

"Do you have contact details for Kat's family?" Adam asked as he chewed. "We should tell them that she's missing."

"I don't, because she doesn't have any. She was an only child, and her parents died in a car crash when she was ten. She lived in a series of foster homes until she was eighteen, and she's struggled to put roots down ever since—I think that's why she keeps moving from place to place."

"What about Mo?"

"I don't even know his surname, but somebody must. What about Samir?"

"I bet guys at the sports club would. But while we're in town, let's try Samir first."

At the Octopus, we found Samir in an even grouchier mood than before.

"Sorry, but I cannot help."

"Can't? Or won't?" I was done taking shit from the locals.

"Ma'am, I have my own family. I don't want to cause any trouble for them with the police."

The police? Why were the police involved? They wouldn't even give us the time of day when we tried to report Kat and Mo as missing.

"What do you mean?"

Samir shifted from foot to foot as if he wanted to

make a run for it. Adam must have had the same thought because he moved sideways to block the door.

"The police say not to look for the tourist. That she went to Cairo."

"Cairo?"

Could it be true? Mo *did* come from there.

"That's what they say."

How were we supposed to look in Cairo? We'd barely made any headway in Fidda Hilal, and that was a tiny town. Cairo was a sprawling city.

"And Mo? Did he go to Cairo, too?"

Samir shrugged and shook his head. "Mo is Egyptian. He does not concern you. You must leave now."

He spread out his arms and shooed us towards the exit. As soon as we stepped out the door, Samir slammed the metal shutters down on the shop, and a few seconds later, the lights on the Octopus went out and that awful music stopped playing.

"What now? Do we stay here? Go to Cairo? Give up and fly home?"

Adam shook his head. "Not Cairo. There's a distinct smell of bullshit floating around here. We've got two rumours circulating, and they contradict each other. How could Kat be murdered by Mo *and* have gone to Cairo?"

"I don't know. I just don't know. I don't know anything anymore. I can barely even remember my own name."

"Then it's time to go back to the hotel. We both need some rest."

CHAPTER 19

THAT EVENING, I paced around my villa, hoping the monotonous motion would shake something free in my brain. But nothing rattled loose.

After my hundredth pass in front of the sofa, Adam reached out and snagged my hand.

"Sweetheart, wearing the floor out isn't going to help."

"I know, I know. I'm just so... Arrrrgh."

I tore at my hair in frustration as I flopped down beside him. Right away, his arms wrapped around me, holding me in place so I couldn't get tempted to do another circuit.

He kissed me gently on the temple. "I am too, but we need to get some sleep. Neither of us is at our best right now."

I captured his lips with mine. I didn't need sleep; I needed a distraction. And he gave it to me, trailing soft kisses along my jawline as one hand squeezed my ass.

"You want me to take your mind off things, baby?"

"Yes."

I wanted to escape to a world that wasn't this one.

He kissed me again, more deeply this time, and his fingers left fire in their wake as he peeled me out of my shirt. He tried to extinguish the flames with his tongue, but all that did was make things hotter.

I wrapped my legs around his waist as he picked me up, and we both landed on the bed in a tangle of limbs. I wasn't sure where I ended and he began. The Ass was mine. Over the next few hours, he took me on a journey through sweet oblivion, giving me everything I'd been missing in six wasted years with Bryce.

The trip to heaven was a sharp contrast to my day in hell.

With hindsight, perhaps we should have spent more time sleeping, but what were a few dark circles between friends? I needed Adam like a glutton needed dessert.

Our exhaustion wasn't helped by another unproductive day of searching. Although we did manage to track down Simone and Elaine, the two girls I'd met at Kat's when we had that movie night. Simone seemed nervous, and her eyes kept darting around as if just speaking to us could get her into trouble.

"Give me your number, okay? If I hear anything, I'll text you. But I know I won't. That's not how it works around here."

Elaine was a little more positive, maybe because she was several years older with slightly more backbone.

"I haven't heard anything, but I'll keep an ear out. Why don't you try contacting the families of the other missing girls? Just in case the disappearances are linked? Three voices might be harder to ignore than one."

Why hadn't we thought of that? Most likely because my thoughts were so jumbled by then that I could barely string a sentence together.

"Great idea. Do you have any idea who they are?"

"Simone knew the waitress. I'll call her."

"She wasn't very helpful when we spoke to her earlier."

"Then I'll have to be convincing. I'm afraid I never met Irina, but perhaps you could try the watersports club?"

"We'll do that. And thank you—you have no idea how much this means."

A single tear rolled down her cheek. "Kat was my friend, too."

Back at the hotel, Adam and I parked ourselves on a couple of sunloungers next to the watersports club and waited for Grace to go past. Although she didn't leave until dusk, the wait was worth it because she gave us details of Irina's Facebook page.

"You can probably find some of her family on there," she said. "Good luck with everything. Irina was a doll."

Together, Adam and I drafted a message to send to Irina's father, and also to the parents of the waitress. According to a text message from Elaine, she was called Melati and her folks lived in Indonesia.

"This is so hard," I said. "I mean, how do you write a message to a parent explaining that you think their daughter might have been abducted, or worse?"

I'd occasionally had to have difficult conversations with parents at school, but suddenly, telling Mrs. Biggs that little Katie had high-kicked Archie Maitlin in the nuts because she wanted to be Wonder Woman didn't seem so awkward anymore. Mrs. Maitlin had threatened to hire a "no win, no fee" solicitor, but Mrs. Biggs was married to a barrister so she'd said Mrs. Maitlin could bring it on, and I'd had to mediate. Secretly, I thought Archie had deserved the kick.

"Let's just keep it generic," Adam suggested. "We'll say we're trying to get hold of someone who can help us to find Irina. Then hopefully we can get a phone number and speak to them directly."

An hour after we'd sent the emails, there was a quiet knock at the door.

"Did you order food?" I asked Adam.

"Not yet. You stay there, and I'll get it."

A few seconds later, he led a small Egyptian man I'd never seen before into the room.

"This guy says he needs to speak to you." The look on his face said that he didn't want to let him anywhere near me. It didn't escape my notice that Adam kept his body firmly between the two of us.

When the man got closer, I could see he was more of a boy. Everything about his demeanour said "shifty," and he had a nasty bruise spreading across a puffy cheek. I guessed his age at fifteen.

"You are Callie?" he asked.

"Yes, but I don't think I know you?"

"I am brother of Samir. He say you look for Miss Kat and Mohammed."

My heart started to beat faster. "That's right."

"A friend of mine, he was in the prison last night. He hear there is a foreign person locked up and that it is a woman. He hear she have yellow hair."

Which would fit with Kat's blonde tresses.

"Do you know how long she's been there?"

He shrugged. "Short time, probably. People not usually last long in the prison."

"Do you know *why* she's there? What did she do?"

Another shrug. "That is all I know. I hope you find Miss Kat. She used to help me with my English speaking."

"Thank you for coming—we really appreciate it."

His brow furrowed with a lack of understanding.

"Appreciate—it means it's made us happy," I clarified.

He smiled at us, displaying a crooked row of brown teeth. "*Afwan*. You are welcome. It is good that you are happy."

With that, he darted out the door and disappeared into the night.

I turned to Adam. "The police station? Do you really think she's been at the police station the whole time?"

"I don't know, but I'm beginning to believe that in this town, anything's possible."

"Well, we need to go there and find out." I pulled on one trainer and started doing it up.

"Whoa, it's nearly nine o'clock. You can't just march into the police station and demand answers, especially at this time of night."

"Well, I can't just leave her there."

"You won't. *We* won't. But we need to come up with a plan before we rush in there, all guns blazing. I'll have a chat with Gabe in the morning. He seems to have a few contacts."

"But Kat's in *prison*."

"We don't know that for sure. The first thing we

need to do is confirm that, one way or the other."

Logically, I knew he was right. But over the long hours of the night, with little sleep, my anger and frustration built. Someone had to *do* something. And that someone had to be me. Common sense went out of the window, perhaps because I may have been suffering from just a teeny bit of pre-menstrual tension, and I vowed not to leave Kat in jail for a moment longer than I had to.

The next morning, I waited until Adam was in the shower, then pulled on my shoes, scribbled out a note to let him know what I was doing, and ran for the taxi rank outside the hotel. By the time I got to the police station, fury had descended upon me like a pack of hungry wolves.

I marched up the steps and found a different man seated at the front desk.

Hands on hips, I stared him down. "Where's my friend?"

He shrank back and tried shrugging. What *was* it with all the shrugging around here?

"I do not know."

I thumped my fists on the desk, and it tilted alarmingly to the side. Half a croissant slid onto the floor.

"Yes, you bloody do. She's in there somewhere." I jerked my thumb towards the rear of the building.

"Give her back!"

He looked somewhat alarmed as he stumbled backwards in the direction I'd pointed.

"I get the boss."

Guess he wasn't used to being confronted by an angry woman before he'd even finished his breakfast. I paced the room while I waited, anger fuelling my steps. This place was filled with imbeciles, and the building itself had a feeling of malevolence. Dark and dingy, its walls spoke of untold horrors. It gave me the creeps.

"Babe, what the hell are you doing?"

Oops. Adam had got here faster than I thought.

"Something. I'm doing *something*. Which is more than anyone else is."

The door at the back opened, and a tall, thin man sporting a greasy moustache walked out. Desk Guy skulked behind him, looking as if he'd rather be anywhere but in that room. The newcomer wore a pristine white uniform with a row of medals pinned to his chest. The big cheese?

I stomped up to him, almost at snapping point, and jabbed a finger into his chest.

"Give Katerina back."

He glared as if I'd just given him a contagious disease. "You foreigners need to stop meddling with what does not concern you. You are *mushkellah*. You are trouble."

"I know you've got her here, and I'm not leaving unless she leaves with me."

"You think you can come to our country and tell us what to do? Things don't work like that around here."

"Well, maybe they should. You can't just go around kidnapping people."

"You know nothing about what goes on. Stupid Englishwoman."

"Well, perhaps you'd like to fucking enlighten me," I yelled.

Where did that come from? Even Adam shifted nervously.

The cop boss couldn't hide the fury in his eyes, but no matter. I squared up to him and matched it with my own.

"Fine," he snapped, then turned on his heel and marched out the door he'd come through.

Fine? What did that mean? Was he coming back? Desk Guy gingerly tiptoed back to his chair and reversed it into the corner as far as it would go while I resumed pacing.

"Babe?" Adam tried.

"Just leave it, okay?"

Ten minutes later, the door opened again and the police captain marched out. A junior officer followed behind, half dragging a slumped figure. Oh holy hell, was that Kat? He shoved her at Adam.

The captain stood in front of me, an arrogant tilt to his nose. "You take her and you leave. You leave town. You leave Egypt. If you are still here tomorrow evening, you will be back here, all of you, and that is something you will regret. Do you understand?"

My anger had turned to fear at the sight of Kat. She whimpered in Adam's arms, her face a mass of bruises. All I could do was nod.

"Now get out." The captain pointed at the door.

Adam scooped up Kat, and the three of us almost fell down the steps in our haste to get away. That place was evil.

"We need to take her to a hospital," Adam said. "Quickly."

I ran into the road to try and flag down a taxi. Two swerved around the madwoman waving her arms before I planted myself in front of a third. The driver had two choices—mow me down or stop. Thankfully, he chose the latter. Adam bundled Kat into the back seat, and I clambered in behind them.

"The hospital," Adam ordered the quivering driver. "Now."

In daylight, I got a better look at Kat, but I almost wished I hadn't.

"Oh my goodness," I whispered.

"Callie, is that you?" Her voice came out as a croak.

"It's me."

I took her hand and squeezed it gently, trying to give her comfort, but she winced, and when I turned it over, I saw the fresh cigarette burns dotting the palm. Her eyes were so puffy they were swollen shut, and there wasn't an inch of her I could see that wasn't covered in bruises. Her hair was tangled, and a streak of dried blood ran from her scalp down the side of her face.

"Kat, what the hell did they do?"

She had a coughing fit before she managed to speak, and the driver passed a bottle of water back between the seats. I helped her to take a sip.

"They said we killed a girl," she choked out.

"You and Mo?"

A weak nod and another cough.

"They still have him. We need to get him out."

"Save your strength, sweetheart," Adam said. "We can talk about this after you've seen a doctor."

"Who..." Cough. "Are you?"

"This is Adam. You remember I told you about Adam?"

"Your hot guy?"

Adam raised an eyebrow.

"Yes, my hot guy."

At least, I hoped he was still mine after the stunt I'd pulled this morning. I'd deal with the inevitable bollocking later. Right now, we had Kat back, and that was all that mattered.

The taxi pulled up in front of a soulless grey cube, whose sign proclaimed it to be the Fidda Hilal Specialist Hospital. Quite what they were specialists in, it didn't say. Once we'd piled out, the driver sped off without waiting for us to pay the fare.

Adam picked up Kat once more and carried her inside. The reception area was as stark as the rest of the building, just a row of plastic chairs against a wall.

"We need to see a doctor," I told the young girl manning the desk. She seemed a little surprised to see a patient there at all.

"You are sick?"

"Not me." I pointed at Kat, and the girl's eyes widened. "Her."

She jabbered into the phone, eyes fixed on Kat, and a few minutes later, a man in a white coat came out.

"What is wrong?"

Good grief—wasn't it obvious? "My friend's been injured."

He gave her a cursory glance and sighed. "Ah. She has been in the police station?"

"How do you know?"

"This is what they all look like."

The blood in my veins turned to ice, and even Adam reeled at the doctor's words. Kat wasn't the first person to be hurt that way?

The doctor beckoned to us. "Come, I will treat her. But you will have to pay."

Adam fished out his wallet and tossed a credit card at the startled receptionist. "Put it on that. She gets the best of everything."

CHAPTER 20

FOUR HOURS LATER, Kat had been fixed up as well as the staff at the hospital could manage. It was better equipped than I'd imagined it would be, helped no doubt by a liberal application of Adam's money. I'd tried to pay the bill myself, but he wouldn't hear of it.

"We'll talk about it later. Right now, you just need to look after Kat."

I couldn't let him fork out that much money, especially as he wasn't working at the moment. But he was right. We'd deal with that afterwards. Kat's wellbeing took precedence.

Dr. Dawoud had proven to be kind and compassionate, and he'd gently cleaned her wounds up and stitched the worst of them. An X-ray showed she had a fracture in her arm, so she was sporting a white cast. The pale plaster made the rainbow of bruises she wore all the more vivid. Purple, green, yellow, black... An impressionist painting of pain.

But most of all, she was worried about her vision. Dr. Dawoud had managed to open her eyelids briefly and found scratches on her corneas. Now she had a gauze patch taped over each eye, and he'd told her to leave them in place until he reassessed the damage in a few days.

"It must have happened when they pushed my face

into the dirt," she sobbed. "I was trying to get away. I couldn't breathe."

How dare they treat her like that? Red hot fury pulsed through my veins once more. A perforated eardrum and a further constellation of angry red cigarette burns on Kat's back rounded out her list of injuries, and if the police captain had been standing in front of me at that moment, I'd have taken a leaf out of Katie Biggs's book.

It wasn't until we got back to the hotel that we found out the full story of what had happened. Once Kat was settled on the sofa with a cup of tea and pastries Adam had ordered from room service, she began to talk.

"Mo and I went diving. You remember I said we were going to?"

I nodded.

"It was a great day for it. The sunlight lit up the coral, and there were half a dozen milkfish hanging around. No current, no sediment stirred up, visibility was great. We'd been down for forty minutes, and we were hovering by the reef wall for our three-minute safety stop when I spotted a plastic bag snagged on the coral."

"The rubbish really spoils things, doesn't it?"

"Exactly. So I pointed it out to Mo, and we decided to take it back with us and put it in the bin. There was something in it, but underwater, it's hard to tell the weight of things. It was only once we heaved it out of the sea between us that we realised how heavy it was."

"So what was in it? Surely you opened it?"

Of course she did. Kat was as nosey as me.

She shuddered, and even through her bruises, she

looked slightly green.

"It was a head."

"A head? Like an actual head?" Adam asked, incredulous.

"Yeah, an actual head. It must have been down there a while because the skin was all loose and the eyes were gone. And the smell! I threw up twice."

"So what did you do?" I asked.

"Went to the police, of course. Mo didn't want to, but what else *could* we do? Throw it back in again? Some poor girl had been murdered."

"You knew it was a girl?"

"Not from the face. That was all messed up. But she had long hair and dangly earrings with little coloured beads on them. Men don't normally have those."

"It wasn't Irina, was it?"

"No. Irina had curly blonde hair. This was black and straight."

"What about the other missing girl? The waitress? She was Indonesian."

"I didn't know her, but I suppose it could have been."

"What happened when you went to the police?" Adam asked.

"We left the head in the truck and headed inside to speak to the guy behind the desk. After we explained what had happened, the captain himself came out with a bunch of other officers. That guy's creepy as hell. He only had to look at me to make me nervous, but it was a bit late to back out by that point."

Creepy was an understatement.

"He was horrid to me too. When I yelled at him, I thought he'd squash me like a bug."

"You *yelled* at him? *You?*"

"Yeah, well, he'd kidnapped you."

Kat turned to Adam. "Is that true? Did Callie yell?"

"Callie did."

Was it my imagination, or did he sound a tiny bit proud of me?

"Wow. You've really changed in the past few weeks," Kat told me.

Yes, I had. I knew I had. Partly due to Adam, but also from within. Without Bryce around, I was finding a strength inside me that I never knew I had.

"So what happened with the captain?" Adam brought us back on topic.

"We all went out to the truck, and the head was in the back next to the diving stuff. The captain took one look at it and screamed at his minions to arrest us."

"Arrest you? Why?" I asked.

"Since we had the head, he said it was obvious we'd murdered the girl. And when we wouldn't admit it, he tried to make us."

"The police just started beating you?"

"First they split us up. Then yeah, pretty much. Beating, burning, electric shocks." Her voice was flat and detached, as if she was talking about somebody else. "Part of me wanted to say I *had* done it, to sign their damn confessions just to make it stop."

"But you didn't?"

"How did I know it wouldn't get worse if I did? They accused me of everything under the sun. As well as the murder, they tried to say we were running a people-smuggling ring, taking people into Israel. And they must have been to my apartment because they rattled a bottle of my cystitis pills at me and accused me of being a drug dealer."

Kat didn't know about the state of the place yet, and I decided to wait before telling her. That would only be another straw on the camel's back.

"They'd drag me into an interrogation room every couple of hours," she continued. "Mostly they used force, but sometimes they'd try other tactics."

"Like what?"

She stared blankly at the wall over my left shoulder. "One time, they shackled me to a chair, and then they brought the head in and dumped it on the table in front of me. Luckily, I didn't have anything left in me to chuck up."

"Oh my gosh."

"And another time, one of the men, he pulled down his fly and threatened to...he threatened to..."

She dissolved into tears, and I hugged her as best I could.

"He didn't, did he?"

"No," she sobbed. "He told me he'd be back later to finish the job, and he would've come soon, I think, if you hadn't arrived. I lost track of time. I didn't even know whether it was day or night. How long have I been gone?"

"Three and a bit days."

"It felt like three and a bit years."

"I'm so sorry we didn't find you sooner."

"How could you have? They wouldn't let me call anyone, and we didn't think to tell you we were going there. If they'd killed me, nobody would ever have known."

"What about Mo?" I asked quietly.

"I don't know." Her voice cracked. "I only saw him

once after they separated us. Two of them were dragging him down the corridor, and he was unconscious. At least, I hope he was only unconscious." More tears came. "It's all my fault. He said we shouldn't tell the police, but I insisted. Never in a million years did I think they'd do something like this."

If I hadn't seen Kat with my own eyes, I'd never have believed it either. The police here were barbaric. This was a secret they hid from the glossy holiday brochures and the fancy websites. The dark side of Fidda Hilal was shaded from view, obscured by year-round sunshine and that sparkling sea. The town should come with a health warning.

"So, what now?" Adam voiced what we were all thinking.

"We need to help Mo," Kat said, determination overriding the quake in her voice.

"The captain ordered us to leave town by tomorrow," I reminded her. "Do you think he was serious about throwing us in jail if we don't go?"

"Yes, undoubtedly. For a few hours, I was sharing a cell with a young boy. He couldn't have been older than fourteen. He said Captain Ibrahim is as corrupt as they come and he gets off on violence. The boy reckoned he'd have taken a payoff from someone to cover up the girl's murder."

"Just when we thought it couldn't get any worse," Adam groaned. "Now we've got a corrupt police captain who might be working hand in hand with the real murderer."

Suddenly I didn't want to have an adventure any more. I wished I could turn back time and find myself sitting in my little flat with a box of tissues, eating too much chocolate and watching *Friends* reruns.

There was a ping from Adam's phone, and he pulled it out of his pocket.

"It's an email from Melati's father. He wants us to call him."

It was the saddest conversation I'd ever heard in my life. Adam did the hard bit and explained what we suspected.

Melati's father sounded resigned rather than angry. Stoic.

"I know my daughter is dead. If she were alive, she would have called me. Not a week went by without us speaking. Besides, I feel it in my soul. Her light is gone."

"I'm so sorry," I whispered.

His voice came back out of Adam's phone speaker. "I only want justice for my daughter. If the remains are hers, she deserves a proper burial. And this Captain Ibrahim, he must pay. I'll contact the Indonesian Embassy immediately."

"Thank you," Adam said. "We'll keep in touch."

"It is I who should be thanking you. Good luck over there."

As soon as he hung up, a lightbulb pinged in my head. "The embassy! Why didn't we think of that? Where is it?"

"The British Embassy will be in Cairo, same as the US Embassy," Adam said.

"We should call them, see if they can help. Or even go there—if we went in person, they'd have to do something, wouldn't they?"

"Cairo's hours away," Kat said. "Nine hours by bus, and even if we flew, we'd have to drive to Sharm el-

Sheikh first. If Mo's still alive, he won't be by the time we go to Cairo and back."

"Let's try calling them first," Adam suggested. "It would be best if you or Kat do it because you're British citizens. Can you manage that?"

"I'll have to," I said.

We found the number on the internet, and the lady who answered seemed suitably horrified when I described our ordeal.

"I'm sure we can do something," she said. "That really shouldn't have happened."

No kidding.

"So can you send someone? An ambassador? We need help. They're still holding my friend's boyfriend at the prison."

"Is he a British national?"

"No, he's Egyptian."

"I'm afraid we can't assist with that. It's a local matter. But I can certainly have someone call and take a report from Katerina. We may be able to persuade the government to pay compensation."

"Is that all? Can't you arrest Captain Ibrahim?"

She let out a small chuckle. "This is Egypt. Things don't work like that around here."

I barely managed to refrain from throwing the phone across the room, and as soon as I hung up, Kat tried to jump to her feet, then thought better of it and sank back onto the sofa again.

"Compensation? *Compensation?* How can they talk about money when Mo's life is at stake? I'm definitely voting for someone else in the next election."

Now wasn't the time to explain to Kat that diplomats didn't get elected.

"We need to try something else."
"Too damn right we do. But what?"

CHAPTER 21

WE RACKED OUR brains, trying to think of a way out of a seemingly impossible situation. In my head, I cursed Fidda Hilal and everyone who'd turned a blind eye to Captain Ibrahim and his abusive ways.

"How about the media?" Kat suggested. "Maybe we could get some journalists involved. If the story was in the public domain, Captain Ibrahim would find it harder to cover things up."

"I'm pretty sure we can't just call *The Times* and ask them to run a piece." They were far too busy writing about the prime minister's alleged affair and the third runway at Heathrow. "Even if we managed to get hold of somebody and they agreed to do it, it'd probably take them months to send a reporter out."

"I hate to say it," Adam said, "but newspapers aren't going to be very interested in an Egyptian national imprisoned in Egypt. The only way you'd get their attention is because of your ordeal, Kat."

"Then we'll have to try that. I'll do anything to get Mo out safely." She struggled to her feet. "Shit, we should have taken photos before the cuts got cleaned up. I wasn't thinking straight. Can somebody find a camera before the bruises fade?"

"Who are we going to send the pictures to?" I asked. "It's not as if we know any journalists. We'd need to try and find their email addresses."

"Where's your laptop? We can look them up. They must have websites."

I couldn't even begin to imagine how time-consuming that would be. Then I had another thought. "What about social media? Facebook? Twitter?"

"That's a great idea! What's the best way of doing it?"

"I've got..." I pulled my phone out to check. "I've got eleven followers on Twitter. And I think three of those are scammers. Bryce wasn't very keen on modern technology."

"Screw Bryce. What would he do? Announce a list of my injuries from a scroll?" she said. "I have around sixty people, I think. It's a start. How about you, Adam?"

He bit his lip and went a shade paler under his tan.

I put my hand on his. "Don't worry, I'm not going to stop loving you just because you've got less Twits than me."

It took me a few seconds to process what I'd just said. Adam too, because as I clapped my hands over my mouth, his eyes widened.

"You love me?" he asked.

"I didn't mean to... That is, it's too early. I should have waited. It wasn't a good time..."

He kept staring at me.

"Well...yes."

"Oh, fuck."

Not quite the reaction I'd been hoping for. His pained expression had me backtracking as fast as I could speak.

"Please, don't let this change anything. I promise

I'm not going to dash out and start shopping for a wedding dress. I mean, yes, I already have one, but I don't want to wear it, well I do, because it's pretty, but..." I slumped down. "I'll shut up now."

He opened his mouth, but no words came out, and he closed it again. His gaze dropped to the floor. Even without the benefit of sight, Kat must have been able to sense the atmosphere because she tried to help.

"Let's go back to Twitter. Adam, how many people can you reach?"

He ignored her and closed the distance between us in three hesitant steps. My heart seized, crumpling as if a giant was crushing it in his hand. Adam gripped my upper arms, and the tremble I felt in his fingers transferred to me, running through my limbs to my soul.

"W-w-what's wrong?" I asked. Because something surely was.

He leaned down, resting his forehead on mine and letting out a reedy breath. Everything around us ceased to exist. The room, the country, the situation. They all disappeared. At that moment, it was just the two of us and a giant ball of fear interloping in the middle.

"When I came on this vacation, love was the last thing I expected to find. I sure wasn't looking for it."

He made a sound that was a cross between a choke and a laugh and looked away. I closed my eyes. I didn't want to hear what came next. More than anything, I longed to turn back the clock and return to relaxing on the beach. But that time was past, wasn't it? I forced an eyelid open and found Adam looking at me again.

"Callie, I love you. I always will. Whatever happens, please, please remember that."

"What do you mean, whatever happens? You're scaring me."

"Baby, I love you."

It seemed as much a revelation to him as it was to me. Then he straightened and stepped backwards. His face hardened as he came to a decision.

Even though she couldn't see him, he turned to face Kat. The look of fear on her face mirrored my own, and the air in the room had turned claggy with tension.

Adam took a deep breath, the last of a condemned man, and addressed Kat.

"Twenty-four million, give or take."

CHAPTER 22

KAT REGAINED THE use of her tongue first.

"Twenty-four million what?" Kat asked.

"People on Twitter. That's how many I can reach."

What on earth was he talking about?

His mouth was set in a grim line as he fished his phone out, tapped the screen a few times, and slid it over to me. I peered down at it. The Twitter app was open on an account belonging to Scott Lowes. That name sounded familiar, but why?

I flipped through fuzzy thoughts. Scott Lowes... Scott Lowes... Hang on, wasn't he one of the many, many Hollywood hotshots that Kat kept obsessing over?

"Why do you have access to Scott Lowes's Twitter account? Are you his PA or something?"

Kat couldn't help herself, even in the middle of such a dire situation.

"You know Scott Lowes?" she shrieked, and started fanning herself.

Adam sagged back against the wall, and I sucked in a breath. Kat needed to learn how to tone things down, but now was hardly the time to remind her. Instead, I turned my attention back to the phone and squinted more closely at the tiny picture. A swipe of the screen made it bigger. I looked up at Adam, then back down again.

"What the heck...? You *are* Scott Lowes."

He nodded.

"But... But..."

"You said you'd never date an actor again. I didn't know how to tell you."

I stood up, hands on hips. I couldn't believe this. "So you thought it was better to lie?"

"Technically, I didn't lie about anything. I just left some stuff out."

"You told me your name was Adam."

"Because it is. Adam Scott Lowestein. My agent shortened it when I started acting, and Hollywood seemed to prefer it."

I collapsed back on the sofa. My legs wouldn't hold me up. And once she'd got over her initial fangirl moment, Kat leapt to my defence.

"You bastard! You're dating Velvet Jones."

"I'm not."

"Yes, you are. I saw it on celebgossip.com."

He smacked his palm on his forehead. "Oh, so it must be true."

"You went to two premieres with her."

"That was the studio's idea."

"You still went."

"Look, Velvet's whacked. I made one movie with her, and then she wouldn't leave me alone. She called me every damn day. I had to change my number."

Was he telling the truth? I may not have been familiar with Scott or Adam or whoever he was, but I'd seen a picture of Velvet. She was beautiful, thin, petite, and rich—everything I wasn't. How could Adam possibly prefer me? I couldn't even put on a wetsuit without help.

And I certainly couldn't trust him anymore.

So much had changed in just a few seconds. Last night, I dreamed of a future with Adam. Adam the unemployed drifter. And now I had Scott the Hollywood millionaire? Somehow, what was undoubtedly every other girl's dream had turned into my nightmare.

"I don't know who you are," I said quietly.

"Yes, you do. I'm just Adam. Nothing's changed."

"Oh, sure, nothing's changed. Other than the fact that the man I fell for has millions of females lusting after his every move, everything's totally normal."

Suddenly it all made sense. Those girls who thought they recognised him. His discomfort while shopping in town. His incredibly white teeth.

"But baby, I don't lust after them. Only you. You're the first woman in years who's seen me as a real person. To all the others, I'm just a bunch of dollar signs and a ticket to fame."

But baby. He sounded sincere, but he was a freaking actor. How could I believe a word that came out of his mouth? Inside, I was shaking. Outside too.

"I can't do this."

"Sweetheart, Callie, I love you. I can't lose you."

It wasn't his decision. He knew how badly I'd been hurt by Bryce, and now he'd shredded me again. How much of our "relationship" had been genuine? Any of it? I'd slept with him, for crying out loud. Had all the sweet talk been a pretence so he could get his kicks?

"You just did."

With that, I turned on my heel and locked myself in the bathroom, on purpose this time. It was either that or run outside, and I suspected the hotel staff would have smartphones at the ready. One wrong move and they'd be emailing either my mother or possibly Captain Ibrahim.

I sat down on the edge of the bath and dragged a hand across my face. It came away wet with tears. The old saying sprang to mind: *Fool me once, shame on you. Fool me twice, shame on me.*

That was me.

The fool.

Maybe it was genetic. When my mum met my dad, he told her he worked in a bank in the city. He'd show up in a suit and wine her and dine her, take her out to the poshest restaurants. It was only a couple of months later, when she showed up one day to surprise him at the office, that she'd found out his actual job was cleaning floors four through six. She'd given him the benefit of the doubt and married him anyway, and look how that had turned out.

Sure, with Adam it was the other way around, but he'd still misrepresented himself. As with my parents, it was hardly the basis for a lasting relationship.

Outside the door, I heard the sharp lash of Kat's tongue as she fought my corner, and guilt needled at me. For the second time in recent weeks, I'd put her in a horrible position. She was supposed to be focusing on Mo, and instead, she was dealing with my mess.

I was the worst friend in the world. So what did I do? I reached for the toilet paper.

Half an hour later, Kat tapped on the door. "It's me. Can I come in?"

I cracked the door open, and she slipped through.

"You shouldn't be up," I said.

"It helps to move around. Otherwise I'll get stiff."

She took a seat on the closed toilet and stretched out her legs.

"Is he still out there?" I asked.

"Yes. He's calling half of Hollywood. #NightmareInFiddaHilal is already trending on Twitter."

"I can't believe he didn't tell me the truth."

"I can't believe you were dating Scott Lowes and you didn't even realise."

"Why would I? I've only ever watched those types of films with you. I'd be more likely to recognise some obscure Romanian actor with a penchant for Shakespeare."

"But still..." She shook her head in disbelief.

"I'm sheltered Kat, live with it."

I rolled my eyes, then realised she couldn't see.

"Wait, wait... Did you do it?"

Even in the throes of a crisis, Kat couldn't resist a good bit of gossip.

"Just once."

She squealed in delight. "Ooh, I want all the details. Was he big? Did he know how to use it?"

"Kat, I'm not rehashing every sordid thing. But yes, and most definitely yes."

"I knew it! Damn girl, you're lucky."

Really? Right now, I didn't feel as if fate was on my side.

"What should I do, Kat?"

"Besides the obvious answer of march right out there and screw him senseless?"

"Kat, be serious for a minute. Please?"

"Sorry, sorry. What should you do? I don't honestly

know. I mean, Scott seems like a genuinely nice guy. He's not at all how I imagined he'd be."

"But he wasn't truthful. He had so many chances to tell me who he really was, and he didn't take any of them. When I asked what he did for a living, he said he was between jobs."

"Well, he kind of is. His next movie doesn't start filming until early next year. He's going to play a detective investigating a murder in a tropical paradise." She snapped her fingers. "Hey, I bet that's why he needed to learn to dive."

I recalled his initial lack of enthusiasm over the course. Kat was probably right.

"Well, he got a little more than he bargained for in Fidda Hilal, didn't he?" I laughed hollowly. "Probably he can chalk this whole trip up to research and get a tax write off."

"He really cares about you, Callie."

"If you care about someone, you don't hide your freaking identity from them."

"He wanted to tell you who he was, but he was so happy being Adam the average bloke rather than Scott the megastar, he was scared to spoil it."

"Scared? Yeah, right. Kat, I fell in love with a man, and now he's turned into somebody completely different."

"Maybe they're actually the same?"

My brain was a jumble of emotions. Anger, hurt, and disappointment were doing battle within, and I wasn't sure which was winning.

"I need some time."

"If you can't face Scott, will you be okay on your own for a while? I really need his help with Mo."

"Of course, but I should be helping too."

"Callie, you're my best friend and I love you dearly, but Scott knows, like, three million people and you don't." That was Kat, blunt as always. "We're doing okay if you need some time to think."

"Call me if you need anything?"

"I will. And I'll be here for you whatever you decide with Scott."

"Good luck out there."

"Thanks," she mumbled into my hair. "And thank you for rescuing me. If you hadn't gone psycho on the captain, I'd still be in jail. At least this way, Mo stands a chance."

At first, I tried to stifle the sobs that clawed their way up my throat as Kat went back to Adam. But it was a hopeless task.

In the end, I surrendered and let them come.

CHAPTER 23

DARKNESS HAD FALLEN when the voices finally stopped, and it was surprisingly cold sitting on the tiles. My bottom had long since lost all feeling, but that only merged into the numbness that had spread through the rest of me. I tugged the bath towel around me tighter, like a shield. I'd thought my heart would be in agony, but there was so little of it left intact, I'd gone beyond that.

Kat opened the door and used her good-ish arm to help me to my feet.

"Look at us," she said. "We're a pair of crocks."

I managed a small smile. "When you said I wouldn't be bored on this trip, I have to say this wasn't what I imagined."

She flopped down on one side of the bed, and I took the other. I felt a sharp stab between the ribs when I thought about the man who'd slept next to me the night before.

"I'm so sorry. Honestly, I could never have imagined this. I've been in Fidda Hilal for months and never seen this side of it before."

"Perhaps you didn't want to? We all fall in love with a dream, and it's depressing when we have to wake up."

"I think you're right. And you know what? Everybody here's guilty of wearing rose-tinted glasses.

Captain Ibrahim didn't become as powerful as he is overnight. Too many people buried their heads in the sand while he scaled the mountain."

"Let's hope his downfall is a little bit quicker."

"For Mo's sake, it had better be."

We both tossed and turned for most of the night. Sleep came fitfully, and at four, I woke up and couldn't get back to sleep again.

What should I do? This time yesterday, I'd been... well, not happy, exactly—how could I have been when Kat was missing—but I'd had the man of my dreams by my side.

"You awake?" Kat asked.

"Yes. I can't sleep."

"Me neither. Have you thought about what you're going to do?"

"About Adam?"

"Unless you're dating any other members of the A-List that I don't know about."

"As if. I've gone over and over things in my head, but I just can't think. It's like his aura punches through the wall and scrambles my brain. What I really need is space. Kat, I can't wait to go home."

"So go."

"And leave you here alone? No way."

"But I won't be alone." She squeezed my hand in the darkness. "Elaine's coming to help me first thing, and by the looks of it, there's going to be a media circus starting tomorrow."

"They're really coming?"

"Scott woke up his agent and told him to start earning his damn money. Apparently he's been on the phone to everybody, from Steven Spielberg to the Pope.

You can't get a flight to Sharm tomorrow for love nor money."

"Wow. Captain Ibrahim's going to be pissed."

"Good. I'll be in a front-row seat to watch him go down. I want fireworks, ticker tape, the whole shebang."

And Adam would no doubt be in the middle of it. Hollywood's golden boy.

I started shivering. "What if the reporters find out about us? Me and Adam, I mean? I don't want my picture to be all over the internet. I can just see the headlines now: *A-lister slums it with schoolteacher, what was he thinking?* My pupils' parents would be horrified."

"All the more reason for you to get out of here and let things blow over."

"But—"

"Hear me out. I can't wait to get out of this place either, and I'll be back in England as soon as I can get there. And if..." She choked out a sob. "If we find Mo, I'm hoping he can get a visa too."

"*When* we find Mo."

"When..." I could tell she had her doubts, and quite frankly, so did I. "We've got nothing, Callie. Scott said they wrecked our home. I don't even have clean underwear."

"You can use anything of mine you need."

"We'll need more, if we get back to England. Clothes, shoes, somewhere to stay. Could you help?"

"Of course." I'd max out my credit card if needs be.

"You should be able to get a flight back to England. It's coming the other way that's a problem."

"Could you tell Adam for me? That I need a few

days? I don't think I can face him myself."

"I'll tell him."

"Do you think he'll understand?"

"If he doesn't, then he's not worth crying over."

The next morning, I stepped out onto the terrace to get one final look at what I once thought was paradise. I breathed in the sea air, now tainted by the smell of fear, and turned my face to the sky to soak up a few last rays.

Should I try talking to Adam before I left? Yes, I'd been shocked at the big reveal yesterday, but I'd also been a tiny bit rude when I ran off to the bathroom. Could there really be a future with him? My head told me I was stupid to even consider it. That I'd just been a convenient holiday fling.

But my heart asked, "What if?" What if he'd been telling the truth when he said he loved me? What if fairy tales really did come true?

As the sun rose higher and my skin started to tingle in the heat, I came to a decision. I needed to speak to him.

Except Kat got in first. I heard her voice, still hoarse, through the screen of fragrant oleander between Adam's terrace and mine.

"Callie asked me to tell you goodbye."

"She's really leaving?"

He sounded calm, matter-of-fact. There was none of the anguish he'd shown yesterday evening.

"This morning. She's taking the first flight out."

"It's probably for the best."

For the best?

I ran inside before I burst into tears and they realised I'd been eavesdropping. My head had been right, and my heart was an idiot.

It's for the best.

I had my answer. Adam was glad to see the back of me. Fine. Half an hour, and I'd be out of his life for good.

CHAPTER 24

THE JOURNEY FROM Fidda Hilal to Sharm el-Sheikh seemed eons longer than the drive the other way. Then, I'd been lamenting the breakup of a relationship with a man I now understood had taken me for granted.

From the weeks I'd spent with Adam, I saw how little effort Bryce had put into our time together. He'd expected me to run around after him, making dinner and washing his clothes. Ironing his underpants had seemed so normal at the time.

Now I knew better.

But you know what Bryce didn't do? He didn't lie.

As I wiped a tear from my cheek, I mourned the death of a person who'd never truly existed. Adam had shown me what I wanted from a man. A friend, a companion, someone who'd have my back no matter what. He'd given me that. But what he hadn't given me was something I realised I needed above all else.

Honesty.

I needed a man who gave me all of himself. Adam claimed he hadn't been dishonest, but he hadn't been forthcoming with the truth either. Except when he was talking with Kat. He'd been quick enough to tell her that he didn't want me there.

Well, he'd got his wish.

Traffic on the two-lane highway was far busier than

before, but ninety percent of the vehicles were on the other side of the road, all heading towards Fidda Hilal. Trucks carrying boxes, cars with suitcases strapped to the roof, and even a couple of coaches whizzed past. And in keeping with Egyptian tradition, my driver tooted and waved at every single one of them.

I still couldn't help feeling I was taking the coward's way out, but even as she hugged me beside the taxi, Kat had insisted I was doing the right thing.

"Honestly, I'll be fine. There are plenty of people here to help now. If you can keep yourself out of the spotlight, so much the better."

"If you want me to come back, just call, okay? I'll get the next flight out. Well, the next one I can get a ticket on."

"I'll see you soon, but it'll be in England. Just make sure you stock up on chocolate. I can't wait to get my hands on a giant bar of Cadbury's."

"It'll be waiting, I promise."

As we drove into Sharm el-Sheikh, a symphony of hoots serenaded us. There was traffic everywhere. It was only when we finally reached the terminal that I understood the reach of Scott Lowes.

Had I walked into an airport or a movie set? Harried-looking runners wheeled stacks of boxes, people shouted into phones, and two hipsters nearly came to blows over the last pain au chocolat at the kiosk. In the background, a make-up artist painted a stunning brunette's lips as she prepared to go live for the camera. Out on the tarmac, heat haze simmered around a row of private jets, and airport staff frantically tried to herd crowds in the right direction. One of the security guards manning the X-ray machine was asleep.

A fuzzy monitor told me I needed desk eight, and I skirted a guy snapping pictures of the chaos. The EasyJet check-in was manned by a pair of blondes close to my age, and as I reached the front of a very short queue, they gawked as another gaggle of photographers sped past, heading for arrivals.

"Flying out, love?" one of them asked.

"Yes, back to England."

"You're going the right way. You can pick any seat you like. The plane's almost empty."

"I dunno what's going on," piped up her friend. "It's gone mental. It wasn't even this bad when Indigo Rain came to Sharm to film a music video."

"Have you looked at Twitter?" I asked.

"Nah, the boss don't like us using our phones while we're on duty. Why? Who's 'ere?"

"I believe Scott Lowes was spotted in Fidda Hilal."

"O. M. G!" she shrieked, turning to her friend. "Tracey, we've got to go there. I love him. I want to have his babies."

"Let's call in sick tomorrow. But I need to get me roots done before we go. And me nails."

Good luck to Captain Ibrahim trying to lock Adam up while those two were in town. They'd scratch out his eyeballs then batter the door of the jail down with their stilettos.

"I need to get a new outfit," Not-Tracey said. "Or I could wear that white skirt I bought last week. D'ya think it goes with my tan?"

"Everything goes with a tan."

"Uh, I'm sorry to interrupt, but do you think I could finish checking my bag in?" I asked.

"What? Oh. Yeah." Tracey slapped a label on it and

sent it down the conveyor. Would it make it back to Luton? I gave it a fifty-fifty chance. But even if it ended up in Timbuktu, what did it matter? I wouldn't need a bikini at home, anyway. No, I'd soon be back in front of my class, more worried about toilet training and teaching the alphabet than whether I was getting a muffin top.

For the two hours until my flight, I watched the people arriving with morbid fascination. The floor-to-ceiling windows gave a great view of the rich and famous as they flew in for their five minutes of glory.

An elderly janitor pushing a trolley full of cleaning supplies stopped next to me and peered out.

"Is that the girl off the news?" he asked me.

"I should think so, yes." One of them, at least.

"This is very exciting. It's good to have so many visitors."

At least Kat's ordeal was helping the economy. If there was one small piece of good to come out of this nightmare, it was the influx of much-needed foreign visitors into the region. I hoped that some of them would see beyond Captain Ibrahim and his corruption to the locals, most of whom were lovely.

"Yes, the hotels will all be full, that's for sure."

"I've heard that the president of Egypt himself is coming. It would be a great honour for him to visit our town."

A politician chasing after TV cameras? That didn't surprise me. "I'm sure he'll be here soon."

I didn't see the president, but I did count the logos of twenty-seven TV stations. Everybody liked a good scandal. I only hoped Adam's efforts produced the outcome we all wanted.

Even with the added activity, a minor miracle happened and my flight was less than an hour late. True to what I'd been told, it was only a quarter full. It felt almost eerie, and worse, it meant I actually had to pay attention during the in-flight safety briefing. As soon as the drinks trolley appeared, I chugged back five gin and tonics, bagged myself a row of three seats, and passed out for the duration.

I'd planned to catch a taxi home from the airport, but when I walked into the arrivals hall, thankfully with my suitcase in tow, I heard my name being called.

"Cooee! Callie!"

I knew that voice all too well.

"Hi, Mum." I swallowed a groan. Kat must have called her.

She squashed me in a hug. "Kat said you'd decided to fly home early. I can't say I blame you, what with all the drama. I wouldn't have wanted to stay there either."

How much had Kat told her? I really hoped she hadn't said anything about Adam.

"All those dreadful policemen, turning a blind eye like that," Mum continued. "It's just not safe. Kat's even been on the telly, dear. And that awful man, the one who did that to her face. He was wearing handcuffs."

Captain Ibrahim? Already? "What did they say?"

"Kat did an interview—with the BBC! It was on the lunchtime news. She was standing next to that hunky actor. You know, the one out of *Forever Black*. They showed a picture of him without his shirt on. Oh, if only I was forty years younger."

Even my mum was a Scott Lowes fan? *Someone save me now*.

"Did they say anything about Kat's boyfriend?"

"Hmm, I'm not sure. I was distracted by the young man's teeth. They're so very white."

Mother! And to think Adam used ordinary toothpaste.

"You've lost weight. At least now you're back you can get some proper English grub," she carried on. "None of that foreign muck. And I've brought your new house key."

"Did you give Bryce his script back?"

"Of course not, dear. When he called me, I just pretended the lock was jammed. And I don't think you should give it back to him either. That boy hurt you. He doesn't deserve a thing."

As soon as I got home, I turned on the TV. Yes, yes, I know I shouldn't have, but I was like a moth drawn to a flame.

When I found the twenty-four-hour news channel, the first thing I saw was a worried-looking Kat, limping along beside a stretcher. While the cameras rolled, she disappeared into a building I recognised as the hospital.

Had that been Mo with her? How bad were his injuries?

I turned up the volume.

"A young man named as Mohammed El Masri was rescued from Fidda Hilal's notorious jail as officers from Cairo arrived to take the police captain, Anwar Ibrahim, into custody. The extent of Mr. El Masri's injuries remains unclear, but we'll provide further information as soon as it's available."

At least Mo was alive. That was something to be thankful for.

"None of this would have happened without the efforts of Hollywood star Scott Lowes, who stumbled across this injustice while on a scuba diving holiday. Scott, how does it feel to have brought this abuse of human rights to the world's attention?"

The camera cut to Adam. A very different Adam. Clean-shaven, wearing an artfully distressed T-shirt that probably cost three figures, and having somehow fitted in a haircut overnight.

The sight of him set my heart off in a wild staccato.

He gave his trademark smile, the one that made him millions. I squinted at the screen. Perhaps I was imagining it, but today's smile didn't look as if it reached his eyes.

I missed him already.

There, I admitted it. I missed him.

Was there any chance that he was missing me?

Then the camera panned back, and I saw who he was standing next to. This time it wasn't Kat. No, Adam's arm curved around the waist of none other than Velvet Jones.

My eyes narrowed. Well, it didn't take long, did it?

Even in the oppressive heat, her makeup was perfect, and her thick golden mane swished around her shoulders as if she'd just stepped off the set of a shampoo commercial.

I scraped my fingers through my own brown locks. How could I even consider competing with her?

On screen, Adam started speaking, waffling on about how justice had been served and he was only doing what any civic-minded person would have done, but I barely took in his words. I was too busy watching his fingers as they gripped Velvet's hip through her flimsy cover-up.

In turn, she leaned into him and gazed up adoringly.

He'd said she wouldn't leave him alone, but had that been another fib? At that moment, it very much looked as if he was enjoying her attention.

Then the interviewer turned to Ms. Jones. "So, Velvet, you must be very proud of Scott?"

"Who wouldn't be? He's achieved so much in his life, both here and with his charity work back home. I'm thrilled to be dating somebody with such a kind and generous heart."

I clenched my jaw together so hard, it was a miracle I didn't crack a tooth. *Relax, Callie.* No point in racking up a fortune in emergency dentist fees. When I'd called Adam The Ass, I hadn't been wrong, had I?

The heads on the screen kept talking, but I didn't hear anything else they said. My sobs drowned out the words, and when the news anchor popped back on the screen, muttering some insipid rubbish, I jabbed the off button and threw the remote across the room. It hit an arrangement of dried flowers and knocked the whole lot off the sideboard.

The vase hit a table on the way down and shattered.

My heart shattered with it.

CHAPTER 25

I SPENT THE next two days holed up in my bedroom, ordering stuff for Kat on the internet. Toiletries, underwear, clothing, shoes, a ton of chocolate...all the essentials. Mum had offered up one of her two spare rooms, so at least that was the accommodation sorted. I took the batteries out of the TV remote and turned off my mobile. Kat's phone had gone AWOL, but she'd promised to text me when she got a new one. In the meantime, she had my landline number, and I didn't want to speak to anyone else.

Every time Adam popped into my head, I gave myself a mental slap, and when my virtual cheeks were smarting, I got my emergency bottle of wine out of the cupboard and chugged the whole thing. Tesco would deliver more, and then I'd be free to wallow in misery until I went back to school.

It was a good plan until I remembered—too late— that when my mum got the locks changed, she would of course have got herself an extra key cut.

"Callie! Callie!"

Just what I didn't need. Sympathy. I'd rather have had a dartboard and pictures of Velvet bloody Jones.

"In the bedroom, Mum."

She flung the door open and switched on the light. "Goodness, child, what on earth are you doing in here with all the curtains drawn? It's a beautiful day outside."

"I don't feel well."

She stood back and studied me in the way a scientist would examine particularly interesting bacteria.

"I knew the food out there would disagree with you. Have you taken some Imodium?"

I didn't know what was worse—Mum thinking I had the trots, or having to admit that once again I'd managed to make a complete hash out of my love life. I decided the former would be easier to live with. At least she wouldn't have leaflets made informing everyone I was suffering from an upset stomach. If she found out about Adam, she'd be out looking for a replacement before I could chain her to the radiator.

And I knew there would never be anyone who could compare.

"Yes, Mum. I think the pills are starting to kick in now."

She leaned over and felt my forehead. "You're a little clammy, but you don't have a fever. That's good news, isn't it?"

Fantastic. Nothing could be better.

Mum bustled around, straightening the bedclothes and rearranging the trinkets on my dressing table.

"Have you been drinking plenty?"

I didn't get a chance to reply before she answered her own question.

"I'm sure you haven't. I'll get a jug of water for your nightstand."

Phew. I felt a sense of relief as she left the room, but I knew it would be short-lived. I wouldn't be safe from her questions until the front door closed behind her.

"Have you got enough toilet paper?" she called from the kitchen.

"Yes."

It was just my sanity that was in short supply.

She came back with the water and poured me a glassful. "Drink up, dear."

I wasn't thirsty but I obliged, ever the dutiful daughter.

She pulled the curtains open and studied me. "Are you feeling sick?"

"No, it's just my tummy."

"What else can I do to help? Do you need me to go to the pharmacy for rehydration salts?"

I faked a yawn. "I think I just need some sleep."

"Of course." She patted me on the hand. "You do look pale. I'll pop over again tomorrow to check up on you."

I let out a groan. I didn't need to fake that.

"Thanks, Mum, but you don't have to. I'll be perfectly all right by myself."

"Nonsense, dear. I'll be round right after my Zumba class."

Fantastic. I could hardly wait.

After she'd departed, all I wanted to do was turn over and cry, but I couldn't. It was high time I called Kat to find out how she and Mo were. I'd do it straight away, I decided. Right after I'd made a cup of tea.

Three cuppas later, I'd done the washing up, emptied the airing cupboard, and alphabetised my CD collection. I couldn't put it off any longer.

I turned on my mobile, and as soon as it found a signal, it went crazy. My emails, text messages, and voicemails were in double figures, but I ignored everything except the first text from Kat and programmed her new number into my phone.

She answered on the second ring.

"Callie! Are you okay? I've been so worried about you, but I knew you wouldn't feel like talking for a day or two."

A day or two? Try a month or two. Maybe even a year. I tried to put a brave face on things.

"I'll be okay, as long as you don't mention Adam. Scott. Whatever his name is."

"I just need to tell you something first. It's…"

"Is it about Adam?" I interrupted.

"Well, yes, but…"

"I don't want to hear it."

"But—"

"Just don't."

There was a resigned sigh from the other end. "Okay, fine."

"How's Mo?"

"He worried everyone to start with, but he's stable now. The bastards broke both his legs, and he had internal bleeding. The doctor said he wouldn't have lasted another day."

"That's…that's…" *Unfathomable.* The police were meant to uphold the law, not break it themselves. "That's horrendous."

"Yes, but we got there in time—that's the important thing. He'll recover. It'll take a while, but he'll recover. He needs a plate in one of his legs, though."

"It was a bad break?"

"One of the cops hit him with a metal bar when he wouldn't admit to dismembering Melati. But there is some good news. He's coming back to the UK with me as soon as he's well enough to travel. A surgeon in London offered to do the operation for free."

"Mum says you can both use her spare room for as long as you want."

"Really?"

Mum may have driven me around the twist at times, but she had a heart of gold.

"I've ordered your clothes, plus a wardrobe and a chest of drawers from IKEA. Dave said he'd put them together this weekend."

"Poor Dave. He'll probably move out to the potting shed permanently."

"Nah, I reckon he'll like having another bloke around for company. Is there anything else you need?"

"I can't think of anything. And people keep sending us random stuff in the hope that we'll endorse it."

"Endorse it?"

"We're insta-famous now. I've got forty thousand followers on Instagram and another twenty thousand on Twitter."

"I didn't even know you had an Instagram account."

"I forgot about it myself. Before this week, I'd posted a handful of pictures, and my only followers were Mo, Elaine, and somebody's cat. Now people are sending me moisturiser, trainers, beachwear, food supplements, you name it, in case I'll take a photo of it. EasyJet's even offered to waive the excess baggage charges so we can bring all the stuff home with us."

That was perhaps the biggest miracle so far.

"Did anyone send wine?"

"No, but I've got a whole crate of SupaBoost Smoothies."

"Before I forget, I put your jewellery and money in the hotel safe."

"Adam— Sorry, he who shall not be mentioned told me. Thank goodness you looked in the chickpea tin— everything else in the apartment can be replaced, but I'd have been devastated if I'd lost my mam's necklace."

Now that we'd sorted out the logistics, I asked the question that had been on my mind for days. "So, I'm dying to know—what happened with the police after I left?"

"Well, first Twitter crashed. Then a joint delegation from the British and Indonesian Embassies arrived within hours and started raising hell. The Egyptian government had no choice but to send in a special police squad from Cairo to start cleaning house."

"I'm surprised they acted so quickly."

"The response floored me. It goes to show that not everywhere in Egypt is a hotbed of corruption. The new guys dragged Captain Ibrahim out of his beachfront mansion in handcuffs, and there must've been a hundred reporters watching."

"I bet he was cross."

"Oh, he was furious." I heard the glee in Kat's voice. "Even better, once his minions realised he'd been taken down, they queued up to tell the investigators about all the terrible things he'd done. With him out of the way, there's almost a party atmosphere in town."

"What things *had* he done?"

"I don't have all the details, but I know they found the bodies of three torture victims in freezers at the jail."

Those poor, poor people. "Were Irina or Melati among them?"

"No, but they did find what was left of Melati's head in a bucket. The rats had been at it, but there was enough for a DNA test."

My stomach turned as Kat continued. "It turned out her father's some sort of business magnate, quite well known, so the story's caught the attention of the Indonesian media as well. People all over the globe have been up in arms."

"There's no sign of Irina?"

"I didn't say that. That was another scandal. A bigger one."

Bigger? What could possibly be bigger than a head in a bucket and crashing Twitter?

"Go on..."

"Once they'd hauled the captain off, I think they must have given him a dose of his own medicine because he admitted he'd been paid to cover up both killings."

"Who by? Tell me they know who by."

"It'll freak you out."

Would it? After what I'd seen and heard over the last few days, I thought I'd become remarkably resilient.

"Will you just tell me already?"

"Okay, okay. It was Eid's father. He was protecting his son."

It took me a moment for Kat's words to sink in.

Eid was the murderer? Eid? *Eid?* Suddenly, I felt sick, and I rushed for the bathroom. At least I hadn't totally lied to Mum. I knelt down in front of the toilet and gripped the sides as I lost the glass of water I'd just drunk, and once I'd wiped my mouth, I retrieved the phone.

"Are you okay?" Kat asked.

"Not exactly. Eid? You're kidding me."

"Nope. Apparently he didn't take too kindly to unrequited love."

I shuddered at the narrow escape I'd had. I mean, I'd eaten dinner with the man. He'd wanted me to meet his family, for crying out loud. That could have been *my* head floating in the sea. If it hadn't been for Adam, coming along when he did...

Stop thinking about Adam.

He and Velvet could do whatever they liked. I didn't want to see either of their faces ever again.

"Did Eid say what happened?"

"Oh, yes. He didn't like the idea of being tortured, so when he was arrested, he confessed right away. Both girls rejected his advances, so he killed them in his house. Because he didn't have a car, he had to chop the bodies into little pieces to get rid of them on his moped."

I heaved again. Good thing I didn't have anything left to hork up.

"Are you all right?" Kat asked.

"Just feeling slightly queasy."

"I can understand that. Anyhow, Eid admitted he threw both of the girls into the sea in chunks. There's a team of technical divers going down tomorrow to see if they can find any sign of the packages. The Indonesian government have sent a naval vessel to support them, and the Russians are helping too."

"At least they're taking it seriously."

"Believe it or not, it's done wonders for international relations. Everyone's joined forces to work together, and Fidda Hilal looks like a cosmopolitan version of the G20. I'm hoping they'll have negotiated world peace by the time we leave."

I breathed a sigh of relief. All that could be done was being done. At least two families would find closure from their tragedies, and the town of Fidda Hilal would become a safer place for its inhabitants. I said as much to Kat.

"It's all thanks to you. I haven't mentioned your name to the reporters, but I made sure they knew Adam and I didn't do this alone. If it wasn't for your tenacity, there would have been a couple more bodies in those freezers. There aren't enough 'thank yous' in the world for what you did."

"Nonsense, I only did what anyone else would have done."

"No, they wouldn't. They didn't. That's why Captain Ibrahim got away with as much as he did for so long. You're a true friend, Callie Shawcross."

Tears prickled the corners of my eyes. At least I'd managed to repay some of the kindness Kat had shown me while we were growing up.

"I'll see you soon, okay?" I told her. "I could do with a hug."

"I'll bring all the hugs in the world."

Chapter 26

SPEAKING WITH KAT left me feeling a little better. At least I knew Mo would be okay, and I couldn't wait to see them both back in England.

That still left one giant elephant in the room. Adam. I stuck a lampshade on his head and tried to ignore him.

The next morning, I still didn't fancy getting out of bed, but the room had started to hum a bit, so I changed the sheets and washed the old ones. Then I figured I'd better sort out the dirty laundry from my suitcase since I'd just wheeled it in and dumped it in the lounge. I'd already stubbed my toe on it three times, and I was sick of tripping over it.

Immediately, I wished I hadn't bothered. Every item in there was a reminder of a trip I'd rather forget. That old saying, "It's better to have loved and lost than never to have loved at all?" It was rubbish. Utter rubbish.

First Bryce, then Adam. The only thing I was ever going to get close to in future was the pet goldfish I decided at that moment to buy. Having something to care for would take my mind off them both.

Things got worse when I shook out a kaftan and realised I'd picked up one of Adam's T-shirts by mistake. I lifted it to my nose and inhaled, and the musky scent made me weep all over again. I folded it up and stuffed it into the back of my underwear drawer. It could stay there until I decided what to do with it.

I was just shoving the dark garments into the washing machine when I heard a rap at the door. Had my mother finally learned to knock? I set the machine going then scrambled to my feet. At least by unpacking, I'd achieved something. Baby steps, eh?

"Hi, M—"

Oh. It wasn't my mum. I really needed to remember to use that little peephole thing. Mum was always lecturing me about it.

I managed to curb my initial response of "What the bloody hell do you think you're doing here?" and instead went with, "If you tell me where you left your papers, I'll go and get them."

"Could I come in for a second, Callista?" Bryce asked. "I need to talk to you."

I wanted to say, "No way," but my assertiveness lay in tatters on the floor of the police station in Fidda Hilal.

"Make it quick." I swung the door open and gestured for him to enter.

Bryce perched on the edge of the sofa, a far cry from before when he'd sink into the cushions as if he owned the place. Today, he looked haggard, weary, as if he hadn't slept for a week. And his clothes were crinkled. Unusual for a man who used to insist I ironed his socks.

"What do you want, Bryce?"

"Would you like a cup of tea?" he asked.

It was *my* flat, and he was offering me a cup of tea?

Did he not understand how this worked? But he never normally made the effort, and I found myself saying yes, more out of morbid curiosity than anything else. I followed him into the kitchen, and he opened three cupboards before he found the mugs.

"How do you turn your kettle on?"

"The switch at the bottom. No, you need to put water in it first."

Good grief.

Bryce splashed water all over the place, and of course he made no move to wipe it up. Then once the kettle was going, he reached for the sugar canister.

"I don't take sugar," I reminded him just as he was about to drop a spoonful into my cup.

"Oh. I thought you did?"

We'd dated for six years, and he didn't know how I took my tea? That honestly shouldn't have surprised me, but I still sighed as I leaned against the counter.

"Is there a point to all this?"

"You said you were thirsty."

Actually, I didn't. I'd said yes to a cuppa, but Bryce had always heard what he wanted to hear.

"I meant the visit. Why are you here?"

He fiddled nervously with a teaspoon. "I just wanted to see how you were. I saw Katerina on the news, and she said you were in Fidda Hilal too."

"She told me she didn't mention my name."

"Yes, she refrained from doing so, but anybody familiar with the pair of you would have been able to guess. Callista, it sounds as though you went through incredible hardship."

"It was nothing when you consider what Kat went through."

How could he compare my ordeal to hers?

"I understand, I understand," Bryce said hastily. "But she has people assisting her. Who's here to support you?"

"Mum came over yesterday."

"Is that it? One visit from your mother? Callista, you need to start taking care of yourself. I mean, look at the place. It's unkempt."

"Thanks. That makes me feel so much better."

"That's why I'm here—to make you feel better."

"Do you still keep a dictionary in the cereal cupboard?"

"Of course."

"When you get home, try looking up the word 'sarcasm.'"

"Sarcasm?" The penny finally dropped. "So my comment *didn't* make you feel better?"

"No, Bryce, it didn't."

"Then I suppose I should apologise. Uh, do you want a hand with the cleaning?"

Bryce was apologising? And offering to clean? This I had to see. He'd never so much as picked up a duster in our entire relationship, and a cleaning lady did his flat.

"Well, if you're offering, the lounge needs vacuuming."

"I'll start right away."

Two seconds later, he poked his head back around the doorjamb.

"Where do you keep the vacuum cleaner?"

This was going to be a long morning, wasn't it? And he hadn't even made the tea. Not for the first time, I finished something Bryce had started. In fact, I'd kept a vibrator in an empty tampon box in the bathroom for that very purpose.

By lunchtime, he'd abandoned the vacuum cleaner in the middle of the lounge and flopped onto the sofa.

"Gosh, that was backbreaking."

He'd only done one room, for crying out loud, and he hadn't even done that very well. He went around things rather than lifting them out of the way. Mind you, it was better than it'd been before, so I couldn't complain. And he *had* made an effort.

But what he hadn't done was answer my question. Why was he here? I took a seat in my favourite armchair, a pale green leather affair with squashy arms Mum had bought me when I first moved in that also happened to be as far away from Bryce as I could get without reversing into the kitchen.

"Bryce, why did you come over today?"

He sighed theatrically and gazed at the ceiling. Looking for divine inspiration?

"Callista, I've realised I made a mistake."

"Just the one?"

He ignored my snippiness.

"Before our wedding, I panicked. My feelings for you overwhelmed me, and I couldn't imagine I'd ever live up to your ideal. Now, my eyes have been opened, and I know nothing will ever triumph over my love for you."

"And?"

"What I'm trying to say, my darling, my Ophelia, is that I very much want to marry you."

My heart started pounding. My head too. A month ago, I'd been praying I'd hear those words, and if I had, I'd have fallen straight into his arms.

But so much had happened since then. I'd travelled to a different continent and met a very different man. A man who'd swept me off my feet and shown me what it was like to be cherished.

But that man no longer existed. He'd lied to me, then let me leave without so much as a murmur. I could still hear his words to Kat echoing in my head: *it's for the best*. Worse, the image of his hand resting on Velvet's hip swam in front of my eyes. It had only taken him a few hours to move on from whatever we'd had.

At least Bryce had never lied to me. He may not have been the best boyfriend in the world, but he was on my level. Adam was floating on a cloud somewhere far above my head, sharing his harp with a harpy.

Maybe my time in Egypt had been a lesson, designed to teach me one thing; that my judgement lately had been appalling.

Had I been too hasty in writing off Bryce? Had a taut butt and a six-pack messed with my mind?

What if it was Bryce and not Adam who was my destiny?

After all, I was just a primary school teacher from Berkshire, not a global phenomenon.

I'd never got closure with Bryce. I'd lost my head rather than thinking things through. It was entirely plausible he'd freaked out over the wedding. I mean, he was a man. Men were terrified of commitment, weren't they?

Was Bryce truly as bad as my troubled mind had made him out to be?

"I don't know what to say."

"Say yes, my beautiful little nymph." He dropped onto one knee in front of me.

When Adam had referred to the origins of my name, it had sounded so much sweeter.

"I'll have to think about it."

The climax of my trip to Egypt may have been traumatic, but I'd learned one thing in my time away—I wasn't going to let Bryce walk all over me again. If he wanted to step back into my life, he'd have to put as much effort into things as I had.

If he proved himself, then we'd see.

"He who knows, does not speak. He who speaks, does not know," Bryce said.

"Sorry, what?"

"It's Lao Tzu, Callista. It means thinking is overrated."

Oh, of course.

"I'm still going with the thinking. And I must say, you'll need to buck your ideas up if you're serious about this."

"Whatever do you mean?"

"Well, for starters, you'll have to help more."

"I did."

"Once. You helped once. I mean if I'm cooking dinner, it might be nice if you did the washing up. Or if I do the laundry, perhaps you could hang it up?"

"I suppose I could strive to make an attempt."

"Plus you could take me out occasionally, and not just to your friends' supper parties."

"Anything, my darling. I'll do anything." His knees cracked as he got up, and he brushed his trousers down. "I'll be back at seven to take you to dinner."

He kissed me on the hand, and then he was gone.

My nerves jangled as I waited for the knock on the door that evening, which was crazy because I'd known Bryce for years. Was going out with him a good idea? I still wasn't sure. I hadn't told mother when she'd stopped by with homemade chicken soup this afternoon. She'd probably have sent me to a therapist.

And perhaps she'd have been right to do so.

Bryce turned up at twenty to seven, bang on time. For him, anyway. Luckily I was ready.

"Callista, you look ravishing," he told me as he led me down to his Mini.

"Thanks. Where are we going?"

"La Maison Candille. It's French."

With a name like that, what else would it be?

The maître d' looked down his nose at my plain black jeans and purple tank as he led us to our table. If Bryce had warned me we were going someplace where the menu needed a translator, I'd have dressed up a bit.

After snapping a napkin across my lap, the waiter served an amuse-bouche of something-on-toast. Then he left us to make our selections. I played it safe and picked risotto, which at least was a dish I understood. Bryce ordered his meal in French, eager to show off his grasp of the language.

While we were waiting for our food to arrive, he leaned forward, his chin resting on his steepled hands.

"So, darling, tell me about your trip to Egypt."

I choked on the toast and went into a coughing fit.

A passing waiter thumped me on the back while another dashed from the kitchen with a glass of water.

"Sorry," I sputtered.

"Not a problem, my darling. We were discussing Egypt?"

"It was very, uh, hot."

"I should imagine it was. At least sitting on the beach wouldn't have been terribly taxing."

If that was what he thought I'd been doing, I wasn't about to correct him.

"It certainly was pleasant. The view was lovely."

The view. Oh, the view. The ripples of Adam's abs as he lay next to me. The way his hair tumbled into his eyes when he tilted his head. The twinkle in his eye as he said my name.

Wait, did Bryce just say something?

"Sorry, what?"

"I said it must have been a very enjoyable break until Katerina managed to get herself into trouble. Although I can't say that surprises me. She always was a wild one. What exactly did she do?"

How dare he assume it was Kat's fault? She'd only tried to do the right thing. If more people did the same, the world would be a better place.

"Can we talk about something else?"

Preferably before I decked him.

"Of course, darling, whatever you want."

Bryce launched into a monologue about the writings of Aristotle while I stared at the art on the walls. What on earth had possessed somebody to paint a cow with a mushroom growing out of its head? Thankfully the kitchen was efficient, and before Bryce finished explaining the works of Homer as well, our food arrived.

My risotto steamed invitingly. The aroma of garlic made my mouth water. On the other side of the table, the waiter ceremoniously placed Bryce's plate down in front of him, then removed the silver cover with a flourish.

"What's this?" Bryce whispered.

"It is tête de veau, sir. As you ordered."

Bryce still looked confused.

"Calf brains, sir."

Could it be that Bryce's French wasn't as good as he thought it was? He'd gone a little pale. I must admit, it was amusing watching him push his dinner from one side of the plate to the other, picking out the peas one at a time by spearing them on his fork. My meal was delicious.

Bryce insisted we have dessert, which wasn't exactly a hardship in a place where the pastry chef was clearly a genius. I chose the chocolate fondant, and the centre oozed to perfection. Bryce took no chances and ordered a fruity tart.

Afterwards, he dropped me off at the kerb outside my flat and leaned over to give me a peck on the cheek.

"Can we do this again tomorrow?" he asked.

The evening hadn't been entirely unpleasant, and better yet, Bryce had paid the bill. And part of me, the part that still seethed when I thought of Adam and his Hollywood beauty, needed to prove he wasn't the only one who could move on.

Bryce was still Bryce, but he was trying. I owed it to him to play my part in putting our demons to rest, one way or the other.

I managed to muster up a smile. "What time do you

want to meet?"

CHAPTER 27

I WOKE UP the following morning to the overly cheerful sound of Sister Sledge's "We Are Family" coming from my phone. Kat was calling.

"How are you doing?" she asked. "I tried calling last night, but you didn't answer."

"Oh, I think I left my mobile at home," I said without thinking.

"Left your phone behind? Where did you go?"

"Uh, out."

"Where?"

"To a restaurant."

"Who with, Callista?"

She knew, didn't she? "Bryce," I answered, cringing into my pillow.

"Callie! How could you? After the way he treated you?"

It was a testament to modern technology that I could hear every inflection of her pissed-offness. I didn't need to stand in front of her to see the peeved look on her face.

"He came over, and he was nice to me. He vacuumed."

"He *vacuumed*? Oh, that makes up for everything. Callie, he left you at the altar."

"Technically, it was three days before that part."

"Stop sticking up for him. What he did was indefensible."

"I was feeling lonely."

"But Adam—"

"We're not talking about him. Ever."

I had to stay strong about this. One small mention, one tiny thought, and I'd tumble down the slippery slope.

"Callie, you can't keep avoiding the issue."

"I can and I will. So, how's Mo?"

She huffed, no doubt stamping her foot in frustration. "Getting better every day. He tried walking yesterday afternoon."

"That's great! He'll be zooming around in no time."

"I hope so. The signs are good. At this rate, he'll be able to fly in a few days, with a doctor along for the ride, of course."

"So I'll see you soon?"

"Yep. I'm missing you."

"Missing you too. Did they find any sign of Irina?"

"They've come up with an arm and part of a leg so far. They reckon Eid dismembered the girls with the replica samurai sword hanging on his living room wall."

Good thing I was lying down when she said that because I'd have ended up flat on the floor otherwise.

Kat carried on, oblivious. "He had to cut them up small to get the bits through the checkpoints without anybody noticing. It was only Captain Ibrahim and some of the higher-ups who were in on the plot."

"Enough, Kat."

"Sorry. Just thought you might like the details."

"That's more Bryce's thing. He wanted to know all

about my trip last night."

Kat laughed. "Nosy bugger. He can watch it on TV the same as everybody else."

"Exactly. I told him I didn't want to discuss it."

We chatted for a few minutes, then Kat said she had to visit Mo. She promised to call again soon. Her phone was now sponsored by Vodafone, apparently, so she could call anyone she wanted for free.

Two hours later, a knock at the door startled me as I was making a sandwich for lunch. The knife clattered to the counter. Surely it wasn't Bryce again?

No, it was the local florist.

"Flowers? For me?" I certainly wasn't expecting them.

"They're roses," she said, quite unnecessarily.

And they were beautiful, or at least I thought so until I cut my thumb on a thorn as I was trying to get the card out.

> *Darling Callista,*
> *Your smile is my light,*
> *Bryce.*

Well, wasn't that sweet? He really *was* making an effort.

I found a vase for the bouquet, then put my shoes on. I needed to buy groceries, and Mum wanted a hand with turning the mattress in the spare room. Dave was busy gardening again.

"I'm glad you're feeling better, dear," she said when I turned up on her doorstep. "It's easy to pick up nasty things abroad."

Like sword-wielding serial killers and men who break your heart? Absolutely.

"It's onwards and upwards from here, Mum. Things

can only get better."

I only hoped I spoke the truth.

Against Kat's advice, I went to a play with Bryce that evening. He clutched my sweaty hand in his clammy one, while we watched two people dressed as World War II soldiers speak mainly in Italian for almost two hours.

"Fantastic, wasn't it?" Bryce said as we left. "They really captured the atmosphere of the battlefield. Such tragedy, such drama."

They were on a battlefield? Where were all the guns? The taller of the pair had been carrying a lamp, and the other had a set of cutlery that seemed to be a metaphor for something or other.

Bryce took advantage of my silence and kept talking. His monologue on method acting in the nineteen forties continued most of the way home, and I tried to block it out as I arranged my thoughts. This date hadn't been fun, and last night's dinner wasn't great either. Just okay. Bryce and I had nothing like the easy camaraderie I'd felt with Adam after only a handful of dates.

With Bryce droning on beside me, I came to the conclusion that I'd rather have spent the evening cleaning the bathroom. Why had I stayed with him for so long? Had I been blinded by love? Was I worried about appearances? Or was I scared of being alone?

Truthfully, it was a little of all three.

"Callista?"

"Huh?"

"You zoned out again. I asked what you did when you first realised Kat was in trouble?"

"I told you, I don't want to discuss it."

"But darling, a problem shared..."

"It's not a problem anymore. It's just something I want to forget."

Why couldn't he get the message?

"I saw Katerina on the news again today. She seemed happy."

"Yes, she is. She's coming home in a few days."

And there would undoubtedly be fireworks between the pair of them.

"You spoke to her?"

"This morning."

"I thought she'd stay in Egypt with that man of hers."

"He's coming too."

"Where are they staying? With you? Isn't your flat a bit small?"

"They're both sleeping at Mum's."

"I should visit. Offer my commiserations. I could take a fruit basket and some tickets to my upcoming play."

I was sure Mo felt quite bad enough already without having that inflicted on him. If it was the one Bryce had been rehearsing for before I left, he was playing a suicidal coal miner. Hardly uplifting.

I murmured something non-committal as we pulled up outside my building, and Bryce got out to open my door for me.

"Shall I come up for coffee?" he asked.

In the past, that suggestion would have made me shiver with delight. But today, I cringed away instinctively, the same way I would have if a wasp was hovering nearby.

"I don't think that's a good idea."

"It's nothing we haven't done before, darling."

"But that was then and this is now. I'm sleeping alone tonight."

If there was any shred of doubt remaining that Bryce wasn't the man for me, his reaction erased it. He stomped back to the driver's side, got behind the wheel, slammed the door, and zoomed off. So much for being a gentleman.

At least the evening had helped to clarify things for me. Given me the closure I needed. My post-aborted-wedding mind hadn't been exaggerating—Bryce really was a twit.

The decision was made. No more Bryce. The right man was out there, somewhere, and I'd wait until I found him. Or until he found me.

I slept soundly that night.

I'd only been up for five minutes the next morning when there was a knock at the door. I glanced at the clock. Almost nine. I wouldn't be able to sleep in like that for much longer—soon I'd have a classroom full of kids waiting for me at half past eight every morning.

I had mixed feelings about returning to work. Unlike some people, I'd never thought of teaching as a calling. It was more that graduate positions were difficult to come by and they'd been having a recruitment drive. I figured I'd teach for a few years before I decided on my dream job, but I was still none the wiser.

I tied a robe around me and padded out of the bedroom. Who was it this time? My mum? Bryce?

I cracked the door open.

The answer was neither of them.

Chapter 28

WHEN I OPENED the door, a vision in blonde hair extensions stood before me. Petite, pretty in an artificial sort of way, and obviously pregnant.

She put her hands on her hips. "Are you Callie Shawcross?"

"Yes—"

Before I could get out "And you are?" she slapped me hard across the cheek.

"What the...?"

"You slut!"

How did having slept with two men, ever, qualify me as a slut?

"Perhaps you'd care to explain?" I said through gritted teeth.

"Did you or did you not go out with Bryce Featherstone last night?"

How did she know that?

"Well, yes, but..."

She raised her hand again, but this time I managed to grab her wrist before she made contact.

"Owwww!" she yowled. "You're hurting my arm."

"Stop hitting me!"

"Stop stealing my fiancé!"

Her...fiancé?

"What the hell are you talking about?"

"Bryce, of course! We're supposed to be getting married in three weeks, and yesterday I found out he'd been seeing another woman. You!"

She glared at me. If looks could kill, I'd have been pushing up daisies. I lifted the hand I was still hanging onto, and sure enough, there was a ring. Three small diamonds in a twiddly gold setting. Almost identical to the one Bryce had given me, in fact. What did he do, get them on BOGOF?

I sighed. Perhaps I should have been angry, but quite frankly, I was out of fucks to give.

"You'd better come in."

The girl stepped over the threshold and stood just inside the door, hostility rolling off her in waves. Should I leave the door open in case I needed an escape route?

"What's your name?"

"Mandi. With an 'i.'"

"And you already know I'm Callie. Whatever Bryce has been up to, I think it's safe to say he's been playing both of us."

"What do you mean?" she asked sulkily.

"Did he tell you we were engaged for three years?"

Her jaw dropped open, then her eyes narrowed. "You're lying."

"I met him when I was sixteen at the amateur dramatics society."

"You're lying," she said again, but with less conviction this time.

I opened my desk drawer and lifted out the photos that had once been displayed on top of it. My life with Bryce was now reduced to a few snapshots in dusty frames.

Mandi's face crumpled as she looked through them.

Bryce and me having Christmas dinner at my mum's. Bryce and me ice skating. Bryce and me on his twenty-first birthday. Bryce and me at my graduation.

"I-I-I can't believe it," she said, and then the tears came.

I could hardly believe it either. I mean, I'd come to the conclusion that he was a slug, but a philanderer as well? How could Bryce have had the gall to take me out last night, knowing Mandi was waiting at home for him?

Luckily, Mum had stocked up on tissues before I went to Egypt, and I still had seventeen boxes left. I fetched one for Mandi-with-an-i.

She swiped at her eyes, then howled louder when she realised one of her false eyelashes had detached itself. It crawled across the wadded up Kleenex like a small, sad caterpillar.

"I'll make us a cuppa, shall I?"

"Y-y-yes, please. And I'm sorry I slapped you."

"Forget it."

I made two cups of tea, plenty of sugar in Mandi's and a dash of brandy in mine. Why did this stuff keep happening?

"H-h-he said he l-l-loved me," Mandi sniffled.

Half of her tea slopped out of the mug and splattered onto the carpet. I blotted it up as best I could, then patted her awkwardly on the back.

"He said the same to me. I guess he was lying to both of us."

"But he was so sweet. He told me I was his Ophelia."

That little shit! Next time I saw Bryce, I was going

to stick pins in him.

"How did you find out about me?" I asked.

Bryce hadn't given the slightest indication that he'd met somebody else on either of our two recent "dates," much less that he'd moved quickly enough to ask her to be his wife. And whose was the baby?

"My friend works at the florist next to the bingo hall. You know, the one with the pink neon sign? It's got 'The Cheapest Way to a Girl's Heart' written in the window?"

I'd been past it on occasion. Bargain-basement flowers, bargain-basement men. No wonder they hadn't taken the thorns off my roses. I nodded.

"He went in there and ordered flowers, and when they were for you and not me, she texted straight away."

My curiosity got the better of me. "So, how did you two meet?"

"I used to work as a waitress in the Starlight Lounge. Bryce used to come in quite often, but it was ages before he noticed me. I put extra olives in his martini." A strip club? They met in a freaking *strip club*? "Then one night we were passing in the corridor outside the toilets, and our eyes met. He said that was the moment he knew he wanted to marry me."

I felt faint. How had I never seen that side of him? And how could he afford to keep visiting a strip club, anyway? He never had any money. Unless... Was that *why* he'd never had any money?

"How long ago was that?"

"About two years."

Two years? *Two freaking years?* Pins were too good for Bryce. I was tempted to borrow Eid's samurai sword instead.

Deep breaths, Callie.

"But he spent at least five nights a week with me. Didn't you think that was odd?" I asked.

"He told me he was in a touring production of 'The Merchant of Venice.' Playing Shylock. I was so proud of him."

Mandi reached for another handful of tissues and blew her nose.

I thought of the excuses he'd used with me. He had to tidy the props cupboard. Jimmy in the lighting department needed somebody to hold the ladder. Another bloody rehearsal. How could I have been so stupid?

"It wasn't only you. He led both of us on."

"I thought he'd changed," Mandi blubbed. "A month ago, he came home and said he'd quit the play. He said he couldn't stand being away from me so much, and he wanted us to be together every night. We went on holiday to Jamaica, and everything was wonderful."

Jamaica? Bryce took Mandi on my bloody honeymoon! I was going to cut off his testicles and put them through the mincer.

"He had a new project he was working on," Mandi continued. "A screenplay. The idea came to him the other morning while he was watching the news, or so he claimed. Something about Egypt. A murder mystery, he said. He wanted to turn it into a movie. Anyhow, when he was out with you, he told me he was doing research for it. Can you believe that?"

I thought back to Bryce's questions about my time away. Yes, unfortunately I *could* believe it. He didn't love me at all. I doubted at that moment that he ever had. He'd just been using me, although it hadn't stopped him from trying to invite himself into my bed, the little snake. "Little" being the operative word there.

Poor Mandi. He'd lied to her too, and she was pregnant. That must be devastating.

"The baby." I gestured at her swollen stomach. "It's Bryce's?"

"Oh yes," she said. "I'm at least eighty percent sure."

Sorry, what? I choked on a mouthful of tea. Okay, brandy.

"Eighty percent?"

"At least. I mean, there were only two other guys, and they both pulled out."

You know what? On second thoughts, Mandi and Bryce deserved each other. I helped her up and led her to the door.

"Do you have any family?" I asked.

"My mum and dad. They live in Kent."

"Why don't you go and stay with them for a while? Clear your head? If Bryce is serious about you, he'll wait. If not, at least you'll know where you stand."

"That makes so much sense. I'm glad I came today —you're a great listener."

Yeah, go figure. If someone had told me this morning that before I'd even had my coffee, I'd be offering relationship advice to my ex-fiancé's pregnant lover, I'd have asked them what drugs they'd been taking.

"Will you be okay getting home?" I asked, keen to get rid of her but feeling a little guilty about casting her out on the street.

"Yes, and thank you for everything."

Once she'd gone, I knocked back the rest of the brandy, drank a few fingers of gin, and went back to bed. Maybe later, I'd try this day again.

By the time the afternoon came, fury had taken hold, fuelled by a pounding headache and no doubt assisted by my alcohol consumption. As my eyes narrowed on Bryce's precious script, still sitting on the chest of drawers in my bedroom, I knew what to do.

First, I took some headache pills, and then I started spring-cleaning. And by spring-cleaning, I mean I gathered everything Bryce had ever touched, carted it downstairs to the communal garden, and set fire to it.

Kat was right. The flames were cathartic.

And so were the firemen.

When old Mrs. Carter panicked and phoned 999, the men of Blue Watch were very understanding, not to mention hot. It was a challenge to fit all six of them into my flat for coffee, but when they left, I had a big smile on my face and the phone number of the sexiest one on a slip of paper in my pocket.

Who knew? Maybe I'd even call it.

When Kat rang me later in the evening, I was feeling almost cheerful.

"How are you?" she asked. "Did you have a good day?"

"I'm just peachy. I started off by giving Bryce's pregnant girlfriend relationship advice and finished off by having a nice chat with six of Blue Watch's finest."

As I heard her choking at the other end of the line, I offered her a mental pat on the back. Thankfully someone seemed to oblige with a physical one because she soon came back.

"Can you repeat that? For a moment, I thought you said Bryce has a pregnant girlfriend?"

"It certainly seems that way. It was either that or a cushion. And it appears she's been ironing his socks for the past couple of years."

Kat sucked in a breath. "Flippin' heck. I always knew he was a weasel, but even I didn't suspect that. What did he have to say about it?"

"I haven't spoken to him yet. I'm saving that joy up for tomorrow."

"Give him a punch in the face from me, would you? Actually, I'll be home in two days. I can do it myself. Nothing would give me greater pleasure."

"Sorry, but that's my treat."

"Fair enough. Did you mention firemen?"

"Ooh, yes. You were totally right about them. Let me tell you about Steve..."

CHAPTER 29

AT ONE O'CLOCK in the morning, I woke up on the floor. I didn't often have nightmares, but there was no other word for a dream starring Bryce. He'd been on stage, playing Hamlet to Mandi's Ophelia, when Adam swept past in a tuxedo and challenged him to a duel. I'd been glued to my seat in the audience, quite literally paralysed, and I'd been struggling to free myself and help Adam when I fell out of bed.

As I lay there on the cool floor, watching car headlights flicker across the ceiling, I had time to reflect.

My initial euphoria about the demise of Bryce had given way to numbness. I felt hollow, as if somebody had scooped out my insides and put them on the bonfire with his belongings.

But it wasn't the loss of Bryce himself that made me feel that way, it was my own stupidity. How could I have been taken in so thoroughly? And not just once, but twice? First by Bryce, and then by Adam. Although on a scale of one to utter dickhead, Adam's deception paled into insignificance compared to Bryce's. It was Adam who'd hurt me most. A tear trickled down my cheek as I mourned the loss of my self-esteem and the man I'd once loved.

The man I still did love, if I was honest with myself.

I padded through to the lounge and fetched the tissues that Mandi hadn't used, and soon I had a pile of them scrunched up beside me. My ears still rang with Adam's last words—his relief at me leaving. *It's probably for the best.*

Over and over again, they echoed in my head. What if I'd never heard them? What if I'd spoken to him the next morning? Could things have been different, or would it only have prolonged the inevitable?

I'd never know.

All I could do was hope that in time the hurt would fade, and that one day I'd be able to think about our time together with fondness.

I was still exhausted when I heard a knock at the door the next morning. Bryce stood on the doorstep wearing a button-down shirt and maroon skinny jeans. Both were wrinkle-free. Had he picked up an iron himself? Or did Mandi do them before she left?

Had he even noticed she'd gone?

He was clutching a picnic basket—one of those old fashioned wicker ones that gave you splinters and were super awkward to carry. I spotted a pad of paper sticking out of the top—for notes on his screenplay, obviously.

"Callista, darling, I thought we'd go to the park for lunch. I got a selection of delectable nibbles from the Italian delicatessen."

"I'll pass, Bryce, but before you go, I just have to give you this."

I handed him a small plastic baggie filled with grey dust. I'd been looking forward to this moment all night.

"What is it?"

"Your stuff."

Once I'd explained what I was doing and why I was doing it, the firemen had kindly helped me to sweep up the remains of the bonfire before they left yesterday.

"Stuff? What do you mean?"

I ticked off the items on my fingers. "The script for your play. That green shirt that you liked. Your school yearbook. Some plectrums for your guitar."

He just couldn't help himself. "You mean plectra."

"Whatever." I smiled and carried on. "A stripy cashmere scarf. Your Paul Smith messenger bag. A tub of hair pomade. Ferdie."

Bryce gasped. "Ferdie's in here?"

Ferdie was Bryce's Steiff teddy bear. He'd bought him after reading a magazine article titled *Why All Men Should Own a Cuddly Toy*. Ferdie *had* been kind of cute, but once I'd made the decision, the bear had to go. The button from his ear had made it through the inferno, and now it was sitting on top of the ash.

"How could you? Ferdie brought out my feminine side."

"It was easy. I just sprayed a bit of lighter fluid on the pile and lit the match."

Bryce clapped the back of his hand to his forehead and took in a deep breath.

"Why, Callista? Why?"

"Does the name Mandi ring any bells?"

He went white. Or at least, he went mostly white. I

peered more closely at his face. When had he started wearing blusher?

"I can explain. It was a one-time thing. A single night. I lost my creative inspiration, and it devastated me. I'd had one too many white wine spritzers, and it just happened."

A one-time thing? The lying git. They'd have done it more than once on my honeymoon, that was for sure.

"Jamaica? The baby too? That just happened?"

Bryce paled a shade further, and his cheeks looked even more ridiculous. Think eighties music video. He began pacing.

"But I don't love Mandi. She's infatuated with me. It's been an incredibly difficult time. I didn't want to cause her any psychological harm, so I've been trying to let her down gently." He sighed dramatically. "You're the only woman for me, Callista."

He opened his mouth to carry on, but I held up a hand to stop him. He looked surprised, probably because I'd never interrupted him before.

"Bryce stop talking. At least do the honourable thing and look after her."

"Well, of course I'll pay something towards it. You know how these things work. Young girls are always trying to trap desirable men into marriage."

It? He called the baby *it*? What had I ever seen in Bryce? How had he managed to keep this side of himself hidden? I'd wasted almost a quarter of my life with him. Six years I'd never get back. It was a sobering thought.

Did he speak to Mandi the same way he spoke to me? What had he told her about his ex-girlfriends? That we were hopeless groupies blinded by his talent?

You know what? I didn't care anymore.

"Just leave, would you? I haven't got another word to say to you."

"I'll give you the time you need, Callista, but understand I'll stop at nothing to get you back. We're soulmates."

I slammed the door in his face and went to get on with my life. It was too short.

Just after lunch, I arrived home to find a huge bouquet waiting on my doorstep. The florist must have had fun getting that up the stairs. I took a closer look. Uh-oh. It was full of pink lilies, and I started to sneeze. At least I still had eleven boxes of tissues left.

I shifted my packages into one hand and plucked out the card.

Callista,
Your eyes are blue as time, your soul white as the purest snow.
I will love you forever and a day,
Bryce.

I screwed up the card and left the whole lot in the hallway. Six years, we were together, and he couldn't remember I was allergic to lily pollen?

And why was time blue?

Inside, I cleared a space on the sideboard, and an hour later, my shiny new goldfish bowl took pride of place. Bob swam around in it, picking up bits of gravel and spitting them out again. It must be nice to be a fish. Nothing to do all day, and only the last seven seconds to worry about.

Another hour, and my Bob-watching was rudely interrupted by my phone ringing.

"Hi, Mum."

"I'm cooking dinner, dear."

"Thanks, but I'm okay. I picked up something from the supermarket earlier."

"But it's lasagne made from scratch. And sticky toffee pudding."

Damn, she played dirty. I'd never been able to resist her sticky toffee pudding.

"I'll be there in an hour."

"I didn't want you moping around at home," Mum said as I walked through the door. "You need to get over Bryce."

Oh, believe me, I was over him. In fact, right then, I couldn't believe I'd ever been under him.

"Can we not talk about Bryce?"

"Okay, dear. That new fellow you met on holiday, he didn't work out either?"

Tears pricked my eyes as I busied myself getting salad out of the fridge.

"Just a holiday fling."

"That's a shame. Still, I hope he gave you plenty of romps in the bedroom. You looked as if you needed it."

"Mum!"

"Do you have any pictures? Kat said he was very good-looking."

Just look at the nearest billboard. Scott would be up there, advertising his latest movie. Or maybe some toothpaste.

But Adam? All that was left of Adam was captured in a few candid snaps on my phone. I couldn't bring myself to look at them yet.

Instead, I kept my head down and concentrated on shredding lettuce and spinach, then added oil and balsamic vinegar before I carried the bowl through to the dining room.

"I'll lay the table," I called out. "How many places? Is Dave joining us for dinner?"

Before she could answer, the doorbell rang, the scratchy sound of Für Elise echoing through the house.

Guests? Mum hadn't mentioned anything about guests. Surely she hadn't...? No, not again...

"Tell me you haven't been meddling again?"

Mum stepped out of the kitchen, wiping her hands on a tea towel. She looked as bewildered as I must have looked peeved.

"I didn't invite anyone else." She saw my face. "Honestly. Kat told me to leave it alone for a while. Although I met Mildred Wilson's son the other day, and he's a doctor. A real catch. Mildred said his last girlfriend ran off with the man who was building their new extension."

"Stop! There's somebody at the door."

"Oh, yes. Would you mind getting it? The lasagne's ready to come out of the oven."

I peered through the glass privacy panel in Mum's

front door, but all I saw was a crinkled silhouette. Who was it? I eased the door open, prepared to slam it if Bryce had decided to stalk me.

"Persephone? What on earth are you doing here?"

"Surprise," she said, then burst into tears.

She shuffled into the house with Annie on her hip while I rescued her little wheelie suitcase and Annie's changing bag from the kerb. This woman looked like my sister and sounded like my sister, but she sure didn't act like her. As I closed the front door behind us, there was a clatter from the kitchen as Mum dropped the tray she'd been carrying.

She asked the same question as I had. "Persephone, what are you doing here?"

"He left us, Mum. Pierre left us."

She gave a most unbecoming snort and smeared mascara across her face. I ran for the tissues.

Her perfect husband had run out on her? How? Why? Persephone and Pierre were made for each other. Both were snooty, materialistic, and enjoyed trampling lesser mortals who got in their way as they climbed the social ladder.

"What happened?" I asked as I deposited a wad of Kleenex into Persephone's hand.

"He moved in with a dancer. From the Moulin Rouge. We went there for his birthday treat, and three months later, I found out he'd taken more away with him than a souvenir program."

Baby Annie decided to follow Persephone's lead and started bawling too. Since my sister made no move to comfort her daughter, I picked Annie up and bounced her in my arms. Then the smoke alarm joined in, screeching above the din as acrid clouds billowed through the open kitchen door.

"The garlic bread!"

Mum leapt up as Dave wandered in from the garden, brushing dirt off his hands.

"Is dinner ready yet?" Then he noticed Persephone. "Is that the new thing in Paris?" he asked, gesturing at her streaky face.

A little later, we managed to get dinner onto the table, minus the garlic bread, which went into the dustbin. Dave shovelled lasagne into his mouth like a man possessed, no doubt planning his escape from the horde of emotional females.

Persephone stared into space while I fed some sort of mush to Annie. Vegetable casserole, according to the label, but it was bright orange and had a distinct lack of recognisable vegetables.

"What can we do to help?" Mum asked.

Nothing.

"Persephone?"

"Huh?"

My sister was on a different planet. The jacket of her tailored suit hung askew, and her chignon had come loose. Not at all like the sibling I knew and tolerated.

"Do you want me to call Pierre?" I asked. "Try to make him see sense?"

"You can't. He and Stéphanie have gone on a month's trek to Namibia. He said he needed to 'find himself,' whatever that means. He left me a note."

Pierre didn't do anything by halves. What an asshole. Bryce may have been a prick, but at least he'd had the guts to tell me personally.

And Adam? Adam had just faded into the sunset.

I squeezed Persephone's hand. Yes, she was a bitch, but nobody deserved this.

"Maybe he's having a mid-life crisis?"

"No, he already had that last year when he bought the Porsche." She blew out a breath. "Perhaps it was my stretch marks? Do you think a tummy tuck would help? I should join a gym."

"But you're a size eight."

"My thighs still jiggle. See?"

She got to her feet and bounced on the spot. The only thing that moved was her ponytail.

"Nothing's wobbling."

"Nonsense. You just don't know how things should look. Where's the nearest fitness centre?" she asked, then she looked me up and down. "Oh, sorry. You obviously wouldn't know." She turned to Mum. "Where's the nearest fitness centre?"

I sighed. It promised to be a long few weeks.

Two hours passed before I managed to escape. I put Annie to bed and left Persephone shopping for shape-wear on the internet. Probably she thought she was being nice when she offered to buy some for me too, but the thought of squishing myself into Spanx left me more depressed than ever.

When I unlocked the door to my flat, I should have felt happier. After all, I wasn't sharing space with my sister any longer. But I didn't. Despair kicked in. If Perfect Persephone couldn't keep a man, what hope did I have?

CHAPTER 30

"PERSEPHONE'S AT YOUR mother's?" Kat asked.

I nodded, and she leaned forward to tap the cab driver on the shoulder.

"Could you take us to the nearest hotel instead?"

"Ignore that," I told him. "Kat, you're not chickening out. What do you always tell me about facing up to my fears?"

"I'm not scared of Persephone. She just drives me around the flipping twist."

"It's character building."

"I just got out of prison for murder. I don't want to go back in."

Mo shifted uncomfortably beside Kat. "If it's not too much trouble, I'd like to lie down."

Kat sat back and folded her arms. "Fine, you win. We'll stay there tonight. But if Persephone makes one snide comment about my hair, my outfit, or my lifestyle, I'm not being held responsible for the consequences."

Sometimes, I wished I shared Kat's lack of self-restraint.

When we pulled up outside Mum's, Kat and I helped Mo out of the car and into his wheelchair. His two casts stuck out in front of him at an awkward angle. Dave took the cases while mum fussed around, getting in the way.

"I'm so glad you managed to get here, Mo. Callie's told me all about you, haven't you, dear? I'm Brenda, by the way."

Mo stuck out his hand, and I winced as I saw the line of cuts winding their way up his arm. They'd scabbed over now, but the surrounding skin was still an angry red.

"I'm pleased to meet you, Brenda. Thank you for allowing me to stay in your home."

Mum nudged Kat, beaming. "Isn't he polite, Kitty Kat?" Kat had never outgrown her childhood nickname, in Mum's eyes at least. "Once he's healed up, you'll make such a handsome couple."

"Where's Persephone?" I asked, surprised she hadn't come out. Normally she couldn't resist being nosy.

"She signed up for some kind of boot camp. Lots of men in uniform shouting at her, she said."

Kat shuddered. "I've had enough men in uniform shouting at me to last a lifetime."

"Oh, you poor dear. Do you want a cup of tea?"

In Mum's eyes, tea was the answer to all the troubles in the world.

"Please."

"Mo, would you like a drink?"

"Tea as well, thank you."

I helped Kat to unpack everything, hoping we wouldn't need to pack it all back up again when Persephone made an appearance. By the time darkness fell, Mo was settled comfortably on the sofa, talking about motorbikes with Dave. Kat walked down the path with me.

"How are you holding up?" she asked. "I still can't believe what happened with Bryce."

"I was such an idiot, and for so long. The only saving grace is that I found out what an utter pillock he was before I married him."

"There is that. And how about the other thing?"

Inside, I crumpled. "I'm trying not to think about him. If I do, well... I just can't."

"You know I'm here if you need to talk."

"I do, and I appreciate it more than you could ever know."

So much for not thinking about Adam. As soon as I walked away, he monopolised my thoughts. I ached for his touch, his words, his closeness.

When I got home, I did something I said I wouldn't. I took out my phone and looked at the few photos I had of him. The two of us grinning sleepily in his hammock. One of him lazing on a sunlounger. A snap taken by the waiter in the Italian restaurant with the sea glimmering in the background.

The one that hit me hardest was the very last picture I took. Adam stood on his own, gazing straight at me as I aimed the camera. His gleaming smile lit up the screen. His eyes lit up my soul. And not so many hours afterwards, his fingers had lit up my body.

I missed him. I'd *always* miss him.

"Do you think it's going okay?" Kat asked for the

hundredth time.

"Somebody would tell us if there was a problem."

Mo had been in the operating theatre for six hours, and the surgeon said the procedure to repair his right leg would take most of the day.

Kat had said a heart-wrenching goodbye just after eight, and since then, we'd been sitting in the waiting room. At least I'd been sitting. Kat had mostly been pacing.

"I can't believe two weeks ago we were strolling together on the beach. Now look at us."

"A lot's happened, hasn't it?" I offered her a bottle of water. "Drink?"

She took the bottle, but rather than taking a sip, she began picking the label off with what was left of her fingernails.

"He's the one, you know."

"Yes, I do know. I saw the way he looked at you on the first day we met."

"We nearly didn't make it."

"Don't think like that. You *did* make it. You're here, you're together, and you have your whole future to look forward to."

"It taught me a lot, being in that dungeon. Life's too short—I never realised that before. I'm only twenty-two, and I figured I'd have forever to tick off all the things on my bucket list. It never occurred to me that I might never finish."

"Carpe diem." Seize the day.

"With both fucking hands, Callie." She checked her watch. "Where *is* he?"

Another hour passed before the surgeon appeared, looking haggard and a little bit blood-stained. Ick. I sat down fast when I realised whose blood it was.

"The news is good, Miss Rawlins. Mohammed should make a full recovery as long as he listens to his physiotherapist."

"Can I see him?"

"An orderly will take you through shortly."

The intensive care unit was another reminder of my own mortality. Mo looked frail, but he still smiled when he saw Kat. Yes, he was definitely the one. It wouldn't surprise me if the next wedding I went to was theirs. We stayed until a militant nurse kicked us out, and it was only when my stomach grumbled in the car park that I realised neither of us had eaten all day.

"Do you fancy cooking?" I asked Kat. I knew I didn't.

"I'd probably die of starvation before it was time to dish up."

"Takeaway?"

"We'd still have to eat near Persephone. She's got a diet app on her phone now. When I went downstairs for a snack last night, she insisted on telling me the calorie and fat content of my packet of crisps. I almost throttled her."

"Pub?"

Kat grinned. "Perfect. Let's find one on the way home."

The flowerpots outside The Jolly Lion gave it a cheery

feel, although the lion pictured on the sign looked more ravenous than happy. Perhaps it was the knife and fork he was waving.

There was an unseasonable chill in the air, and I huddled into my thin cardigan as I curled up on a squashy leather bench in the corner. Kat had gone to the bar for drinks.

"Coke for you, lemonade for me."

She dropped two menus on the table, then threw a newspaper on top of them. I quickly averted my gaze, but it was too late. I'd seen the headline. The sleazy tabloid was open to the entertainment page, the bombshell stamped across the top in thick black text.

Scott Lowes takes out restraining order against Velvet Jones.

I devoured the rest of the article before I could stop myself.

"Do you think it's true?" I asked.

The paparazzi weren't exactly famed for their accurate portrayal of facts.

"Bloody right it is. He said he was calling his lawyer as soon as he got home. Velvet drove him nuts in Egypt."

"I saw them on TV right after I left. They looked pretty into each other then."

Kat rolled her eyes. "Scott's an *actor*, Callie. He does that shit for a living. Velvet sprinted past the TV crew just as he was about to go on air and threw herself at him. All he could do was smile and get on with it. He didn't want to overshadow what happened to me and Mo by having a spat with Velvet live on TV."

"So he didn't choose to stand next to her?"

"Quite the opposite. As soon as the camera turned

away, he was furious."

A small, hysterical giggle escaped my mouth.

"But that wasn't the best part," Kat continued. "She bribed one of the hotel staff to let her into his room that evening so she could wait for him in bed. Thing was, she got the wrong room. I'm not sure which of us was more surprised—me or her."

"Are you serious?"

"Yup. And *she* was starkers."

"No way."

"Yes way. And all those bikini pics are definitely Photoshopped."

"So then what happened?"

"She started screaming, I started yelling, and Scott heard the noise and had her escorted off the premises by hotel security. The woman's cuckoo."

"I had no idea."

"Well, I tried to tell you, but you wouldn't let me."

A horrible feeling washed over me. Horror and fear and regret and dread all rolled into one. A fist that pummelled my guts and seized my throat. Adam had said Velvet was crazy, but I hadn't believed him at the time. If he'd been telling the truth about that, what else had I got wrong?

"He wanted me to leave," I whispered to myself. I hadn't misheard those words.

"What are you talking about?" Kat asked.

"Adam. He wanted me to leave."

"What on earth makes you think that?"

"I heard him talking to you the morning I left. You told him I was leaving, and he said it was for the best."

"Did you hear the rest of the conversation?"

"No, that was quite enough."

"So you didn't hear him say that it would be selfish of him to try and stop you, no matter how much he wanted to? That because he loved you so much, there was no way he could inflict the media shit storm onto you?"

I swayed a bit, and Kat leaned over and shoved my head down between my knees.

"Don't faint on me," she ordered.

When the blood stopped whooshing in my ears, I slowly sat up straight again.

"What have I done?" I croaked.

"You've been a complete idiot."

"Thanks for that startling observation."

"Just telling it like it is."

"Remind me again why you're my best friend?"

"Because I'm wonderful and you love me."

My insides were doing backflips. I'd managed to screw things up royally with the most amazing man I'd ever met, and I had no idea how to fix it. Or if it even could be fixed.

"What the hell do I do?" I asked Kat, hoping she'd come up with a miracle.

"Call him?"

"I can't do that! What on earth would I say?"

"Duh, how about admitting you've been incredibly stupid, then telling him you've come to your senses and you still love him?"

"I can't just phone him up and say that. I barely know him."

"You spent weeks practically joined at the hip."

"With Adam. He's Scott now. I don't know *him*."

"He's still the same person."

"Physically, maybe. But Adam was so...so down to

earth. Scott... Now that it's sunk in, I feel like I should bow at his feet."

"That's the last thing he'd want. I spent some time with him after you'd left, and we talked. He fell for you precisely *because* you treated him like an average Joe. Underneath all the glitz and glamour, he actually seems very lonely."

"I need to give this some thought, okay? I don't want to make any more stupid mistakes."

"Well, don't take too long. Carpe diem, remember?"

I staggered into my apartment building in a daze. Nothing made sense anymore. I had some serious thinking to do, and for that I needed wine. A bottle, maybe two. And chocolate. Chocolate always helped.

I tramped up the stairs, cursing the maintenance team for failing to replace the broken lightbulb on the landing yet again. The hallway was in perpetual gloom, and my life was quite depressing enough. Wait. What was that? I got halfway to my door and stopped short. Outside, a shadowy figure sat slumped against the wall.

My heart stopped, then started hammering. The crazy rhythm made me wonder if I should head back to the hospital for an ECG. I took a step closer, squinting.

Was that...? No... Surely it couldn't be...?

CHAPTER 31

I CREPT CLOSER to the dark figure. Who was it?

Or rather, *what* was it?

I got near enough to poke it with my foot, and it keeled over sideways, furry legs sticking up in the air.

After two attempts, I got my key in the lock and opened the door. Light flooded out. A giant teddy bear lay sprawled on the floor, looking like a murder victim. All that was missing was the chalk outline.

I detached the frilly heart it was holding in its outstretched hands and read the message.

Callista,

You will always be my one true love,

Bryce.

Oh, please. I threw it down in disgust. But what the hell was I meant to do with the oversized monster? The bear was bigger than me and weighed about as much too. I couldn't leave it in the hallway. Somebody would trip over it, and I didn't want broken bones on my conscience.

I nearly gave myself a hernia as I dragged the furry freak into the flat and hauled it onto the sofa. It sat there, staring creepily at Bob. Tomorrow, I'd take it to a charity shop, although carrying it would be a challenge. Would it need its own bus ticket?

The alternative would be to take a leaf out of Eid's

book and dispose of it piece by piece, but I didn't have a handy samurai sword. I wasn't sure I could bring myself to hack Paddington up with scissors either. No, I'd have to do it the hard way.

Why me?

And where was that wine?

A bottle and a half later, I felt much better about things, and I'd also come to a clear decision. Which was... I'd consider the problem tomorrow.

Adam starred in my dreams again. This time, he was standing in the middle of a bridge with me on one side and Velvet on the other. As we raced to the centre, a hole opened up, and Adam fell away from our outstretched fingers into the raging torrent below.

We'd both lost him.

In the morning, I ignored the dark circles under my eyes and pushed Brian, as I'd named him, down the stairs. He landed at the bottom with a soft *thunk*, and one of my neighbours took pity and helped me to drag him to the bus stop. The kindly old driver of the 409 service into town consulted his handbook, and when he couldn't find any reference to giant teddy bears, he let Brian ride for free.

The first two charity shops I tried were a bust. One said they didn't have space, and the lady manning the till in the second took one look at Brian and said, "Thanks but no thanks, love. He'll scare the kiddies."

I could see her point. In daylight, his yellow eyes were a bit alarming.

"Please?" I begged the guy in the third store. "He's very, uh, fluffy."

"I'm not sure he's what our customers are looking for."

"If I have to take him home, I'll probably die from exhaustion. Or heatstroke. Do you want that on your conscience?"

"No, but—"

"And I've run out of wine. Do you know how difficult it is to share a flat with a giant bear when you've run out of wine?"

"I guess we could sit him over there in the corner."

I smiled sweetly. "Thank you."

Sweat was still trickling out of my pores when I got home. I climbed the stairs, picking bits of acrylic fur off my top as I went, then tripped near the top. Brilliant. Now my knee hurt, and I'd probably have a bruise too.

Oh. No.

What was that? That new box outside my door? I tiptoed closer and plucked the card out from under the big red bow.

Callista,

I saw this and thought of you,

Bryce.

A vacuum cleaner. He'd bought me a new bloody vacuum cleaner. Gnashing my teeth, I rolled the card up really tightly. That would make it easier to insert it where I planned to later on.

I'd never sold anything on eBay before, but surely it couldn't be that difficult? Hopefully I'd make enough to buy another crate of wine.

As I walked into my bedroom, I caught a glimpse of myself in the mirror. Good grief—I looked like a hybrid of Brian and an out-of-shape beetroot. Hospital security would turn me away at the door. A shower was desperately needed.

Afterwards, I was rummaging around for a pair of knickers when it happened. My hand clasped around something else instead. Adam's T-shirt. Before I realised what I was doing, I'd brought it to my nose and inhaled. It was faint, but still there—the sweet, musky smell of the man I was hopelessly in love with, along with a hint of Hugo Boss Orange.

My phone sat on the nightstand, taunting me.

Did I dare to call him?

What should I say?

"Hi, it's Callie. From Egypt? Look, about the whole Adam/Scott thing, I've thought it over and decided it doesn't matter. Can we just pick up where we left off?"

No good. I needed an apology in there.

How about, "I'm sorry I abandoned you to Velvet. I should have stayed and clawed her eyes out for you. Will you ever forgive me?"

I flumped onto the bed. Why couldn't I think of the right words? When Bryce had walked out on me, I'd been speechless, which sure had made things easier.

Kat's words came back to me. *Carpe diem*. She was right—I had to seize the day with both hands, come what may.

I dialled Adam with shaking fingers. My heart was thumping so loudly I was surprised the lady next door didn't knock on the wall and shout for me to turn the volume down.

His phone rang once, and then his voice came

through, soft and sexy. "Hey."

"Hi, uh, it's Callie. I-I-I..."

"Just kidding. I'm not here. Leave a message, and I'll call you back."

I hung up and flung the phone away as if it had burnt me. Making that call had taken every last shred of my courage, and leaving a voicemail would have taken a whole lot more.

And what if he'd diverted me on purpose?

I didn't want to think about it. And not only that, I'd spent so much time agonising over whether to make the call in the first place, I was late. If I didn't hurry, I'd miss the bus.

Mo looked decidedly perkier than the day before. The top of his bed had been raised into a sitting position, and Kat perched on the edge beside him. He'd pushed his plate of hospital-issue food to the side in favour of a box of chocolates.

Just seeing them made my mouth water. Between having to deal with Brian and worrying about Adam, I hadn't had time for breakfast.

Kat saw me eyeing them up and pushed the box over. "Go on."

"Is it that obvious?"

"You're looking at them as if you've been stranded on a life raft for six months and they're your last chance at salvation."

I plucked one out and popped it in my mouth. "These are delicious."

"I know." Mo grinned at me. "Adam brought them."

I stopped mid-chew. "Adam brought them?"

"He means Adam *sent* them." Kat patted Mo on the hand. "Don't you?" She turned to me. "Sometimes Mo's English isn't perfect."

"Ah, yes. Sent them. That's right. Yes."

The delicious truffle turned to sawdust in my mouth. I forced it down my suddenly dry throat, another reminder of what I'd lost.

"Are you all right?" Kat asked. "You look as if you've seen a ghost."

"I'm fine, honestly. Mo, how are you feeling?"

"Very happy."

"They've been giving him morphine," Kat explained. "Last night he thought Kylie had come to visit. He was singing and everything, so the nurse said. They had to reduce the dose."

"I wish I'd seen that."

"When Mo's out of the hospital, we can have a karaoke night."

Would that involve me singing as well? "I'm not sure that's a good idea."

"Come on, be adventurous."

"No way. I tried that before, and look where it got me."

"That's settled then—a karaoke night. I'll set it up."

Tell me again—why was I friends with Kat? We chatted for a while longer, but when the nurse started tapping her foot, we had to leave.

"Do you fancy getting lunch?" I asked Kat once we'd escaped the glare of Nurse Frosty.

"Sorry I can't. I need to run some errands."

Rats. Even with Bob on the sideboard, my flat felt lonely. I didn't want to go back there yet.

"I'll come and give you a hand."

"I couldn't ask you to do that. It's going to be really boring."

"It's fine, honestly. I don't mind."

"I only need to buy socks and stuff. And, er, shampoo. I'll be fine by myself. You should get home. Doesn't your flat need a clean?"

First Bryce, and now Kat. My flat wasn't that dirty, was it?

Kat gave me a quick hug and stepped back. "Ooh, look. Here's the bus into town. I'll see you tomorrow, yeah?"

I didn't have time to answer before she leapt on board and disappeared.

What had I done? Why didn't Kat want to spend time with me? I gave my armpits a surreptitious sniff just in case. Nope, they were good.

I still hadn't worked out the answer by the time I trudged upstairs to my flat. Please, say Bryce hadn't left any more "gifts."

Oh, thank goodness. The hallway was empty. Had he finally got the hint? I sure hoped so because I didn't want to spend the rest of my life listing things on eBay. I hadn't yet worked out how to mail the bloody vacuum cleaner—I'd have to arrange a courier somehow—but that was a problem for after lunch. Was twelve o'clock too early for a glass of wine? I'd picked up a bottle of Cabernet Sauvignon on the way home, and the grapes were calling my name.

Wait.

No, tell me he hadn't...
What was that on the coffee table?

CHAPTER 32

MY TEETH CLENCHED as I stared down at the single red rose that definitely hadn't been on the coffee table when I left. And what was that beside it? A ring box?

At least it wasn't a steam cleaner or an iron.

"Bryce! Who the hell gave you a new key?"

The door clicked shut behind me. "Baby, it's not Bryce."

What the...? I recognised that voice. Pivoting around, I caught my heel in the rug and lurched forward, right into Adam's arms.

"That's better. I was worried it'd take a bit of work to get you there."

I craned my neck up, unable to move in his tight embrace.

"What are you doing here?" I whispered.

"Kissing you."

What could I do but kiss him back?

I'd missed this. I'd missed everything about him. His gentle embrace, the way my body moulded to his, the little zings of electricity that zapped through my veins. He tasted delicious, a mix of mint and coffee, and even after we came up for air, he didn't loosen his hold on me. I slid my hands down to his ass. Yes, I'd missed that too.

"You came all the way to England to kiss me?"

"No, I came all the way to England to ask you to marry me."

What?

I came round on the sofa. Adam knelt in front of me, fanning me with a magazine, and there was no faking the look of panic on his face.

"Baby, are you okay?"

"I had a really weird dream. Wait—am I still dreaming?"

I heard the rattle of a key, and the front door crashed against the wall. My sister walked in like she owned the place, dressed in a pair of yoga pants and a sports bra.

What the...?

She paused, blinked a couple of times, and continued into the kitchen. I scrambled to my feet and hurried after her.

Give me strength.

"Persephone, what are you doing here?"

"I need a jogging buddy, and who better than my favourite sister? I mean, you could do with losing a few pounds. You'll have to hurry up and get changed, though—I've got an appointment to have my fat frozen off at two o'clock."

What could I even say to that?

"But I don't want to go jogging."

"Nonsense—look at the size of your bottom. Just wear something baggy and you'll be fine."

I forced myself to move away from the knife block as she clattered around the kitchen.

"What are you looking for?"

"A glass. Not one of those ugly plastic things. I need water. Those herbal slimming pills I bought on the internet are disagreeing with me. I felt nauseous earlier, and now I'm hallucinating."

"Hallucinating?"

"When I walked in, I could have sworn I saw Scott Lowes on one knee in your lounge."

Adam appeared in the doorway. "Lady, I don't know who you are, but this isn't a good time."

"There he is again!" Persephone shrieked. "And this time he's talking."

I put my arm around her shoulders and led her to the door.

"If you're not feeling right, it's probably not a good idea to go jogging today. I mean, what if you embarrassed yourself in public by trying to have a conversation with someone who wasn't there? Hallucinations aren't something you want to mess with."

"I suppose you've got a point."

"Why don't you go back to Mum's and have a nice lie-down?"

"You think that would help?"

I tried my best to sound sympathetic. "I'm sure of it."

I guided her out of the door and closed it behind her. Where was Satan? Surely he was missing her down below by now?

"Who the hell was that?"

"My darling sister."

"Damn, she's a piece of work. And just for the record, your bottom is perfect."

He squeezed it for emphasis, and I tipped forward into his arms. He kissed me again, on the forehead this time.

"I have to admit, that wasn't quite how I'd planned on proposing to the woman of my dreams. It's not like that in the movies."

"You should know."

Today, Adam was every inch the movie star. Gone was the shaggy hair and the washed-out T-shirt, replaced by a slicked-back crop and a cashmere sweater. His eyes hadn't changed, though. They were still the same gorgeous blue, although this afternoon they were tinged with worry.

Carpe diem, Kat had said. Seize the day.

I wanted to seize Adam.

Even with the new hairstyle, the smart clothes, and the Hollywood moniker, it was clear the man standing in front of me was indeed Adam.

Soon to be *my* Adam.

"Yes," I whispered.

"Yes? You'll marry me?"

I nodded, my throat suddenly tight.

His smile came back, big time. I think I gave him a run for his money, even if my teeth didn't glow in the dark.

He picked me up and spun me around. My legs narrowly missed Bob's tank, but a potted plant went flying. Hey, perhaps I'd have a use for that vacuum cleaner after all?

Adam set me down and hugged me tightly. Hmm. It seemed that other parts of him were happy with my answer too, if what I felt against my stomach was any indication.

I gazed up into his hooded eyes. Adam's pupils dilated, I felt a rush of heat between my legs. Clearly we were reading from the same script.

He let me go and held a finger up. "Hold on one second."

With superhuman strength, he heaved the sofa in front of the front door.

"Not taking any chances," he told me. "Hold this."

He handed me the ring box, then scooped me into his arms and carried me to the bedroom. Slowly, slowly, he unbuttoned my shirt, and as the thin cotton slid down my arms, the cool air perked up other parts of me. Or perhaps that was partly Adam. Oh, who was I kidding? It was all Adam.

My bra followed my shirt to the floor, and Adam dipped his head and went to work. A shiver ran through me, and I practically purred.

"I've missed you so much, baby."

I smushed my face into his chest. "Missed you too."

The cashmere was lovely, but I'd still rather it wasn't there. I peeled the sweater over Adam's head and took a moment to admire the man standing before me. He was every bit as sexy as I'd remembered.

His hands moved to my belt, and I hastily sucked in my stomach. Maybe I *should* go jogging? There was a definite pooch, probably caused by my excess alcohol consumption over the last few days.

Adam tugged my trousers off, then stood back to look at me the way I'd looked at him. I wasn't expecting gushing compliments, but did he really have to start laughing?

I put my hands on my hips. "What's so funny?"

He pointed, and I groaned out loud when I realised what I'd done. One time, *just one time*, could I not embarrass myself totally?

In my haste to get dressed that morning, I'd put on

the first pair of knickers that came to hand. And they happened to be the comedy pair Kat had given me for Christmas last year.

EAT ME, they instructed. I tried desperately to cover them up.

"It's no good. I've seen them now."

"I can explain…"

Adam silenced me with a kiss. "After I've done as I'm told."

He peeled them off, and the next twenty minutes showed me that novelty panties were definitely the way to go. I returned the favour, and it wasn't long before the rest of our clothes went flying.

Two hours later, we both lay spent in a pile of tangled sheets. I barely had the energy to raise my head, but I managed to lift my hand and admire the ring Adam had slipped onto my finger between rounds one and two. A thousand colours sparkled on the ceiling as a beam of sunlight caught the diamond.

It was beautiful, much like the man who'd given it to me.

"What now?" I asked.

"You want to take a turn on top?"

"You'll have to give me a few minutes to recover first. But I meant after today. We can't stay here forever."

"We could. You have a pizza place that delivers, right? I'd just need to get up and move the couch."

I gave him a squeeze. "Be serious. Pizza doesn't have enough vitamins."

"Sure it does, if you add enough toppings."

"I'd need some chocolate as well."

He chuckled. "Anything for you, baby."

For a moment, I actually considered it. Becoming a hermit with Adam, just the two of us and takeout every night. But it wasn't really practical. We both had jobs, for one thing.

"What about the future?" I asked.

They say love conquers all, but had love ever come up against thousands of screaming groupies?

"I'm contracted for one more movie. There are others in the pipeline, but nothing's been confirmed. I don't mind taking a step back. Hell, I'll quit completely if that's what it takes."

Adam was offering to end his glittering career for *me*?

"Tempting though it is to keep you all to myself, I think your fans would lynch me."

I had visions of besotted women sticking pins into Voodoo-Callie dolls and spit-roasting my effigy over an open fire.

"They'd soon move on to the next guy."

"How about you just take time off between each lot of filming? Maybe I could fly out and see you in the school holidays?"

"If you want to carry on working as a teacher, I'll support you one hundred percent, but you know you don't have to, right?"

"I don't?"

"Baby, I earned $20 million for my last movie."

My eyes saucered. I'd realised he must earn a lot, but that much?

"Oh!"

"If you want to travel with me, I'd like that very much."

A life without lesson plans? Without having to do

something I didn't love, eight until five every day? Without having to clean up after the tiny tots had those "little accidents?"

"I think I'd like that too. Actually, I had this idea..."

He laughed. "When women say that, I'm never quite sure I want to hear the rest."

"In Egypt, when Kat and Mo went missing, we didn't know who to turn to. I'd love to be able to offer some kind of help for people in the same situation, maybe a website or something..."

Would he think it was dumb? One woman trying to get justice for the world's missing people?

"That's a great idea, and I know plenty of people who'd help. Everybody in the industry wants to get more publicity for themselves, and charity work always makes them look rosy."

A contented glow blossomed in my heart, and as I lay there watching my future husband, it spread out to every extremity. I had what I'd always wanted. A man who believed in me, who cared about the person I was inside. And he just happened to be rich and good-looking. I gave a soft sigh.

"What was that for?"

"Because I love you. I'll start purring again in a minute."

"Lie back, baby. Let me give you something to really purr about."

I loved the way that when Adam said something, he totally meant it.

After rounds three and four, neither of us wanted to get out of bed, but there came the point when we were both starving.

"What do you want for dinner?" Adam asked.

You.

Or perhaps a nice can of Whiskas. I'd purred so much I figured I must be part feline.

"Uh..."

"How about pizza? And ice cream? I can think of a couple of things I'd like to do with that."

"Perfect."

As was he.

It took two of us to heave the sofa back to where it belonged. How Adam had managed to move it on his own, I had no idea.

My stomach grumbled, and I looked at my watch. Fifty minutes had ticked by since Adam ordered the food, and I was starving.

Finally, there was a knock at the door. I jumped up and flung it open.

"Thank good..." The words died in my throat. "Bryce, what are you doing here?"

"I came to pledge my undying lo..."

I stepped back hastily as Adam's fist connected with Bryce's nose. There was a satisfying crunch, and blood went everywhere.

"Sorry about the carpet, babe, but I've been longing to do that since you first told me about this prick."

I gave him a high five. "Is your hand okay?"

"All good. I knew the fight training I did for the movie before last would come in useful one day."

Adam's knuckles looked pristine, thankfully, but Bryce rose to his feet and swayed a bit.

"I know who you are. You're that actor. That Hollywood actor."

"Well spotted," Adam said.

Bryce gingerly touched his face and winced. Was it my imagination, or was it starting to swell already?

"You broke my nose."

"I'm so glad. For a moment there I thought I might just have bruised it."

The rest of Bryce's face coloured to match his nose. "I'll sue!"

Wow, that was the most dramatic I'd ever seen him.

"What are you going to say, Bryce?" I asked. "That you walked into a cupboard door? Because that's exactly what I saw you do."

He narrowed his eyes at me. "You can't say that. It's lying."

"Lying? *Lying?* I'd say I learned from the master on that one, didn't I? How *is* Mandi today?"

Bryce turned back to Adam and offered a sickly grin. "How about we settle for a part in your next movie?"

He nearly got his nose broken again when Adam slammed the door in his face.

EPILOGUE PART 1

THE SHIMMERING SEA stretched out in front of me, azure blue. A small sailboat floated past on the horizon, no haste, no hurry. The captain had all the time in the world. I trailed a hand over the edge of the sunlounger, letting a handful of near-white sand slip through my fingers. The sun beat down relentlessly from a cloudless sky as the straw umbrella over my head fought to keep me shaded.

My iPad pinged. I had a lot of emails to answer these days, but at least I could do it from some of the world's most stunning locations. I was just about to send a reply when a shadow fell over me.

"A beautiful woman should never be alone."

The voice was Russian, and the man it belonged to had to be at least seventy, although his budgie smugglers would still have looked dodgy on a man half his age. I struggled up to a seated position.

"Uh..."

"I'm having a party on my yacht. Please, join us?" He gestured to the row of scantily clad women lined up behind him.

Six months had passed, but nothing had changed. We might be in the Maldives rather than Egypt, but the men didn't get any less sleazy, they just got richer.

A growl from my side saved me from having to

answer. "She's taken."

The Russian guy put his hands up in a half-hearted apology and backed off, trailed by his half-naked harem. Phew.

I shuffled across so Adam could sit beside me. He hadn't put a shirt on. Good.

"I love it when you go all caveman on me."

He nuzzled into my neck, dropping a row of sweet kisses across my shoulder.

"I can't leave you alone anywhere."

The tablet fell into my lap as I turned to kiss him. So far, his security team had done an excellent job of keeping the beach clear of paparazzi, but unfortunately, Russian oligarchs were beyond their remit.

"Then don't."

"Are you finished there?" He gestured at the iPad. "Because I've got something I'd like to do before we go out for dinner with the others."

"And what's that? Do you want me to run through your lines?"

"No."

"Give you a hand with your positioning?"

"No."

"Advise on wardrobe choices?"

He picked me up and threw me over his shoulder, and I grinned like an idiot as he carried me up the path to our villa.

"Ah, you want me to help with your fitness training."

"Keep your mouth shut, sweetheart. At least until we get inside."

I leaned on Adam's arm that evening as we climbed up the steps to the restaurant. Hopefully the other patrons wouldn't notice I was having trouble walking. Adam had introduced me to the pleasures of the reverse cowgirl, and I couldn't get enough of it.

He guided me through the door, one hand on the small of my back. Even though I was used to it now, his touch still made me shiver.

As did a lot of things about Adam. I was a mess of goosebumps. Thirty degrees Celsius, and people kept asking if I was warm enough.

Oh, I was warm enough, all right. Quite hot, in fact.

We'd eaten at Monty's a few times since we arrived on the island, and the food never failed to disappoint. The relaxed atmosphere reminded me of our time in Egypt, back when we'd just been Callie the schoolteacher and Adam the drifter.

How things had changed since then. In just six short months, my life had gone from mundane to extraordinary.

Had I truly found my paradise?

Women the world over would say yes, but I couldn't shake that niggling feeling that something wasn't quite right.

Adam had come home late on a couple of occasions, including once when he said he was staying overnight with a friend. But the friend was a fellow actor, and he'd been pictured falling out of a nightclub with a Zlist starlet at three a.m that same morning.

Then there were the times he hung up the phone when I walked into the room, and the emails he carefully shielded from my view.

Was he as into me as I was into him? Days like today, I'd say the answer was absolutely. But could it last forever?

Dammit, I needed to stop thinking about this before it consumed me. It wasn't easy, though. Bryce's betrayal had left me with trust issues, and Bryce had been a frog compared to Adam's prince.

Just enjoy your dinner, Callie. Focus on the good things.

Like Kat coming tomorrow. I'd been looking forward to her visit since she told me her plans two weeks ago.

"Mo's legs are well on their way to being fixed now," she'd said. "And we could both do with a break from the British winter. What better way to get it than to come and see my best friend in the whole world?"

I'd jumped at the idea. Secretly, I got a bit lonely while Adam was busy filming. The movie business sounded glamorous, but in reality, it was just a whole lot of standing around while the director kept changing his mind. I'd spent a few days on set, but people kept staring at me. Not just the crew, but Adam as well. Then he forgot his lines and the director got cross.

Yes, I was better off keeping out of the way.

Kat and Mo arrived by taxi in the evening. Mo seemed slightly nervous, but Kat was her usual bubbly self.

"I can't wait to spend some time on the beach," she said. "Look at me, I'm so white I could star in a washing powder advert."

I hugged her tightly. "I've found a nice peaceful corner, right by the sea. And the waiters don't interfere with my life either. Not like in Egypt. Speaking of people interfering, how's Persephone?"

Kat and Mo had moved into my flat, but my sister popped over regularly to irritate them. Somehow, she was under the impression that Kat liked her.

"Actually, she's not been too bad these past couple of weeks. She's started dating her new boot camp instructor."

"Seriously? Since when does my sister like beefcake?" She'd always been into the tall, rich, and preppy type. Suits, button-down shirts, fat wallets—that sort of thing.

Kat shrugged. "I guess when he yelled at her to drop to her knees and give him five, she took it the wrong way."

"Well, as long as she's happy."

Persephone may have been the bane of my life, but I still wanted her to find a way of mending her broken heart.

Mo balanced on a leg and a crutch to give me a hug as well. His recovery was going well, but he still needed a little assistance from time to time.

"How are you feeling?"

"Much better, thank you. I'm still having physio every week, but it's not so painful now."

"That's great news."

"And it was very kind of Adam to send a jet for us. The seats were so much more comfortable."

Adam, Kat, and Mo had become good buddies. There was none of the awkwardness that had festered between her and Bryce, which certainly made life easier. When Adam heard they wanted to visit, he'd insisted on making the journey as painless as possible.

"Made it much easier to join the mile-high club, too," Kat whispered into my ear.

"Kat!"

She rolled her eyes. "What? Tell me you haven't."

Well, I could, but I'd be lying. Heat rose up my cheeks.

"I knew it!"

Time to change the subject...

"I told Gabe we'd meet him for dinner tomorrow. He's been looking forward to seeing you as well."

Adam had got Gabe a job as a diving consultant on his new movie. He said there was nobody he'd trust more to keep him safe underwater. And he'd made damn sure that Gabe had a work permit this time.

"I can't wait to see him. Is Adam coming too?"

"He said he was."

Even to my own ears, my voice sounded flat. Yes, Adam had said he was coming, but he'd cancelled our plans more than once recently.

"Callie, what's wrong? Is something up with Adam?"

"I'm just going to unpack," Mo said, then bolted from the room.

"He doesn't handle girl-talk very well," Kat explained. "It scares him. Now, tell me what the problem is."

Sometimes, there were downsides to being so close to someone. Kat knew something was wrong, and she wouldn't stop pressing until she'd pried the details out of me. I might as well get it over with.

"I'm worried Adam might be having an affair."

Her incredulous expression told me exactly what she thought of my suspicions.

"Why on earth would you think that?"

I told her about his last-minute changes of plan, his surreptitious phone calls, and his general evasiveness. Lately, he hadn't even mentioned our wedding. We'd discussed a few ideas, but that was ages ago, and I'd been so busy setting up the charity... Did he even want to get married anymore?

"Maybe it's something to do with work?" Kat suggested. "He could be in talks for a new movie."

"But what if he's cheating on me? Bryce did."

"Adam isn't Bryce."

"Don't I know it—Adam has beautiful women throwing themselves at him night and day. I've had to remove three pairs of panties from the hotel veranda already this week."

"You're beautiful. And Adam only has eyes for you —everyone can see it."

"But he's not here most of the time. And his co-star's stunning."

"She's also fifteen years older than him. And isn't she married?"

There was that, and she'd only ever been nice to me. But appearances weren't everything. She could be a cougar disguised as a Siamese.

"You think I'm overreacting, don't you?"

"I *know* you are."

But even though I wanted to trust Kat's judgement, I couldn't stop the worries from clouding my mind.

I'd planned to sit on the beach for a while the next morning, but like they had so many times over the last few months, events at the charity took over. A girl had gone missing in Thailand, and after speaking to her distraught parents, I mobilised my fledgling network to publicise her disappearance.

By the time social media the world over was doing its thing, I was so hungry I resorted to snarfing down a bar of chocolate and a packet of salted peanuts from the minibar because I couldn't wait until dinner.

Kat had checked in at lunchtime to see how I was doing and re-tweeted the details of the missing girl to the thousands of Twitter followers she'd gathered over the past few months. Now that the furore over her ordeal had died down and Mo was getting better, she wanted to get more involved with my work.

"I can stay and help if you want," she offered. "Mo will be okay on the beach by himself."

"Don't be silly—this is your holiday. I've had enough sun to last me for months."

"If you're sure."

"I am, absolutely. Now get back out there so Mo can top up your sunscreen."

As we got ready for dinner in Kat's villa, I received

word that the teenager we'd been searching for had been found in a local hospital. One of the nurses had seen a tweet from her favourite pop star and recognised the unconscious patient who'd been brought in after a road traffic accident. It wasn't the best outcome we could have hoped for, but at least her parents could be with her now. I fired off a "thank you" message to the singer in question to let her know how much she'd helped and went through to Kat's bedroom. She was rummaging through her suitcase for a dress.

"I need to find something pretty. What if there are photographers?"

"You can make all the effort in the world, but they'll still manage to get a shot of you with your eyes closed or your mouth open."

I knew that because it had happened to me many, many times. Adam told me not to look at the gossip websites, but I couldn't help myself.

"They only make you miserable, baby," he said.

"I know, but it's worse knowing that people are gossiping about me without knowing what they're gossiping about."

Truthfully, the gossip was the least of my worries. Every day, I trembled as I checked for evidence of his suspected infidelity. And my fears only grew when he phoned me right before we were due to meet for dinner.

"Babe, we've been delayed again. One of Dana's false eyelashes fell off in the middle of a scene, so we have to go for a retake."

An eyelash? Really? I closed my eyes and leaned back against the wall.

"So you're going to miss dinner?"

"I'll make it up to you, I promise."

"I love you," I whispered.

"Love you too."

My heart stuttered as I hung up. How many more times would I hear him say that?

How long before he decided I was no longer good enough?

EPILOGUE PART 2

KAT CALLED ME at seven the next morning, a few minutes after Adam had left.

"It's our last day on the beach," he'd told me as he dashed out the door. "We need to make an early start to get the lighting right."

My spirits plummeted as the door closed behind him. There were three days of filming left, and I was marking the time off on a calendar in my head. I'd have liked nothing more than to bury my head in the sand until it was over, but no way would Kat allow me to do that.

"Get up, sleepyhead," she said, way too perky for that time in the morning. "I've booked us massages in the main building at eight."

I stifled a groan. "Sounds great."

"Careful, don't show too much enthusiasm."

"Sorry. I'm not feeling myself at the moment."

"Tell me you're not still clinging to that crazy notion that Adam's doing the dirty?"

Yes. "No, of course not."

"Callie, I know you're my best friend, but sometimes I want to shake you. I'll be over in half an hour. Make sure you're dressed."

I sighed and rolled out of bed. At least if I was busy with Kat all day, it would keep my mind off other things. With that in mind, I took a quick shower and twisted up my hair, then threw on a pair of shorts and a T-shirt. I'd just shoved my feet into a pair of flip-flops when Kat hammered on the door.

"You'd better be up," she yelled.

There was no subtlety about Kat. Not only was I wide awake, but the guests in the villas either side undoubtedly were too.

"I'm ready," I said, opening the door. "And your cheerfulness is hurting my brain."

"Today's going to be a good day," she insisted. "Trust me, you'll love it."

The last time she'd said those words—two years ago when she'd talked me into going dry-slope skiing with her in England—I'd ended up with a twisted ankle and a scraped elbow.

I trailed behind her as she walked to the long, low building that housed the hotel reception, a couple of meeting rooms, and the health suite. She turned right when we entered and started down a corridor.

"I thought the beauty rooms were that way?" I pointed in the other direction.

"Nope, this is definitely right. I checked last night."

Except we didn't end up in a treatment room. Kat flung open a set of double doors and...

"Surprise!" she shouted, bouncing up and down and clapping her hands.

I stared at her like she'd gone quite mad.

"What's all this?" I hissed.

People were milling around everywhere. Racks of dresses took up one side of the room, and what appeared to be a beauty salon had been set up on the other. An intimidating lady with a clipboard and an earpiece strode towards us.

"It's the stuff for your wedding. Isn't it great?" Kat couldn't keep the grin off her face.

"My what?"

She lifted my left hand and pointed at the ring. "Your wedding. You know, to the man you've been engaged to for months?"

What? I felt faint.

"We need a chair over here," the clipboard lady yelled.

One was thrust behind me, and I collapsed into it. A wedding? But we hadn't even set a date.

"I don't get it. What wedding? Kat? What wedding?"

Kat crouched down in front of me. "Adam wanted to get married sooner rather than later. He knew how busy you were with the charity, and he could see how important that was to you. So he thought he'd organise everything himself as a surprise."

"I'm getting married?"

"Yes."

"Today?"

"Yes!"

I was speechless. During these last few weeks, I'd begun to fear we'd never get married, and Adam had arranged *this*? A whole freaking wedding?

"Callie? Are you okay?" Kat asked.

I barely heard her.

Planning a wedding was a mammoth task, and Adam had done it all himself as well as starring in a feature film. I hadn't lifted a finger to help. Logic said I should be thrilled, but what I felt was guilt.

Kat gripped my arm. "Say something, Callie. You've

gone pale."

Hysterical laughter bubbled from my lips. "Is this what Adam was doing? All those phone calls? The late nights? The emails?"

She nodded.

"I've been thinking such awful things about him."

I couldn't help it—I burst into tears.

Panic flashed in Kat's eyes. "If there's anything you don't like, I'm sure we can change it."

Kat wasn't the only person worried. Behind her, the clipboard lady stood wide-eyed in horror, and most of the other people were staring at me too.

"It's not that. I just feel terrible that he did so much work by himself."

"It's a good thing I'm here to shake some sense into you. Adam's been having a great time with this. We all have."

"What do you mean, 'we all have?'"

"Uh, me, Mo, your mum, Dave. Even Persephone's been sticking her oar in."

"Persephone made me wear a bright yellow dress when I was her bridesmaid!"

I still had nightmares about that dress. I couldn't go past a field of buttercups any more without having palpitations.

"Don't worry, we didn't let her near the outfits. We gave her party favours and invitations."

"Invitations? Who's coming? What about my family?"

Just then, I heard a commotion in the corridor.

"Look at the chandelier, Dave. Isn't it huge?" my mum exclaimed.

"This place is so hot. I'm sweaty already."

Oh, great. Persephone had come all the way to the Maldives.

"I like you hot and sweaty, my little munchkin."

Who the heck was that? And why did Persephone giggle? My sister never giggled. Maybe she'd removed the stick from her ass to get through airport security.

"They're all here," Kat said. "Your mum and Dave, Persephone and her muscle man, and Adam's family."

"What about—"

"Even your father. Adam had a detective track him down. He and your mum have promised to be nice to each other."

I sagged in relief. I hadn't seen much of him over the years, but it wouldn't have been right to get married without him there.

"What about a dress? I haven't tried anything on."

"Adam measured your clothes, and there's a seamstress here to do the final fitting. You've got three dresses to choose from."

I clapped my hand over my mouth. The thought of Adam rooting through my closet with a measuring tape made *me* giggle.

"I can't believe this is happening? Is this really happening?"

Kat grinned at me. "It really is."

The clipboard lady stepped forward, glancing at her watch. "Are we good to go?"

Kat raised her eyebrows at me, I nodded, and all hell let loose. A swarm of beauticians, hairstylists, and make-up artists descended, and two hours later, I'd been plucked, coiffed, and polished to perfection.

My fingers came to my mouth as one of the stylists held the dresses up in front of me. Kat smacked my hand away.

"Stop biting your nails. You'll ruin your manicure."

The dresses were all beautiful. "Did you choose them?" I asked her.

"I shortlisted six, and Adam picked the final three."

It was a difficult decision, but I picked the ivory strapless one with a floaty skirt and delicate beading on the bodice. I held my breath as Kat helped me into it behind a screen.

"Will it do up?" I asked.

"Of course it will. Have faith."

It was ninety-nine percent perfect. A quick alteration or two later, that grew to a hundred.

As I stood in front of the mirror, my thoughts turned to Adam. Where was he? What was he thinking? Was he as terrified as me?

Nica—the clipboard lady—turned out to be a wedding planner extraordinaire. Honestly, her efficiency scared me a little. Soon, Kat and Persephone stood beside me in thankfully tasteful peach dresses, and Mum held Annie in a matching outfit.

"Pretty!" She clapped her tiny hands and made a grab for my tiara, but I managed to dodge out of the way.

Then my father stepped into the room, dressed in a morning suit with a corsage stuck neatly into his buttonhole. The others melted away to give us a few minutes.

"My little girl. You look beautiful."

"Hi, Dad."

He gave me a sad smile. "I know I haven't been much of a father, but I couldn't have hoped for a more perfect daughter."

Mum always said he wasn't cut out for fatherhood. A wandering spirit, she called him, never destined to stay in the same place for long. But he was still my dad.

"I'm glad you came," I whispered.

He squeezed my hand. "So am I."

Nica appeared, and she looked as if she meant business. "Are you ready?"

"I think so. Is it normal to be this nervous?"

She chuckled. "Absolutely. Every bride is. This is the start of the next phase of your life."

I tried to smile, but it came out as more of a grimace. "I can't wait."

"That's the spirit. I'll just call the photographer. We want to get some shots of you in the hotel gardens before you get into the water."

"I'm sorry, what? The *water*? What water?"

"Nobody's told you yet?"

"Nobody's told me anything."

Kat rematerialised, and I wondered if there was a good reason she'd been keeping out of strangulation range.

"Your ceremony's going to be underwater," she told me. "Isn't that exciting?"

My blood slowly trickled down to my feet. "How on earth can we get married underwater?"

"The minister's going to be diving with you, and you'll write your vows on diving slates," Nica explained.

"Is that legal?"

"Yes, one hundred percent."

My first reaction was one of shock, but then I took a moment to think about it. We'd come full circle. I'd fallen in love with Adam underwater, and now I'd marry him there.

"When I met Adam, I *did* say I was going to be more adventurous."

Kat gave me a hug. "Here's to another adventure."

Half an hour later, I stood on the beach. I may not have looked like your typical bride, but the white fins I was wearing did add a certain something to the outfit. Nica had even managed to find me a white BCD and regulator to continue the theme.

As the wedding march played from hidden speakers, I started my walk across the sand with my father at my side. He took me up to the water's edge, then handed me over to Mo, who'd agreed to swim the rest of the way with me underwater. Kat would be my underwater bridesmaid, and Adam was already down there with Gabe as his best man.

I waved to my family and Adam's too—his parents and brother had made the trip—and my pulse rocketed as I sank beneath the waves. Someone had marked out the way with shells, and up ahead, I could make out a metal altar decorated with pink and cream roses to match my bouquet.

The sight of Adam watching me as I floated down the makeshift aisle made my breath hitch. Then I remembered my training and made myself exhale. Having my lungs explode on my wedding day would be all kinds of awkward.

Adam wore a grey suit, and he took out his regulator to grin. Show off. When I got close, he grabbed my hand and helped me to hover beside him.

The minister held up his first slate, and we were off. All I had to do was hold up my vows in turn and then write "I do" at the appropriate moment. My handwriting wasn't usually that bad, honest. Adam gripped my hand tighter as he mirrored my words and added a wobbly heart at the end.

As with everything else he'd chosen, my ring was perfect, a simple white-gold band patterned with roses. As he slipped it onto my finger, I knew it would stay there for life.

The minister held up his final slate, and we got to the part I'd been waiting for.

You may now kiss the bride.

I spat out my regulator and threw myself at Adam. As we ran out of air, I felt a tap on my shoulder and saw Kat had brought a slate of her own.

Get a room.

Oops.

Before long, we walked out of the sea as man and wife, wearing matching smiles. Our families were waiting for us, and rose petals fluttered through the air as we shrugged out of our BCDs.

"Thank you," I whispered to Adam, as he swept me up in his arms and carried me along the beach.

"Anything for you, babe."

"*Any*thing?"

"Uh, yes? What did you have in mind?"

I leaned forward and whispered in his ear.

He squeezed me tighter. "Definitely that. How do you feel about skipping the reception?"

"We can't. Kat wouldn't let us miss our own party. She'd set off the fire alarm or send the clipboard lady to fetch us."

"You mean Nica? Yeah, I see your point—we'd better go."

We managed a few moments alone in our suite— okay, an hour—and I wished I'd still been wearing my veil when we finally made it to the reception. Even a coat of foundation couldn't hide my red cheeks.

Adam's brother was outside the marquee, lounging against a palm tree. He was a blonder but more dangerous-looking version of his more famous older sibling. Having the pair of them here together had raised the temperature on the island a couple of notches.

He gave us a knowing smile as we passed.

"Not a word," Adam told him.

Luckily, I soon forgot my embarrassment when we started dinner. It had been ages since all my family and friends were together in one place, and even Persephone seemed half-human. If I'd known going to boot camp would have such an effect on her personality, I'd have enlisted her in the army years ago.

Mum spent most of the time dabbing at her eyes with a hanky. Dave had brought a supply with him and dished them out at regular intervals. She had him well trained.

"It was so beautiful, dear," she gushed. "Like something out of the movies."

"Thank fuck we didn't need a retake," Adam's brother muttered from the other side of the table.

Despite the heat, the cake was stunning. Each of the tiers was decorated with hand-painted fish and shiny pearls made out of icing, and it even had a model of a bride and groom in scuba gear. Adam and I held the knife together as we cut through the bottom tier, and when the knife hit the board, his lips met mine.

Guests? What guests?

Only when Kat yelled, "Have you found her tonsils yet?" did we stop. My cheeks burned once again, but

Adam didn't care. Far from it. In fact, he looked quite pleased with himself.

Later, as the sun went down on the most amazing day of my life, the waiters dished out champagne and Adam proposed a toast.

"Here's to the future." He held up his glass. "And to my beautiful wife."

"To the future," everyone echoed.

I couldn't wait to see what it would bring.

BACK TO PARADISE

From time to time, I like to write extra short stories that go with my novels. These are FREE to members of my reader group. If you'd like to read an extra story about Adam and Callie's return to Egypt, plus find out a little more about the other Lowes brother, you can get a FREE book, *Back to Paradise*, by following this link:

www.elise-noble.com/trouble-in-paradise-bonus

WHAT'S NEXT?

The Trouble Series continues in *Nothing But Trouble*...

When Ella Goodman's surrogate grandma died, her last wish was simple—she wanted Ella to get off the sofa and have an adventure. Ella's not the impulsive type but she's left with little choice—if she doesn't complete Edith's wish list, she'll end up homeless.

As Ella drifts from one disaster to the next, she has one goal: finish the challenge. She's not going to enjoy herself and she certainly isn't going to fall in love...is she?

For more details: www.elise-noble.com/nothing-but-trouble

If you're in the mood for some darker humour, why not try my Blackwood Security series, starting with *Pitch Black*?

After the owner of a security company is murdered, his sharp-edged wife goes on the run. Forced to abandon everything she holds dear—her home, her friends, her job in special ops—assassin Diamond builds a new life for herself in England. As Ashlyn Hale, she meets Luke, a handsome local who makes her realise just how lonely she is.

Yet, even in the sleepy village of Lower Foxford, the dark side of life dogs Diamond's trail when the unthinkable strikes. Forced out of hiding, she races against time to save those she cares about.

Pitch Black is currently available for FREE:
www.elise-noble.com/pitch-black

If you enjoyed Trouble in Paradise, please consider leaving a review.

For an author, every review is incredibly important. Not only do they make us feel warm and fuzzy inside, readers consider them when making their decision whether or not to buy a book. Even a line saying you enjoyed the book or what your favourite part was helps a lot.

Want to stalk me?

For updates on my new releases, giveaways, and other random stuff, you can sign up for my newsletter on my website:
www.elise-noble.com

Facebook:
www.facebook.com/EliseNobleAuthor

Twitter: @EliseANoble

Instagram: @elise_noble

If you're on Facebook, you may also like to join Team Blackwood for exclusive giveaways, sneak previews, and book-related chat. Be the first to find out about new stories, and you might even see your name or one of your ideas make it into print!

And if you'd like to read my books for FREE, you can also find details of how to join my advance review team.

Would you like to join Team Blackwood?

www.elise-noble.com/team-blackwood

END OF BOOK STUFF

Thank you to my diving buddy for putting up with me being surgically attached to my iPad for so long.

Thank you to Michelle, for being my cheerleader when I first started sharing my work, for giving me feedback when I needed it, and for letting me borrow your wedding planners for the Trouble books.

Thank you to Amanda, for helping me fix the plot (and being so nice about it), the commas, the spelling errors, the speech marks, the list goes on...

Thank you to SayIDidIt for your sharp eyes.

Thank you to the good folks in the WPRH for the advice and for being there when I needed to let off steam. And of course, for the wine.

Thank you to Team Blackwood for your endless support, cake pictures, and memes.

Finally, a huge thank you to you, the reader, for taking a chance on me and buying this book. I hope you've enjoyed it.

While Kat's story has a happy ending, some events in Trouble in Paradise were inspired by a tale I heard on one of my trips to Egypt. Shan Na died in Dahab in 2013, and for her, justice wasn't quite so swift. It took years for a man to be jailed for her murder, and was it the right man? Nobody knows. To this day, her mother remains missing. Her story serves as a stark reminder that paradise is sometimes an illusion.

OTHER BOOKS BY ELISE NOBLE

The Blackwood Security Series
For the Love of Animals (Nate & Carmen - prequel)
Black is my Heart (prequel)
Pitch Black
Into the Black
Forever Black
Gold Rush
Gray is my Heart
Neon (novella)
Out of the Blue
Ultraviolet
Glitter (novella)
Red Alert
White Hot
The Scarlet Affair
Quicksilver
The Girl with the Emerald Ring (2020)
Red After Dark (2020)
When the Shadows Fall (TBA)

The Blackwood Elements Series
Oxygen
Lithium
Carbon
Rhodium

Platinum
Lead
Copper
Bronze
Nickel (2020)

The Blackwood UK Series
Joker in the Pack
Cherry on Top (novella)
Roses are Dead
Shallow Graves
Indigo Rain
Pass the Parcel (TBA)

Blackwood Casefiles
Stolen Hearts

Blackstone House
Hard Lines (TBA)
Hard Tide (TBA)

The Electi Series
Cursed
Spooked
Possessed
Demented

The Trouble Series
Trouble in Paradise
Nothing but Trouble
24 Hours of Trouble

Standalone

Life
Coco du Ciel (TBA)
Twisted (short stories)
A Very Happy Christmas (novella)

Printed in Great Britain
by Amazon

58645445R00203